DEAD
CARNAGE

THE LIFE AFTER SERIES

DEAD CARNAGE

AMANDA FASCIANO

4 Horsemen
Publications, Inc.

THIS BOOK IS DEDICATED TO

To my wonderful husband, Anthony, who continues to push me to strive for my dreams.

To my friends, too many to name, who have helped support me along the way.

To my kids, who help me at every convention, and help keep me from being too much of a fuddy-duddy.

To my readers, who surprise me every day with their support and kindness.

Table of Contents

CHAPTER 1

Coming Clean

Cadence was growing weary of the crowd around her. The office that she and Will shared was the fullest it had ever been. Snow was there, in his usual stuffy-looking tweed suit, his ice-blue eyes showing concern. Ramon, the doctor, was there, a pillar of support and warmth for the woman he loved and who loved him. Whitfield was still there, too, though the man with the wild ginger hair was the last person she wanted to even acknowledge right now.

An hour had passed since Will and Cade had returned from the disastrous investigation at Scarecrow Farms. Cadence was angry, hurting, and tired. She felt the support from Ramon, standing behind her with his hands resting comfortably on her shoulders. He meant well, but all she wanted to do was rage and throw things. And while there were people there, she was not about to break down. She brushed the stray dark blonde hairs that had escaped her ponytail out of her face in annoyance.

Whitfield was sitting on the floor in the middle of the room, his legs crossed. He deserved every bit of rage Cadence could throw at him, and he knew it. He had thought he had been doing the right thing, or at least the wrong thing, for the right reason. But things had gotten so far out of control, and now both the living and the spirits had paid the price. And with X'Haldzos free, there was certainly more danger ahead for them all.

Snow sat at his old desk while Will perched on the top of it. Cadence sat at her desk, her head in her hands, counting to ten.

"So let me try to get this straight," Cadence said, her voice tense, but even. "You occupied the well at Scarecrow Farms. When that … thing … got there, it kicked you out. Kind of a version of the bigger fish taking over the pond. You then did your best to sate its hunger so it would stay at the farm and not move on. That would keep its evil in one place. You were, in your words, doing evil for the greater good."

"Yes," Whitfield said. He understood one wrong move by him, and Cadence would likely jump over her desk and tear him apart. That or Will would be using more of the toys he invented to hurt him. He had meant well when he started, but he wasn't sure he would ever convince them of that.

Cadence nodded; her jade eyes cast at her desk as her mind focused on working through the issue, glad to have something to focus on other than what had just happened at the farm. She also didn't trust herself to look at anyone else. She was too raw.

"I understand that," Cade said. "Agreement or disagreement aside, I understand the motive. Moving on. You were using Captain Rodriguez for a long time. I get the positive side of having a police captain to hide the bodies and control any word of serial killings. But you said you encountered him when he was young. He said something about your plan. Please explain what Captain Rodriguez, these plans you lied to him about, the portal to Barrington Prison, the child ghosts, and Scarecrow Farms have in common." She had yet to mention the loss of Lauren or Sam.

Whitfield pressed his lips together for a moment as he thought of the best way to phrase things. "In the beginning, I was shocked to find someone as adept at seeing and communicating with spirits as he was. I helped him hone that talent. I had hoped he would grow strong enough to be able to destroy X'Haldzos. When he went into the police, I will admit I saw an opportunity. By that time, I had given up on a single human being gaining enough power to destroy the creature. But by then, the lies I had told him had already clouded his vision.

"I had told Rodriguez that with non-human creatures on his side, he would be able to use them, control them, in order to help punish the corrupt and the criminal. The non-humans would strike fear and people would fall in line. He could find others like himself, train them, and make an army. All of that stemmed from the idea that I could use them to get rid of X'Haldzos.

"As for the girl, Ava, Rodriguez found her. I'm not sure how. He wanted to get her away from her parents so he could train her on how to use her gifts. He summoned the child ghost to try to aid in that. I was not involved in that plan. That was his own brainchild, so to speak. My only part in that was not showing up for the investigation because I didn't want to be involved, or more to the point, I guess, for him to see me involved.

"Now on to Barrington Prison, Scarecrow Farms, and the portal. That stone portal has existed on the land since old man Chalmers died. His son, who inherited the farm, was married to a woman who was a practicing occultist. Together, they constructed the portal. When activated, the power of it called to X'Haldzos which is one reason why I tried to keep him sated in the house. And that is why I am so scared now. He is free. The sacrifices that had been made had been done to keep him there. To keep him fed so that he wouldn't seek anywhere else. With that portal, he could go anywhere, even here.

"Pruitt knew he was working with Shaldoxz. He didn't know the truth about me, just the non-human I showed him. He was bitter and the other officers had been neglectful. I used it to set up a situation where Rodriguez and the cult he was trying to build would get someone to sacrifice on the stone. He would then open the portal to Barrington and once a prisoner had come through to possess the body, the body with both souls would be sacrificed. It was like a feast for X'Haldzos. Pruitt thought he was sending the souls out to possess the bodies and live again."

"What I need to know now, is, can you help end this?" Cadence's voice was still terse as she asked the question, her gaze still focused on her desk.

"I would like to be given the chance to," Whitfield said. "Ending this, ending X'Haldzos, is what I have been working toward for a very long time. And yes, I do realize that if I survive the fight, I will be sentenced to imprisonment afterward. I have no illusions about what I've done and the lies I've told. I don't have any illusions about the punishment I deserve, either." He took a chance and lifted his eyes to Riley. "Especially from you."

The room was still with a heavy silence for a moment. They all had their own opinions on the matter, but every one of them knew that Cadence was the deciding factor. After what had just happened, she had the right to decide if she was willing to work with Whitfield again. They all were also silently in agreement that if she wanted to tear his throat out, they would politely look the other way. Whitfield was right. He deserved any and every punishment she could mete out.

"Fine," she said. "You can help us. But no more bullshit."

"Of course," Whitfield said.

Cadence finally lifted her eyes from the desk and looked over at Snow. "He can help, but I am not going to be the one responsible for him. You and Will can work it out between you two about how to handle it. But I can't... I can't even look at him right now."

"We'll handle it," Snow said, getting a nod from Will as well. Snow then paused and fished his phone out of his tweed blazer pocket. A silver eyebrow lifted in curiosity as he saw the caller ID.

"Snow," he said, answering it. His eyes closed tightly, then he winced. "I'll be right over."

"What is it?" Cadence asked, having noted the change of expression and tone from Snow.

"Nothing for you to worry about," Snow said.

"Don't coddle me, Snow. What is it?" Cade's tone was clear in that she was not taking no for an answer.

Snow sighed. "It was Bethany. Lauren is there."

"Right," Cade said, bowing her head.

Ramon felt her shudder under his hands and frowned. "Cade, it's okay to let Snow handle this on his own. Or with Will."

"No," Cadence said, turning to face Ramon. "I owe it to her to be there, too. As much as Whitfield is right in thinking he deserves punishment from me, I feel the same way with Lauren. I'm the reason her ex-husband has no afterlife. I've put her and her friends in danger time and again. I intend to face her. Let her rage at me if she wants."

Ramon didn't like how pale she was. Nor did he like how she was keeping herself so tightly reined in. He could see the chaos of emotion behind her eyes, waiting for the dam to break and her resolve to weaken. But her face was like etched stone. She was set on this path, and she wouldn't waver. He leaned down and kissed her cheek as he squeezed her hand. "Do you want me there?"

"No, I can do this," Cade said. "But thank you," she added, her voice softer. "I'll come home after."

"Yes, you will," Snow said. "That's an order."

Bethany's office was small, so Snow had called her back to invite her and Lauren to his office. Cade and Will followed Snow back to his office, and they took seats on the couches there. The office had changed. The somewhat-modern office with Egyptian flair had transformed into a traditional study with hard woods and rich fabrics. Although the bookshelves had stayed, the tomes on them were different. Cadence allowed herself a small smile when she saw the collected works of Sherlock Holmes on the shelf. It truly was Snow's office now.

Bethany and Lauren arrived not long after. Lauren looked shell-shocked, which was understandable. Bethany looked confused.

"Where's Croft?" Bethany asked.

Snow blinked in surprise before realizing that no one had told her. "It's a long story. Let's just say he got a promotion, and I took his position."

"Congratulations," Bethany said, gesturing for Lauren to have a seat on the couch. "I must ask. What happened? Why is Lauren here? And where is Sam?"

"Sam," Lauren said, her voice quiet. She was staring at the carpet, not seeing it. "Sam," she repeated.

Cadence shuddered visibly at the mention of her brother's name. Her practiced stone façade was beginning to show cracks. She turned away from them all for a moment, gathering her composure once more.

Bethany looked from Lauren to Snow and Cadence. "A couple of hours ago, you brought me two children. Now Lauren is here and from her reactions, I am guessing something happened to Sam. What's going on?"

"Sam's gone," Cadence said, her voice flat.

"Your fault," Lauren said, looking over at Cadence. "Dan was your fault. Aiden getting hurt is your fault, Sam is your fault..." Lauren's voice was growing louder and shriller.

Cadence got up and walked over to Snow's desk, her control over her emotions threatening to crack. She crossed her arms over her chest as if she could physically hold herself together.

Bethany reached over and touched Lauren on the shoulder. "No, none of that was Cadence's fault. Dan's death was his own fault. Aiden is a grown man and can make his own decisions." Bethany did make a mental note to ask about Aiden getting hurt when they had time to discuss it, but now there were more pressing matters.

"Mrs. Kurtz," Snow said to get Lauren's attention. Her eyes had been fixed on Cadence, but she let her attention drift to Snow as he said her name. "I am very sorry about what happened to you. And what happened to Sam. None of us had any idea that the non-human creature from the house would come charging to the portal."

"Portal?" Lauren sounded confused.

"The stone circle," Will said.

Lauren turned her attention to Will. "I know his voice," she said, pointing to Snow. "I know who Cadence is. I know Bethany. Who are you?"

"He is Cadence's new partner," Snow said. "It's a long story.

"Lauren," Cadence said from across the room. Her back was still turned toward them as she spoke. "Sam is not my fault. Not when he was murdered in college, not now. He made his own decisions. No one feels the pain of his loss more than I do. Including you."

She then turned to face Lauren before continuing to speak. "I know you like to blame me. I'm an easy scapegoat for your anger. And for your guilt. And in some respects, maybe I do deserve it. I know you feel guilty for Sam. You also feel guilty about what happened to Dan. Listen to me. You are NOT responsible for either of them. What happened to them is awful. But it happened. We need to deal with it and move on in whatever way we can. I'm pretty sure you're going to be given some choices. That's for you and Bethany to talk about. All I can say is that I'm sorry that Sam and I couldn't protect you from what happened to you. And I'm sorrier than you can imagine that Sam is gone."

Lauren cracked, the numbness of her death wearing off. Tears began falling like rain from her eyes before she hid her face behind her hands. Bethany reached over and rubbed Lauren's shoulder. Snow and Will sat there, trying to politely ignore the emotional blackmail, but be attentive as well.

Cadence moved across the room and kneeled on the floor in front of Lauren. "I can promise you this," Cade said. "We will be putting an end to the thing that killed you and Sam. I will personally see to it. And if I die doing it, so be it. But that thing is not getting away scot-free with all the damage it has done."

Snow looked over at Will and leaned in, whispering to him. The teenager nodded, rose, and left the office. Cadence stayed on the floor, putting a comforting hand on the woman's arm. Snow rose without a sound and went over to his desk. At length, Lauren began to calm down. The tears slowed, then finally stopped. The plump woman wiped the back of her hand across her cheek to erase the tears. She then did the same with the other cheek.

"You're right," Lauren said. She lifted her brown-eyed gaze to Cadence as she spoke. "You're right. I do blame myself."

"But there is nothing you have to blame yourself for," Bethany said, her voice soft and gentle. "Dan was a grown man. He chose what happened."

"As for Sam, he took the job of being your guide and guardian with full knowledge of what that entailed," Snow said as he rejoined them in the couch area. He had a white cube in his hand that was the size of a Rubik's Cube. Unlike the puzzle toy, it was solid. He retook his seat and tucked the cube between himself and the arm of the sofa.

A knock on the door sounded, and they all looked at it.

"Enter, Will," Snow called out.

Will opened the door and brought Whitfield in with him. Cadence's eyes widened, and she looked over at Snow. "Are you kidding me?" she asked in disbelief.

"They need to face each other," Snow said.

Will marched Whitfield in and Cadence got up off the floor for Whitfield to stand in front of Lauren. For her part, Lauren looked confused.

"Go on," Will urged. "Come clean."

Whitfield sighed. "I am the non-human that commanded Wolf. Wolf was the one who recruited your husband to summon the chaos being at Lexington Hills. I was also responsible for your death as well," he said, looking at Bethany. "I was responsible for Overton, both in his early days as a mortal and as a spirit once he was freed from his prison. The chaos being, the murders, all of that was in order to try to keep the non-human at Scarecrow Farms there. I wanted him to stay put. He is a being of pure evil who feeds off blood and pain. I was hoping to keep him full enough to just get lazy and stay where he was. It worked for a long time. Tonight, it failed. He is free, and he is stronger due to what I have done to feed him. This is my doing. I take responsibility for that."

As angry as Cadence was at Whitfield, she gave him credit for being so composed as he accepted the blame for all that had happened.

Lauren looked down at her hands for a moment, then rose. She was shorter than Whitfield, but her presence was still imposing.

"I want to know your name," Lauren said.

"They call me Whitfield," he responded. Any other name wouldn't have mattered. He was fond of the name and preferred to be called by it, for better or for worse.

"Whitfield," she said, as if measuring the taste and sound of it. She turned as if to sit back down, but then whipped back around in a flash, slapping Whitfield across the face as hard as she could. His face turned fully to the side with the force of the blow and a brilliant, red, hand-shaped welt immediately formed on his cheek. The sound of the slap reverberated in the room, which then fell silent.

Cadence let one side of her mouth curl up into a slight smirk. She had been wanting to do that for hours.

Whitfield turned back to face Lauren. He stood, without saying a word, bracing himself for another hit. Instead of continuing her attack, Lauren sat back down. It was like that slap had released all the pent-up anger she had been holding on to.

"If you all don't mind, I'm going to get her settled into a guest room," Bethany said. She cast a sideways glance at Whitfield, the ultimate cause of her own death. She then looked back at Will, Cadence, and Snow. "It's been a long night for all of us. She needs some rest. We can work on figuring out her next steps tomorrow."

Snow nodded. "That sounds quite reasonable," he said. "I would imagine you have a few things to sort through yourself right now, as well. We'll reconvene tomorrow."

"Wait, what are you doing about him for now?" Cadence pointed to Whitfield as she asked this. "You can't just let him go on his own recognizance."

"Calm down," Snow said as Bethany led Lauren out of the office. He picked up the cube he had tucked between himself and the sofa arm. "This is a portable prison cell, much like Overton's urn. And like Overton's urn, it is a null space. No magic or spirit power can be used in there. I'm told the inside is a small version of our prison cells, just a white box. But it is portable. To use if a prisoner still has use to us." Snow then turned his attention to Whitfield. "Do you agree to this?"

Whitfield nodded. "Yeah. It will be easier for you guys to have me around this way." Whitfield then turned to Cadence. "You will never know how deeply I regret how this turned out."

"Why? Because you got caught?" The anger in Cadence's voice was as palpable as her grief.

"No," Whitfield said. "Because of Sam. Because of Overton and what he did to you. Because of Lauren's ex-husband. Because of Bethany. If you want your pound of flesh from me, I won't fight back."

Cadence stood there, staring at Whitfield for a minute. Her jade eyes were still blazing with anger and hatred. "Not right now. But maybe later," she added.

Whitfield nodded. He then reached out a hand and touched the cube that Snow was holding. The cube lit up and Whitfield began to drift apart as if he were a creature made of smoke and steam. The cube drew in the smokey, dissolving form of Whitfield. Once he was gone, the cube's light changed from white to red. Snow moved to his desk, opened a drawer, and put the cube in the drawer.

"Safely tucked away," he said as he locked the drawer and put the key in his pocket.

"Cool," Will said. "I always thought that one would be handy."

"You made that?" Snow asked.

"Yeah," Will nodded. "I wanted to do a Rubik's cube and have each little cube be its own cell, but I couldn't make it work any smaller than that."

"Very inventive of you," Snow said with a smile to the young man.

"We should probably go check in on Aiden and the others. See how they're doing," Cadence said.

"No. You are going home," Snow said. "This is a case that isn't just going to snowball out of control; it's going to avalanche. We are all going to need our rest. Aiden and Derrick are going to have to deal with a lot, but for the next few hours, they are going to have to deal with it without us."

"I agree, for what it's worth," Will said. "I have a feeling that this is going to get a hell of a lot crazier before we put it to bed. We should all get some rest."

"Go home," Snow said gently. "Ramon is waiting for you. You won't be alone."

Cadence blinked a few times in succession, fighting back the tears and emotions she had been struggling to control. Unable to find her voice in that moment, she nodded. Then she teleported home.

"Think she's actually going to go home?" Will asked.

"I do," Snow nodded. "She lasted longer than I thought she would, given everything that's gone on. She knows she needs to get those emotions out."

"She's tough, I'll give her that," Will said. "I'm not sure if I would be able to do all of this after seeing my sibling get vaporized. And I know I wouldn't be able to hold back from whaling on the guy responsible."

"Oh, I have no doubt that in a day or two, we'll be calling in Ramon to stitch up Whitfield," Snow said with a tired smile. "She'll exact her punishment. You were superb tonight, Will. I know this was a test of fire for you."

"The test is still going on," Will said with a grin. "This was just part one. But thank you. I'm gonna go. I need to get some rest and work on some things."

"I'll check in with you both tomorrow," Snow said. Both teleported out of Snow's office.

Snow arrived in the hallway in front of his apartment door. He stood still for a moment, listening. He could hear the low timber of Ramon's voice through the door of Cadence's apartment, which was right across the hall from his. He could hear her sobbing. He clenched his jaw, his chin quivering for a moment before turning and heading into his own apartment. He had his own emotions to deal with as well.

CHAPTER 2

The Day After

Aiden's van was parked in the lot outside Lauren's new-age shop. Aiden, Derrick, and Teeny were all sitting there in silence. They were all exhausted and drained. It had taken a few hours with the police, though Andy Halleran had taken the brunt of the questioning. Andy had made sure that they had gotten their stories straight before the police and ambulance arrived.

Andy had been working security for the group. They were doing a ghost investigation of the farm. That was easy enough to confirm with Paul Phillips. A large wild boar had charged through the trees and, before anyone could react, flung Lauren into the air. She cracked her skull on the stone when she landed. There was nothing anyone could do.

All of it was true. Except for the boar part. But a wild boar would be more believable than a huge non-human creature had opened a portal and disappeared. And for now, Andy wanted to keep the part of his captain's involvement under wraps. He had some figuring out to do about that and needed time to think.

"What the hell do we do now?" Derrick broke the silence to ask the question.

"We try to cope," Aiden said, rubbing his face.

"How?" Derrick had tears in his eyes as he looked at Aiden. "How the hell do we cope with this?"

"I don't know," Aiden said, his voice quiet. "We'll have to figure it out."

"The ghosts you guys work with," Teeny said from her seat behind them in the van, "can they answer questions?"

"Maybe," Aiden said again. He then pointed to the green, felt, four-leaf clover on the dashboard. It had been there since they had parked fifteen minutes ago. It hadn't moved. "But I don't think they're here. Remember, she lost her brother tonight. For good."

"Shit, I hadn't thought of that," Derrick said. He had been so consumed with Lauren's death he hadn't thought of the loss of Sam.

"Who lost their brother?" Teeny asked.

"The female ghost we work with. Her brother was Lauren's guardian angel in a way," Aiden said.

"The one we saw briefly against the dome shield?" Teeny hated asking all these questions at a time like this, but she was desperately trying to catch up. This night had been catastrophic, even more so than the Barrington Prison investigation.

"Yeah," Aiden said with a sigh. He was just staring straight ahead at the shop. "This shouldn't have happened. I don't know how it happened." He slammed his hands against the steering wheel, causing both Derrick and Teeny to jump. "Dammit," he growled. This was the first time he had shown his anger. "What the fuck happened?" He bellowed the question, his voice filling the van and extending beyond. He panted from the force of his yell and felt weak and tired. It was like he had used the last reserves of his energy for that yell.

Teeny reached forward and put her hand on Aiden's shoulder. "We'll figure this out."

"Shit," Derrick said. "I have to call Professor Phillips."

"I texted him when we left," Aiden said. "Told him that we were leaving and that I would be in touch about what happened, but to expect a call from the police."

"What did he say in response?" Derrick asked.

"He didn't," Aiden said. "He's probably asleep."

"Something we should all probably be doing," Teeny said.

"Yeah," Aiden agreed.

Derrick opened the door to the van and got out. "I'll get my backpack from you tomorrow. I don't feel like digging around in the van for it."

"No problem, bro," Aiden said with a nod. "Be careful."

"I will. You too," Derrick said as he slid out of the van and closed the door. He gave Aiden a wave, then walked across the parking space to his car.

Aiden and Teeny watched him go, then Teeny climbed up into the passenger seat.

"Hotel or hospital?" Aiden asked.

"Neither," Teeny answered. "If it's okay with you, I would like to stay with you. I don't think you should be alone."

"I'll be okay," Aiden said.

"Are you saying you don't want me to come home with you?"

Aiden turned in his seat and gave Teeny a look. "No, that's not what I'm saying. But I'm not gonna be great company right now."

"I'm not asking for company," Teeny said with a shrug. "I'm trying to be company."

Aiden thought about it for a moment and then nodded. He started the engine of the van and drove back to his apartment.

The rain was cold, and the sky was gray. Aiden found that appropriate. He hadn't really slept, though it had been nice to have Teeny there. They had both stayed up all night just talking. And crying, if he was being honest. He parked his van outside the New-Age shop. Professor Phillips was meeting him there in an hour. But Aiden needed to begin going through Lauren's files to find things. He had dropped Teeny off at the hospital to check on Liam before heading to the shop.

Aiden unlocked the door and walked in, locking it behind him. He kept the main store lights off. It was going to be a rough day. He went back and started a pot of coffee, going through the motions as he always did. He then sat down in that tiny back office and sighed.

Shelves filled the wall behind the desk. An assort-ment of books was there, from binders with the store's inventory and vendors to books that just interested her. The topmost shelf had a sealed urn in a sealed box. Overton's prison. That was something he was going to have to take home. He didn't want it getting knocked around in a move.

"Jesus," he muttered, looking around the office. "How do I do this?"

After Dan had died so suddenly last year, Lauren had taken it upon herself to make a will. She probably kept that at her home, but Aiden needed the keys to her home. He knew she kept a spare set here. He turned the office chair around as the rich smell of coffee began filling the room. He rolled the chair forward a few inches and reached over to put in the combination for the safe.

Opening it, he found the register till, several deposit bags for the bank, a few files, and a set of keys. He took out the files and the keys. Once the coffee pot had stopped making noise, he grabbed a cup and filled it. He pocketed the keys, then took the files and the coffee out to the table that they had always congregated around.

The store was silent. No music, no customers. He had sat alone at this back table hundreds of times, but he had never been alone in the store. Lauren had always been there with him. It almost made him feel like he was an intruder.

As he was going through the files, he heard a knock on the door. Looking up, he saw Professor Phillips standing there. Aiden rose from his chair and crossed the store at a jog, quickly letting the man in.

"You should have told me," Phillips said as he entered.

"I texted you when we left, as I said I would," Aiden said. The exhaustion in his voice was evident.

"Yeah, but you didn't text me this," the professor countered, taking a newspaper from under his arm and holding it out to Aiden. The professor turned and stormed back to the table.

"Local Store Owner Killed by Wildlife"

It wasn't the top headline, but it was on the front page.

"Shit," Aiden said.

"Yeah, shit," the other man said, running a hand through his shaggy brown hair. "The police were pounding on my door at 5 this morning."

"I'm sorry, bro," Aiden said, joining Professor Phillips at the back table. "When I texted you, there was no answer, so I figured you were asleep. I didn't think about the police coming to you to verify that we were allowed to be there."

"Look, I'm sorry about Lauren," Paul said, pulling back his irritation for a moment as he looked at Aiden's face. Complaining about the police and possibly being linked to yet another death seemed to pale in the face of Aiden's loss. And it was obvious he was taking that loss hard.

"Thank you," Aiden said.

"What happens next?" Paul asked.

"I've been trying to figure that out all night," Aiden said.

"Let me know about the funeral arrangements," the professor said. "I'm helping with them."

"Dude, you don't have to—" Aiden started, but Paul cut him off.

"No, she died doing an investigation for me. You don't get to tell me no." Professor Phillips crossed his arms over his chest. "It's the least I can do."

"I don't even know where to begin with that either," Aiden sighed, sinking down into a chair at the table. When they lost Dan, Lauren had taken care of those things. "I'm going to do some research on it, though."

"Where's Derrick?" Paul asked, noticing that his former student wasn't there.

"Home, asleep I hope," Aiden said.

"And the TV show people?"

"Teeny is at the hospital with Liam," Aiden said. "Russell is either there salivating at the idea of another lawsuit, or he has gone back to California. He tried to horn in on the investigation last night, and Teeny told him to fuck off. And she's quitting the show."

"Good for her," Paul said. "He seemed like an ass."

"Oh, yeah, he is," Aiden said with a slight smile.

"Well, as soon as the police give me the 'all clear,' I'm going to contact people to destroy that house and everything on the property," Paul said. "But I would like to see the footage from last night. Given the stories, I doubt it was a boar that killed her."

"That's why you're the professor," Aiden said. "You're smart. I don't have any of it with me, and it may take me a day or two to even be able to bring myself to watch it. But you do need to see what happened. And for what it's worth, tear the place down, salt and bless the land. Get anything that was there gone before you try to rebuild or sell it."

Paul nodded and sighed. "I'm gonna go. I have a few things to take care of myself. Give me a call in a day or two when you figure out some of the funeral stuff."

"Thanks, man," Aiden said. He got up from his chair and extended a hand to Paul, who shook it in response. "It's appreciated."

Teeny's eyes stung as she walked into Liam's hospital room. After everything that had happened the night before, she was now faced with telling her best friend she was leaving their show. She hoped he would be sleeping for a while. Maybe the hum of the machines would lull her to sleep since she had been up all night with Aiden.

Liam was not asleep. He was sitting up in bed, TV remote in hand, flipping through the mediocre channel offerings that the hospital TV had. His black hair was wild, having not seen a comb in days, and his normally clean-shaven face was sporting a bit of beard growth. He looked over when the door opened and smiled, but the smile faltered as he saw how bad Teeny looked.

"I can probably get you a discount on another bed in here," he said with a smile, trying to joke. When she didn't smile back, he frowned. "What happened?"

Teeny pulled the chair in the room over to his bed and fell into it as if she were deflating. "This is the most conscious I've seen you in days. What do you know?"

"I know you were doing an investigation with Aiden and the others," Liam answered. "I know Russell wasn't happy when he left. He made some comments about you having lost your sense of direction, but he knew you would come back, whatever that meant. I'll be honest, this is the first day that doesn't feel blurry."

"That's good," Teeny said with a smile. "That must mean they're bringing the pain meds down a bit. Do you hurt?"

"A little bit, but it's not bad," Liam replied.

"Well, it's good to see you awake enough to be getting annoyed about not being able to find something to watch," Teeny said.

"Smooth move McGroove," he said. "I'm not changing the subject. What happened?"

"How awake are you feeling? I have a lot of ground to cover," Teeny said.

"Lay it on me," Liam said with a nod. "If I forget, you can remind me later, like you usually do when I forget things." He offered her a smile. It was a real smile. Like the smiles they used to share before their show took off and he began to care more about the celebrity side of things than the actual work or their friendship.

Teeny began the story with what had happened at Barrington Prison. She filled him in on Russell coming to town and being a sleaze. Then she ended the story with everything that had happened in the last 24 hours. She did leave out the part about finding the footage from his camera and seeing exactly what happened to him. She didn't trust that he wouldn't tell Russell.

"Holy shit," Liam said, resting his head back on his pillow. "You've been through hell."

"Little bit, yeah," Teeny said with a nod. "There is one more thing." She was twisting her hands around each other, fidgeting with her fingers.

"Oh?" Liam lifted his head from his pillow to give her his full attention.

"I kind of quit the show," she said.

Liam blinked. "You did what now?"

"I can't stand working with Russell," Teeny said. "Between you getting hurt and the bullshit he tried to pull down here, it was just the last straw. My contract is up. I'm not renewing it."

"Come on, Teeny," Liam said. "I need you. Who else is going to keep me honest?"

"You'll have to find someone else," she said, shaking her head. "I can't do it anymore."

"What are you going to do?" Liam asked.

"Stay here," she replied. She smiled a little at the look of shock on his face. "I've had a lot of time to talk with Aiden. I'm going to keep going with my research, maybe write a book or something. I don't know."

"Come out to California from time to time to hang out with an old friend?" Liam moved his hand to reach out for hers, which she took.

"Of course," she said with a smile.

The door opened and Dr. Michaels walked in, pushing his glasses up on the bridge of his nose. "It's good to see you up," he said with a smile as he saw Liam sitting up in bed. "How are you feeling? Do you have any pain?"

"A little," Liam said. "The nurses have kept me comfortable."

"That's good to hear," the doctor said. "Your last round of tests from yesterday came back. As I'm sure you can tell, we're starting to wean you off the strong stuff." The doctor had put on latex gloves as he spoke and lifted the sheets at the bottom of the bed. He ran his fingers along the bottom of Liam's feet. "Can you feel that?"

"Yeah, it tickles," he said, his feet twitching, then he winced. "And trying to move hurts, damn."

"Right leg?"

"Yep," Liam answered with a grimace as the pain continued.

"That's to be expected," the dark-haired doctor with a thinning hairline said. He turned and logged into the computer near the door so he could make notes on Liam's chart. "So, there's good news. It doesn't look like we're going to have to do any more surgeries on you. We're going to start tapering you off the pain meds so we can work toward releasing you. Do you have an orthopedist to follow up with in California?"

"No," Liam replied.

"I'll make some calls," Dr. Michaels said. "Find a good referral for you out there."

"How long until you spring me?"

"There are still a couple of variables left to determine it, but it should be soon. Not today, but soon," the doctor said. He gave both Teeny and Liam a smile and a nod, then left the room.

"Congrats on the imminent jailbreak," Teeny said to Liam.

"Thanks," Liam said.

A shrill ringing came from the phone built into the hospital bed's railing.

"That thing startles the crap out of me every time," Liam said. He grabbed the phone. "Hello?"

Teeny leaned back in her chair and closed her eyes for a moment. She was asleep before she knew it.

CHAPTER 3

Go Big or Go Home

Aiden had opened the store. It had felt like the right thing to do. At the very least, there might be some sales, so that he would have less to box up to send back to vendors or to put in storage. Some people had come up to the shop to light some candles and lay some flowers in front of the window in memory of Lauren. He hadn't expected that, but the thought made him smile a little, to know that she was so well remembered and loved.

The bell over the door chimed and Aiden looked up to see Tom, the currently indigo-haired owner of Pho-Q walking in. He stopped, seeing Aiden behind the counter, and shook his head.

"So, the story in the paper was true?" Tom asked.

"Yeah, it's true," Aiden said with a sigh. It was not the first time he had given that answer today.

"Damn," Tom said, shaking his head in dismay. "I'm sorry, man. Anything we can do for you guys?"

"Nah," Aiden said. "I'm going to be working on closing up the shop."

"Why not keep it open?" Tom asked with a shrug as he came over to the counter where the tall, shaggy-haired, grief-stricken man stood. "Can't hurt to have a place with this kind of stock at your fingertips with the kind of stuff you guys get up to. Or are you and Derrick not continuing with it?"

"He and I really haven't talked much since this morning," Aiden said. "I assume he'll come in when he gets up. Unless he has homework or class or something."

"Well, you guys come by when you get hungry," Tom said. "The food's on us."

"Thanks, bro," Aiden said.

Tom nodded and headed out. He held the door open for a woman coming in with flowers. Aiden directed her to put them outside with the candles and other flowers that people had been leaving. He recognized the woman as someone who had been a regular customer of Lauren's. Once she had left the shop and put her flowers in with the growing memorial, Aiden bent over, leaning his elbows on the glass case, and rested his head in his hands. He was beyond exhausted and numb.

"How do I do this, Lauren?" he asked out loud to the uninhabited room.

The bell chimed again, and Derrick walked in. He must have gotten into the van because he had his backpack slung over his shoulder. He looked like he hadn't slept much, if at all. Aiden walked over to him and gave him a hug. That was an action that took Derrick by surprise, but he hugged his friend back.

"Okay, that was weird," Derrick said. "Cool, but weird."

"Yeah, well, I figured we both could use it," Aiden said with a shrug. "We've got each other." It had been in the back of his mind all day. They had lost Bethany, they had lost Dan, now Lauren. Their little paranormal group was down to him and Derrick. Teeny might join them, but he wasn't even sure there was going to be a group left after the next few days.

Derrick nodded and made his way back to the table they always sat at. "How come you have the store open?"

"I have work to do in here anyway," Aiden said, answering Derrick. "Figured I would open it up and see if I can offload some of the inventory. And people have been coming in all day."

"I saw the little memorial out front," Derrick said with a nod.

"How are you doing?" Aiden asked.

"I would figure I'm doing better than you. You knew her longer," Derrick said with a shrug.

"Doesn't mean you don't have your own grief," Aiden said. "Last night was bad."

"Yeah," Derrick said, shuddering a little. He kept hearing Lauren's head hitting the rock. When he closed his eyes, all he could see was her body in the black bag with her head cracked open as they zipped her up. He wasn't about to say any of that to Aiden. He knew his friend would be struggling with the same things.

"So, the question is, where do we go from here?" Aiden let Derrick think about that for a moment as he disappeared into the back office. When he returned, he had two cups of coffee in hand. He sat down and passed one cup to Derrick, keeping the other for himself.

"Thanks," Derrick said, taking the offered cup. "And, that's a question I was going to ask you."

"I figure any decision about the group comes from both of us," Aiden said. "We're the last two left."

"Do I lose points if I say I'm a little scared after last night?" Derrick looked at Aiden, fearing the man's opinion of him saying that.

"No bro, not at all. I am, too," Aiden said, much to Derrick's relief. "What happened last night was scary shit. I'm scared. I'm scared of what happened, what we saw, what we know. I'm scared of screwing up whatever it is that comes next. So no, you don't lose points for being scared."

"Have you heard from them?" Derrick pointed his finger up and swirled it around in the air as he asked the question.

"Not a word," Aiden said. "But given what we saw, I didn't expect to." As an afterthought, he fished the green, felt clover out of his pocket, and put it on the table. He hadn't thought to put it out before.

"So, you're closing the shop," Derrick said, looking around. "It's going to be weird not coming here anymore."

"I know," Aiden said with a sigh as he ran a hand through his hair, pushing it back off his face. "I mean, I could keep it open, but I don't know what I would do with it. I'm not a psychic. I'm an audio/video guy."

"Photo studio?" Derrick had always wondered why Aiden didn't have his own studio. He operated based on business cards, online ads, and word of mouth.

"I don't know," Aiden shrugged. "Never really thought of opening one."

"How long is left on the lease?" Derrick asked.

"I have to find it," Aiden said. "I think it's in a file here. I want to say maybe five or six months. I know Lauren was thinking of closing."

"She was?" Derrick couldn't conceal his surprise.

"Yeah," Aiden said, nodding. "With all the cases we were getting, her hours here were getting weird. She said people had been complaining that they didn't know when to come in. She and I had been talking about whether we should renew the lease for another year or not. She had also talked about turning it more into a paranormal geared place instead of a New-Age shop."

"Which brings us back to the question of if we will be doing any more investigations," Derrick said, leaning back in his chair.

"Yep," Aiden said. "It's a vicious circle, isn't it? I've been going around and around with it all day."

"Come to any conclusions?" Derrick was hoping Aiden had answers.

"Nothing concrete," Aiden said. "I think we both need to think about it. With us being in the papers at Christmas for the college dorm thing, and now with this, who knows? We may not get any more cases. People may be too scared to call us."

"Or they might figure we're really good and we get even more cases," Derrick said.

"Maybe," Aiden said with a slow nod. "I'll be honest. It might be best to table the discussion until we get through the funeral. I have decided one thing, though.

I'm getting a damned haircut. This shaggy crap is starting to piss me off."

Derrick chuckled a little and nodded, then looked at his phone as it rang and winced. "Shit, it's my mom. I'll be right back." Derrick grabbed his phone as he got up and answered it.

"Hey Mom," he said as he made his way out the door.

A cold breeze was filtering in through the broken windows at Barrington Prison. Not that any of the remaining residents there noticed or cared. The ghosts that were still there were far from being bothered by the cold.

They had spent the last several days and nights trying to corral the bits and blobs of sorrow, regret, and anger of all those who had been executed at the end of the hangman's noose when Barrington had been an operational prison back into the gallows building. They were the pieces that had congealed to pull the lever and send Liam crashing down to the concrete floor. With the glass broken, and EMS going in and out, the pieces of souls that had once been contained in that building had gotten out. They had divided and gone all over the prison.

Roland got the chain back on the door to the execution room when he felt the now-familiar tingle that someone had arrived at the prison. He teleported into the lobby of the prison, with its dingy orange plastic chairs. He looked around, but there was no one there. It didn't even look like the door had physically opened. *So, a ghostly visitor then?* He teleported to the rotunda, with its cracked and broken tiles. But there was no one there either. Roland furrowed his brow as he pulled out his cell phone. Checking it, he could see that there had been no missed calls from Riley or Snow, or anyone else, for that matter. However, the feeling that there was someone there persisted.

A crashing sound made him whirl around to face the arm of the prison that housed the rec room. Another prisoner teleported down as the door to the rec room blew out.

"What the hell was that?" the mullet-wearing blond man named Waylon asked as he stopped beside Roland.

"Not sure," Roland answered as two more prisoners teleported in behind him and Waylon.

The doors of the rec room had burst from their casing with such force and hit the opposite wall so hard that they lodged themselves in the concrete. All four of the spirits in the rotunda jumped. An oily black shape stretched itself languidly out of the now-open doorway.

"God dammit," Waylon cursed. "I thought we got all them damn things."

"I don't think that's one of them," Roland said. His eyes were glued to the dark shape, and he blanched as his mind figured out what he was seeing. An arm. The shape coming through the doorway so far had just been one massive arm with thick, taloned fingers at the end.

"Shit, get the others," Roland said, aware that there weren't that many others left to get. He could hear the masonry of the building straining. A couple of spirits disappeared to get those who remained. In doing so, they missed the volley of cinderblocks that exploded from the doorway, widening it enough to let the mon-strosity out.

A soft glow came from behind the creature, indicating that the portal was open. The portal didn't concern Roland now, however. Keeping everyone safe did. Five yellow eyes leveled at Roland, focusing on him as he pulled his phone back out of the pocket of his uniform.

"Where?" The voice of the creature echoed loudly in Roland's head.

Roland staggered under the volume, the reverberations in his head driving him down on one knee. He pushed the speed dial button for Snow. He had no idea that Snow had been promoted and a new number had taken its place. The call re-routed itself to Will.

"B-Barrington Prison," Roland stammered, trying to comprehend what the hell was in front of him other than some monstrous oil-slick dipped toad with way too many eyes and talons and teeth that belonged on no creature. "Who are you?" Roland tried to make the question sound demanding and authoritative, but he had never been one to lead.

With a roar, the creature moved faster than its mass would have indicated it could. The rest of the inmates teleported into the room as X'Haldzos launched himself into the air, hurtling at Roland. The menacing, overlarge talons tore through Roland's chest, severing the man's left arm from his body.

"Hello?" Will's sleepy voice came through the cell phone as Roland screamed. The phone clattered to the floor in the hand of the now severed arm.

The demon wasted no time in tearing into his new prey. He enjoyed the confusion, the pain, and the terror that the man and those around him felt.

"Hello?" Will asked again, his voice louder and sounding far less sleepy now. Silver blood splattered over the phone, soaking into its crevices and holes.

Will could hear general noises of alarm and pain. The remaining spirits were trying to fight the thing off, trying to get it off of Roland. Roland, for his part, let out one more gurgle of pain as the creature pulled him in half like a child trying to split a taffy piece in two.

Seeing Roland fall, the spirits redouble their attack with shards of tile, energy attacks, and anything they could muster in the moment. Some made quick weapons like brass knuckles or knives. Others went barehanded. X'Haldzos could feel their paltry attacks, and his muscles twitched. The demon felt his power flare at the annoyance of their persistence.

He turned, facing the spirits fully, his whole body inflating as he did. He roared. The sound waves not only drove the spirits back, but the walls of the prison buckled and fell outwards. Silver blood poured from the sockets where the spirits' eyes had been. The walls toppled like dominoes after the first few went down. X'Haldzos began eating the now blinded prisoners, even as the spirit body of Roland began to dissolve now that his life force was completely gone.

Dust plumes began to rise from the demolition of the building and drift on the cold breeze. Between the power of X'Haldzos's roar and the state of disrepair the building had been in, the structure easily fell in many areas.

At length, having eaten his fill, X'Haldzos turned and began his trek back to the glowing portal. His hunger was sated for the moment, and his energy was drained from the expenditure of power. He had not found the one he had been looking for, but he had at least found a good meal. He might return to this spot. It might prove a safe place to rest, especially with the portal so close. For now, however, he knew the destruction would draw others. And he was too tired to deal with that right now.

As X'Haldzos disappeared into the portal, Will appeared in what remained of the rotunda. As if to emphasize the destruction, a tile on the far side of the rotunda fell from one of the few walls that remained and shattered into pieces on the floor.

"Hello?" Will called out as the dust began to slowly descend. Will could see silvery blood everywhere in the rotunda. And over to his left, in a pool of it, he saw the monitor's cell phone. He didn't want to call Cadence. She had been through enough in the last 24 hours. But he knew he was well out of his depth here. He pulled out his phone and pressed the speed dial button for his new partner.

An annoying and persistent ringing sound pulled Cadence from her fitful sleep. She could feel Ramon's arm over her, and she didn't want to move. The ringing would not stop. After a moment, she realized it was her phone and reached over to answer it if only to get it to stop ringing.

"Riley," she said, her voice thick with sleep. She hadn't even looked at the caller ID.

"Dude!" Will's voice came over the phone. "You need to get to Barrington Prison, like now."

The urgency in Will's voice brought Cadence fully awake. "What's up?" she asked, her tone sharp as she sat up.

Ramon shifted, sitting up in bed beside her, rubbing her arm, and looking concerned.

"You've got to see this to believe it," Will said. "And I'm sorry to disturb you, but I wouldn't call if it wasn't, like, a big thing. Just get here. Please."

"On my way," Cade said. She swung her feet out of bed as she hung up.

"What's going on?" Ramon asked.

"I'm not sure," she said. "Something's going on at Barrington."

"That sounds ominous. Be careful," Ramon said.

"I will be," Cadence said as she mentally changed from her pajamas to black pants, a pale green blouse, and a black blazer. Her honey-blonde hair went from falling around her face into a neat ponytail. "I'll talk to you later. And thanks for being here for me last night. You have no idea how much it meant."

"Any time, mi amore," Ramon said with a soft smile. "See you later."

A moment later, Cadence was at the imposing front doors of Barrington Prison. Or at least where the imposing front doors should have been. Will was standing amid the rubble of the prison. Bricks, stones, shattered glass, and wood lay strewn in almost every direction. It reminded Cadence of how the roof of the farmhouse at Scarecrow Farms had been blown out. Except this was on a much larger scale.

"What on Earth happened?" Cadence asked.

"I was kinda hoping you could explain it to me," Will said, moving over to her. "No one is here. There is not a single spirit left. And look," he said as he led Cadence over to where the rotunda had been. He pointed and Cadence could see the liberal silvery splashes of spirit blood.

"Holy shit," Cadence said under her breath.

"This is where you and Snow thought the portal at Scarecrow Farms went, right? To this prison?" Will asked.

"Yeah," Cade said with a nod.

"I'd say this supports your theory," Will said. "But if that's true, then where did X'Haldzos go?"

"Back in the portal, maybe? How did you know to come here?" Cadence kneeled in the rubble to touch the streak of blood closest to her.

"I got a call," Will said. "I think it was the monitor. The ID came up here, but then all I heard was a guy screaming, then nothing." Will looked shaken as he spoke. Cadence was unnerved as well. She rose and pulled out her phone. After hitting a couple of buttons, she held it to her ear and waited.

"Snow," Cadence said as the other end was picked up. "I know you love it when I'm redundant, but we have a problem." She paused, then nodded. "We'll be right there."

"Our office or his?" Will asked.

"His," Cade said. "But we might need to go to the observation bay when he hears what happened. They may have footage of what happened. I can't imagine one of them seeing this happen and not sounding some kind of alarm."

The two left the prison and appeared in the waiting area of Snow's office.

"Good morning, you two," Bonnie said. The elderly secretary to the director looked cheerful, as always. Her silver hair was pinned up and her blue eyes sparkled from behind her glasses.

"Morning, Bonnie," Cadence said, trying to muster a smile for the woman. She had always liked Bonnie, but cheerfulness was just not something she could handle right now.

"Snow should be expecting us," Will said.

The door to Snow's office opened, and the Englishman stood there in all his tweed glory. "I am expecting you, yes," Snow said. He nodded to Bonnie and then ushered Will and Cadence inside. "So, what is the problem we have now?" he asked. "In addition to our other ones, of course."

"Barrington Prison blew up," Cadence said, her brows furrowed.

"Is that a euphemism for something?" Snow knew her penchant for modern slang, which he didn't understand half of the time.

"No," Cadence said with a shake of her head. "I mean, it very literally blew up. It's just a pile of rubble now. The whole thing. Gone."

"Did Roland call you?" Snow asked, surprise clear in his voice.

"I think he called me," Will said. "But when I answered, all I heard were screams."

"Spirit blood is all over the place," Cadence said. "It looks like it exploded from the rotunda out. The front entrance is gone, the rotunda is gone, and the parts of the wings that were close to the center are in shambles."

Snow sighed. "So, it sounds like our escaped non-human did go to the prison then. How long ago did you receive the call?"

"About 15 minutes ago," Will said. "I went there and looked around, but there was nothing there. No one left. I didn't want to bother Riley, but I didn't know what else to do."

"You did the right thing, Will," Cadence said.

Snow nodded, knowing full well that Cadence was excellent at walling herself off from her feelings in order to get the job done. "You were right to call her, just as she was right to call me." Snow then moved to his door and opened it. "Bonnie, could you be dear and find out which terminal monitors Barrington Prison, if there is one?"

"Yes, sir," Bonnie chirped.

Snow closed the door once more. He was going to have to tell Bonnie about what happened last night before she asked Cadence where her brother was, but he hadn't had a chance to do that yet. He sat down at his desk and gestured for Will and Cade to have seats as well. He avoided asking Cadence how she was doing. He knew all too well. He could see it in the tightness of her facial expression and the circles under her eyes.

"Was there any kind of track or trail going from the prison?" Snow asked. "When this thing moved from the house to the portal, it broke trees in its wake." *And bodies,* but he wasn't going to say that part.

"No, there was no indication of where it may have gone," Will said.

"The execution building was still standing," Cadence offered. "I don't think it went back that way."

"What about the portal room?" Snow looked between them as he asked the question. "Was it intact?"

"I don't know where that is," Will said with a shrug.

"Give me a sec," Cadence stood up and disappeared. She reappeared in the same place a minute later. "Yes," she said. "It's intact, kind of. The doors are blown off, and there is a demon-sized hole in the wall leading from the room to the hallway. I think the rotunda's where Roland was when he called." Cadence put a phone on Snow's desk. It was the one they had given to Roland when he became the monitor. It was broken and covered in silvery blood.

Snow sighed and pinched the bridge of his nose as he closed his eyes. "Given this, it is possible that this thing used the portal system again and could be anywhere."

"Because today wasn't great enough, right?" Cadence said, her voice sour.

Snow's desk phone buzzed, and he hit the button on it for the intercom. "Yes, Bonnie?"

"I'm sorry, sir," came Bonnie's voice over the intercom. "Because Barrington Prison was monitored, they didn't have anyone dedicated to watching it. There is no footage."

"Thank you, Bonnie," Snow said. He then hung up. "All we have to go on is after-the-fact conjecture and theories."

"Not that I want to see or talk to him again, ever," Cadence said, "but do you think Whitfield would have any information?"

"It's possible," Snow said. "But we have more pressing issues at the moment."

"More pressing than a prison blowing up and all the spirits inside being slaughtered?" Will asked.

"Yes, we have a new soul who is trying to decide what to do with her afterlife," Snow said. "And we do have some direct involvement in her being on this side, after all."

Bethany and Lauren walked into Snow's office. The angelic-looking counselor guided her older, plumper friend to have a seat on the sofa. Cadence, Snow, and Will joined them. Once everyone had settled on the sofas and said their hellos, the real conversation began.

"Lauren, how are you doing?" It was Cadence who asked the first question.

"I'm still kind of numb," Lauren said. "And shocked. I never expected what happened."

"Neither did we," Will said.

"I remember that numbness. It will wear off in time," Cadence said. "Depending on what you decide, for all I know, you may want to continue being that way forever."

Bethany put her hand over Lauren's. "You can choose to go to your personal version of heaven or hell. Moving on to that level, you would meet another counselor who would then determine, from your own values and religion, where to place you."

"Or," Snow countered, "you can choose to help us on this side. I believe your strengths in life would lead you to help someone like you. Become what Sam was to you." Inwardly, Snow winced at having to say the young man's name. He knew hearing it would further hurt Cadence. He had a job to do, though, and he had to be clear with Lauren.

Lauren nodded slowly as she listened. "Bethany, I appreciate the offer of heaven. But I want to help. In whatever capacity I can do so best. Dan gave his life, or afterlife really, to help. As did Sam." Lauren turned her eyes to Cadence, who was sitting very still, trying her best to not react to the sound of her brother's name.

"I owe you an apology, Cadence," Lauren said. "I shouldn't have lashed out at you. I was in a fog last night, and the anger was the only thing that was clearing that fog away."

Cadence hadn't been expecting that. She was used to getting an angry reaction from Lauren. "Thank you," the detective said. "And I do get it. Snow can tell you I wasn't the nicest or easiest person to manage when I got here, either."

Snow nodded, agreeing with Cade. "She was a bit unruly at the start."

"Normal or not," Lauren said, "it was wrong. You lost him too, and he was far more to you than to me. But if you are okay with me staying, I think I would like to help others, like Sam did with me. Is that okay?"

Bethany leaned over and gave Lauren a hug. "That would be wonderful."

"And timely," Snow said.

"Oh?" Lauren turned from hugging Bethany back to focusing her attention on Snow.

"We have a very dangerous non-human out there somewhere that needs to be taken down," Snow said. "We have a group of living people that we work with that just lost their leader. Their new leader has been becoming more and more sensitive due to our involvement and communications with him."

"Aiden is becoming psychic?" Both Bethany and Lauren looked surprised, but it was Lauren who had asked the question.

"Not psychic necessarily," Cadence said. "But it is getting easier and easier to communicate with him without the use of the spirit box. He is a sensitive. Given the fact that your group is the one we work with, and we are the only team right now that works with any breathers, they could use the help."

"We try not to put people who knew each other in life together unless there is a good reason. It can make the acceptance of death harder for both the spirit and the living." Bethany looked between Snow and Lauren as she said this.

"I know," Snow said. "But in this case, I think it might be the best. Aiden and Lauren worked well together in life. Due to her own sensitivity, I would wager she has a good deal of power to be able to protect him. And she is aware of our situation and how this team works, to some extent, already."

"Sounds like a no-brainer to me," Will said.

"Would the counseling section accept the placement?" Cadence asked with a look at Bethany.

Bethany pursed her lips for a moment, her blue eyes cast down to her lap as she thought. At length, she nodded. "Yes, I believe that given the situation, they would accept it."

"Good," Snow said with a nod. "Did you take her for her goodbyes last night?"

"Neither Aiden nor Derrick slept," Bethany said. "We did get the other goodbyes done."

Lauren sighed. The goodbyes had been hard enough for her family and favorite places. But watching Derrick pace his dorm room like a zombie had been harder. Seeing Aiden cry had damn near broken her. The only other time she had seen him that broken up had been when Bethany was murdered.

"Perhaps they will sleep tonight," Snow said. "But the goodbye can be modified."

"Are we about to break more rules?" Cadence asked with a faint smile.

Snow was glad to see that small smile, that sliver of who she was cracking through her carefully composed grief. "Yes, your favorite part," he answered.

"What are you suggesting?" Bethany asked.

"Take her to them, or we can," Snow said. "Then Lauren can explain what is going to happen and that she will be with them. Well, with Aiden in specific, of course, but still. I'm sure you get the idea."

"Well, since we're breaking rules anyway," Cadence began, "could we take her? I need to talk with both, anyway. We still haven't gotten to go over everything at Barrington, let alone Scarecrow Farms. And if we're going to be this transparent with them, they at least should meet Will as well."

Snow thought about that for a few minutes. "We should go. All of us."

"All?" Bethany asked, taken aback by the suggestion.

"If I'm going to break a few rules, I might as well make it worth getting in trouble for, wouldn't you say?" Snow asked Cadence.

A genuine smile crept onto her face. "Oh wow, I am rubbing off on you."

Snow nodded a bit, matching her smile with his. "I want you to go to them. See if you can arrange a slumber party of sorts. Get Derrick to spend the night at Aiden's. That new girl who seems to be sticking around, too, so long as she doesn't put me in another damned box."

"Teeny," Cadence said with a nod. "Okay. What's the plan, though? Are you just trying to get them all together so dream-walking them is easier?"

"No," Snow replied. He was nervous about this plan, but it was the best way to get everyone on the same page. "We're all going to have a meeting together. Bethany, if you would be so kind as to get Lauren settled into a permanent residence. Will, I'm sure you can go to the NHD department and get some protective equipment for Lauren to have on her. Not to mention some for all of us as well."

"If you won't need me until tonight, I may be able to make a few more toys as well," Will said.

"Do it," Snow said with a nod. "We will reconvene at Aiden's apartment this evening. Is that amenable to everyone?" He looked as they all nodded at him. "Good," Snow said. "Cadence, go to Aiden and get this evening arranged. The rest of you have your assignments."

The meeting broke up with Bethany and Lauren leaving first. Will waved to Cadence and Snow as he made his way out of the office as well. Once they were alone, Snow closed the short distance between himself and Cadence to give his old partner a hug. She hugged him back, taking comfort in the bond between them.

"I'm scared," she admitted.

"I can understand why," Snow said. He was glad to see that she was at long last coming to terms with the fact that she didn't have to hide her emotions all the time. Six months ago, she would never have admitted such a feeling.

She let Snow go from the hug and took a step back. Her nose stung as tears welled in her eyes. "I feel lost."

"I know," he said, his voice soft. "It will get better. Hopefully, tonight will ease some of your fears. I'm sure Ramon will help ease others."

Cadence made a face at Snow for the Ramon reference. "I'll go see about arranging this little shindig for you," she said. "I have to say I am impressed. I never thought you would just toss the whole damned rule book out the window."

"What is it you like to say?" Snow said. "Go big or go home?"

That brought a laugh from Cadence, who shook her head. "Well, you are going big, that's for damned sure. I'm glad you're in charge, because it's going to be your ass in the sling if the council finds out and doesn't approve."

"I believe the sway of one of the members will help in convincing them to turn a blind eye to the situation," Snow said. "Given the threat that is looming out there right now."

Cadence nodded. "I hope so," she said. "I'll see you later."

"Oh, one more thing," Snow said.

"Yeah?"

"Do you think you could possibly get your Detective Halleran to join in as well?"

Cadence lifted her eyebrows in surprise. "You want Andy in on all of this, too?"

"He is involved, and could be of great help," Snow said. "Especially with the knowledge that our Wolf is his captain."

"I'll try," Cadence said with a nod. She then turned and left Snow's office.

CHAPTER 4

Slumber Party

The bells to the side of the door tinkled together as Cadence entered the New-Age store. Aiden was at the register, selling someone a bunch of candles. He looked up at the noise, acknowledging it, and finished the transaction. The woman left with her bag of candles. She paused outside to take one out of the bag and light it. She then set it down on the sidewalk outside the shop, adding it to the memorial for Lauren. After the woman was gone, Aiden moved to the door, flipped the sign to "Closed," and locked the door.

"I heard the bells," Derrick said from the back table. He had already gone into the back office and gotten the spirit box.

"You're on your toes," Aiden said as he folded himself into a chair. Out of habit, he pulled the crumpled, green, felt clover out of his pocket and put it on the table.

Cadence chuckled to herself about the old practice. It was just the two of them. He could have just turned on the box. She swiped the clover off the table, and it fell to the floor. Derrick turned on the spirit box.

"Afternoon," Cade said, hearing her voice come out of the static a moment later.

"Hey, Cadence," Aiden said, his voice sounding tired. "Is Lauren with you now?" He was hoping for some sign of her being okay.

"I've seen her, and that's really all I can say about it for right now," Cadence said. "How are you two doing?"

"Not awesome," Derrick said.

"Ditto," said Aiden. "And I'd imagine you're about the same after losing Sam."

"Yeah," Cade said. "It's not been the best 36 hours ever. And I am about to make the king of strange requests." She paused for just a moment to let her words go through the box. "Aiden, how would you feel about hosting a sleepover tonight?"

"I'm sorry, do what now?" Both men looked puzzled and surprised, but it was Aiden who asked the question.

"You, Derrick, Teeny, and Andy if he'll join in," Cadence said. "You would have to call him and ask, but you can tell him it's at my request."

"What's going on?" Derrick asked.

"They want a meeting with all of us," Aiden said to Derrick. He was catching on to what Cade was planning. "The best way to do that would be in dreams."

"Yes," Cadence said. "We need a meeting. I think Snow plans to lay everything out. It's going to be him and me, my new partner, Bethany, and Lauren."

"I thought laying everything out was against the rules," Derrick said.

"It is," Cadence said. "But we're in crisis mode now. And believe me, when Snow starts throwing rules out the window, it's a big deal. When he's voluntarily throwing the big rules out the window, that's momentous."

Aiden whistled low. "Damn. Okay, I'll call Teeny and Andy. See if I can get them to come over. You were right though; this is the king of all weird requests," Aiden said.

"Yeah, I know," Cadence said with a chuckle. "Mind if I stick around for the phone calls? That way, I know what to tell Snow when I go back."

"I thought Snow wasn't working with you anymore," Derrick said.

"He's my boss now," Cadence replied. "He got a promotion."

"Okay, I'm gonna turn off the box now so I can call without a ton of static in the background, ok?" Aiden asked.

"Go for it, I'll be here," Cadence said.

Aiden clicked the box off and grabbed his phone from his pants pocket. He dialed a number and held the phone to his ear, waiting while it rang. "Hey, Andy, it's Aiden." He paused while Andy spoke. "I'm hanging in. Thanks. How are you?" Another pause as Andy answered. Derrick was staring at the table but listening to Aiden's side of the conversation.

"Hey, listen, I have a strange request for you," Aiden said. "I've been requested by our mutual friend to put together a little meeting tonight at my place. Kind of a sleepover." He paused again as Andy spoke on the other end of the phone. "Yeah, I know. I said it was weird. You, me, Derrick, and Teeny. I think our friends want a kind of meeting. Is eight tonight okay? Okay, cool, see you then."

Aiden hung up with Andy. "Okay, he's in. He'll be at my apartment around 8 or so."

"So next is Teeny," Derrick said.

"Yep," Aiden said, dialing her number. "Hey, Teeny," he said when she answered. "Is Liam okay enough for you to leave him for the night again?" He paused as she spoke. It took a few minutes of her talking for him to speak again. "Wow, that's great news! So, this is going to sound strange, and I apologize in advance, but can you come spend the night at my place?"

Whatever Teeny said made Aiden turn tomato red. Derrick saw it and covered his mouth to keep from laughing out loud. Cadence did laugh out loud, but neither of the men could hear her.

"No, that's not what I meant. I'll explain more there. Let's just say I think you are going to get some of the answers you've been looking for." He paused again for her to respond. "Say around eight tonight? Okay, great, see you then." He hung up and looked at Derrick, who was still trying to cover his laughter.

"Oh my God, what did she say?" the younger man exclaimed. "I have never seen you turn that color before."

"None of your business, that's what she said," Aiden grumbled. He reached over and flipped the box on.

"I want to know what she said, too," Cadence said.

Derrick couldn't contain his laughter anymore and he rocked back in his chair, holding his belly.

"So happy I can entertain you both," Aiden said grumpily.

"Alright, I'm sorry," Cadence said, a grin still tugging at her lips. "I take it they are both in?"

"Yep," Aiden said. "Which means I need to go clean up a little."

"I'll give you a hand," Derrick said.

"I'll see you guys later," Cadence said.

"Later," Aiden said and turned the spirit box off.

Aiden was in his kitchen doing dishes. He could hear the air pump as Derrick used it to inflate the queen-sized mattress he kept in case anyone needed to crash at his place. They had already stopped at the store for some food and drinks. Derrick had vacuumed while Aiden had picked the laundry off his floor and changed his sheets. The air pump stopped, and Aiden could hear the telltale squeaking of the mattress being moved around.

"Bed inflated and ready," Derrick said as he came down the hallway that the bedrooms were down.

"Okay, we should be good then," Aiden said as put the last plate in the dishwasher. He closed the machine and dried his hands on a towel. A knock sounded on the door.

"Talk about timing," Derrick said.

Aiden nodded and moved to the door. Teeny was on the other side with a bottle of wine. "I don't know," she said, gesturing to the bottle. "It just seemed like the thing to do."

Aiden took the bottle and bent down to give her a quick kiss. "Thank you," he said. He ushered her in and closed the door behind him.

"Hey, Derrick," Teeny said.

"Hello," Derrick said as he sat down on the couch.

"So, I qualify for answers now?" Teeny was half teasing as she sat down on the couch as well.

"It would seem so," Aiden said. "I was told to invite you."

"Told? By whom?" Teeny asked.

"The woman you saw the other night inside the circle," Aiden said. He knew that would pique her interest, and he was right.

"Really? Interesting," Teeny said.

Another knock drew Aiden back to his door. Opening it, he saw Andy carrying a six-pack of high-end beer. Aiden took the beer as Andy held it up to him.

"I figured we could all use a drink after the last day," Andy said.

"You are not wrong, my friend," Aiden said. "Who wants one?"

They all answered that they did, so Aiden handed out three bottles, took one for himself, and put the other two in the fridge. Aiden took the seat on the couch between Teeny and Derrick, while Andy made himself comfortable in the armchair.

"You're in on all of this, too?" Teeny asked Andy the question as she looked at him.

"I don't know if 'in on it' is the right way to put it," Andy said. "I was Cade's partner when she was alive. She's come to me for help a few times. Getting your security detail was just a coincidence."

"Lucky coincidence," Aiden said.

"Cade is?" Teeny asked.

"The woman you saw in the circle last night," Aiden said. "Her name is Cadence Riley. She died about a year ago…"

"More like eight months ago," Andy corrected.

"Okay, eight months ago," Aiden amended. "She and the guy you captured in the box at Barrington were partners. They try to keep spirits in line at haunted locations. That way, people like us don't get too much information."

"And that guy is the one you call Snow?" Teeny asked.

"Yes," Aiden said with a nod.

"Before Lauren was killed," Teeny said, venturing onto the topic as lightly as she could. "There was a flash against the dome. It looked like a guy around Derrick's age."

"That was Sam," Derrick said, taking over the explanations. "He was Cadence's brother."

"He was murdered when they were both in college," Andy said, chiming in. "About ten years ago."

"Jesus," Teeny said. "Unlucky family much?"

"Yeah, well, I've got fuel to add to that fire," Andy said. "My captain… well, our captain when she was alive… he was the guy that activated that circle."

"What?" Aiden's voice was sharp as he sat up and looked over at Andy.

"Yeah." Andy nodded, taking a sip of his beer. "Captain Rodriguez."

"The same captain from the file of death?" It was Derrick who asked the question.

"Yep." Andy nodded once more.

"Holy shit," Teeny said. "What the hell was he doing there? What was he doing, period?"

"I'm not sure, but I have a feeling I'm in for a really bad Monday," Andy said.

Cadence, Snow, and Will had arrived at the apartment right before Teeny had, so they had heard all the breathers' conversations. Bethany and Lauren arrived just as Andy finished speaking.

"Ah, good. You're here," Snow said to the women as they materialized.

"We got to talking and didn't realize the time," Bethany said. "They're all still awake though, so it looks like we're in time."

"Yeah, they've just been talking," Cadence said. "And drinking, which should help in the falling asleep part."

Given that none of the breathers had slept much, if at all, the previous night, it didn't take long for the alcohol to make them sleepier.

"Alright guys," Aiden said after letting the silence hang between them. "I know they want us to sleep. I've got my bed and a queen-sized air mattress in the room, or we can bring the mattress out here and a couple of people crash on the couch and in the chair."

"I'm good with the bedroom," Andy said. "I don't think this armchair would be too comfortable to sleep in."

"It's not great on the neck," Aiden said with a smile. He had fallen asleep there a few times watching TV and always regretted it when he did.

"I don't know about you guys, but I'm ready to pass out," Teeny said.

"Me, too," Derrick said.

"Yeah," Andy said, echoing their sentiments. "After you, Aiden."

Aiden led them all down the hall to his bedroom. "I figured Teeny and I could have the bed. Derrick and Andy, you've got the air mattress."

Andy gave Aiden a look with a raised eyebrow. "Told you before, man, date." He was referring to when he had interrupted Aiden and Teeny before.

"I guess you were right," Aiden said. Teeny slipped her arm around Aiden's waist and smiled. "Blankets and pillows are right there for you guys," Aiden continued. "So, I guess now we just all get comfortable and lie down."

Derrick tossed the pillows onto the air mattress, then Andy and Derrick each grabbed a blanket. Teeny climbed in on one side of the bed and Aiden the other. Both scooched toward the middle of the bed so they could cuddle together as they fell asleep.

"And now we wait," Cadence said to the other spirits.

"I know you can dream-walk, Bethany," Snow said. "I know Lauren can't yet, which is understandable, given how new she is. I taught Cadence. Will, do you know how?"

"No, Cade was going to teach me, but we haven't had time to get there yet," Will said.

"Okay," Snow said, thinking. "Bethany, you have a strong connection with Aiden. Cadence, you have a strong connection to Andy. Bethany, I want you to dream-walk Aiden, then bring Teeny in. So just sit on the bed and connect to both. Cadence, the same goes for Andy and Derrick. Start with Andy, then bring Derrick in. Will, I want you to keep hold of Cadence's arm or shoulder as she dream-walks. Lauren, keep hold of Bethany's arm or shoulder. I'll be in the middle and Will and Lauren will be holding my hands during this. This will create a line where Bethany and Cade can try to draw in Will and Lauren, and I can push if necessary."

The spirits all nodded and took their places. As the breathers began to drop off to sleep, Bethany and Cadence reached out to have a hold on each of their assigned breathers. Will and Lauren kept a grip on Cadence's and Bethany's shoulders with one hand and had Snow's hand in their free one.

Cadence found herself in Andy's apartment. Andy was sitting on the couch watching a football game. She made her way around the couch and poked him in the arm.

"Hey!" He jumped to his feet and hugged her. "What's going on?"

"We all need to have a talk," Cadence said. "This was the best way we could figure out to do it without repeating ourselves a ton of times."

"So how do we do this?" Andy asked, since it was the first time he had been a part of anything like this. He looked around the dream version of his apartment. "I don't see anyone else here."

"Take my hand," Cadence said. "Don't let go." She was aware of Will's presence, but she wasn't ready to bring him in yet. Instead, she closed her eyes and focused on the other flame of subconsciousness she could find in her mind. Dragging Andy with her, they appeared in Derrick's dream.

Derrick was in class. His head bowed over a sheet of paper, his pencil flying furiously as he wrote. He was the only one in the room.

"Derrick," Cadence called out.

Derrick looked up and saw the figure of the woman he remembered from the circle last night, and from the video Aiden had shown them from Dan's dropped camera at Lexington Hills. "You must be Cadence," Derrick said as he rose, his paper all but forgotten.

"I am," she said with a bit of a smile. "Come with us."

Derrick took her hand, and Cadence turned. The room morphed as they changed locations. Cadence had led them to a place Snow had created in his mind. Cade let go of Andy's and Derrick's hands. She tugged on the line she saw connected to her, and Will followed that line, entering the room as well.

Snow had created a warm room with a sunken, circular seating area. The walls were a sandy color, and the carpet and cushions were black. There were some black and gold art déco pieces around. Cadence nodded to Snow in approval.

Cade and Will stepped down into the seating area and took seats. Cadence was on Snow's right, and Will was next to her. Andy and Derrick settled on the half-circle section of the couch across from them. As they sat down, Bethany, Lauren, Aiden, and Teeny joined them in the room. They descended into the sitting area. The breathers all sat on the same side, across from the spirits.

Teeny's eyes were wide as she looked over at the spirits. She recognized Cadence as the woman from the night before. She also recognized Snow as the man she had captured in her modified Faraday cage at Barrington Prison. In her wildest imaginings, she had never thought she would be in this kind of situation, facing spirits, about to get straight answers from them. She was excited and terrified all at the same time.

"I thank you all for coming," Snow said, his English accent new only to Teeny. "Due to recent events, we are having to break with our rules. Aiden, Derrick, and Lauren. We have been working with you for several months now. We appreciate your help more than you know. That help was a smudge of the line of the rules. Due to how successful that help was, and how you kept it quiet, we were allowed to keep the relationship with you and keep working with you. This meeting isn't smudging the line. It is all but erasing it.

"We all have plenty to go over with everything that has transpired recently, from Barrington Prison on," Snow continued. "I think all together we will be able to answer many of those questions. This little party was arranged to save time. It's easier to do this than it is to keep hopping to and from each one of you to get answers. It also serves as something of a goodbye for Lauren, although not the goodbye you think it is."

"Umm," Derrick said, raising his hand a little. "I hate to ask this, and I have a feeling I know the answer, but… where's Sam?"

Lauren and Cadence both stiffened in reaction to the question.

"Samuel Riley lost his afterlife last night when he was thrown against the energy of the domed circle that Wolf erected," Snow said. He hated saying it. He'd grown fond of the young man. And Snow knew it was breaking Cadence's heart to hear about her brother right now.

"Okay," Aiden said. "So, this must be Cade's new partner?"

"I'm Will," the teenager said, introducing himself. "And yeah, I'm the new partner."

"Wait, you said Wolf was there?" Bethany said. She remembered that name. It was the man who killed her.

"He was, yes," Snow said. "He was at the center of the stone circle, the one who raised the energy circle."

Andy looked at Cadence as he spoke. "He's also Captain Rodriguez."

"I know," Cadence said. "Didn't know until last night," she added. "But now I know." She could still easily recall the shock of cold that went through as she recognized him. And the surprise that followed as he spoke to her as if she were still alive and not a spirit.

"I'm a little lost here," Teeny said. "I know you all know each other, but I'm not in on y'alls working relationship yet."

Cadence and Snow exchanged a look, and Snow nodded to Cadence. He was giving her permission to spill the beans.

"Okay," Cadence began. "Before we get into recapping the last few weeks, let's start with some introductions. I think Lauren is the only one who doesn't need an introduction. I'm Cadence Riley. I've been dead roughly 8 months or so. I was a cop, working with Andy here. When I died, I decided to keep helping and was partnered with Snow here." She gestured to each man in turn as she said their names. "We serve on a kind of spirit police force that does its best to keep haunting spirits at locations from giving away solid proof to the living, especially ghost hunters, that the afterlife does exist. We can throw odd noises or voices, but no definite answers. Will here is my new partner since Snow got a promotion. The woman between Snow and Lauren is Bethany. She was Aiden's old girlfriend who was murdered, and now acts as a counselor for incoming spirits to help them decide what they are going to do. That's the Cliff's Notes version of who we all are, at least.

"We had to blur the line of the rules, as Snow said, a few months ago," she continued. "It may sound strange, but this does all tie together. There was a non-human entity that was summoned by a cult at Lexington Hills Asylum. It's something that was never supposed to have been brought into creation. Dan, Lauren's ex-husband, had been part of that cult, which was put together by Wolf.

"The last time that ritual had been used, it required spirits and humans to work together to defeat it. So, blurring the lines, we did what we had to. We were a little too late. It had already killed Dan. But he sacrificed his afterlife to help us defeat it."

"After that, we ended up on a case that brought the ghost hunters together with Detective Halleran," Snow said, picking up the tale. "The dorm house that Cadence's brother was murdered in had some interesting spiritual problems. In asking the good detective to assist us, he was put in danger. Wolf, who had been working for a non-human entity called Shaldoxz, had a couple of overzealous underlings who thought the detective was putting his nose where it didn't belong. Lauren, Aiden, and Derrick helped to rescue Detective Halleran. Sam was able to get most of the spirits moved on from the dorm house and so he was freed from his position there. That's when he transitioned into being a spirit guide for Lauren."

"That brings us to Barrington Prison," Cadence said. "Congratulations on your Faraday cage working, by the way. Snow was thrown in that direction by an unruly spirit right as you turned it on, and the box trapped him. That left me alone to watch over Liam. That unruly spirit that tossed Snow in the cage was also the one who broke the glass in the execution building."

"Did he make Liam fall?" Teeny had been silent up until then, but she had to know what had happened to Liam.

"No," Cadence said, shaking her head. "I had been protecting him from bits of unhappy spirits. They were the ones making the moaning and screaming sounds. They coagulated like the Blob from that old fifties horror movie. Or eighties horror movie, whichever version you want, the idea is the same. When I went to try to stop Pruitt from destroying the glass, I got drawn into an argument with him. The Blob saw its chance and pulled the lever that opened the trapdoor, dropping Liam. I'm not going into specifics about how I did it, but I contacted Andy and got him to come in to help.

"There is also another side to that night," Cadence said, plowing ahead with the information train. "The family investigation with the little girl that Derrick and Lauren were doing. Wolf, we have learned, is very talented at seeing and communicating with spirits. So is the little girl from that family. Wolf found out and was trying to lure her away. He had summoned the spirit of a dead little girl to befriend Ava and draw her to him. This backfired a little bit as the girl was a sociopathic little southern belle who died in a fire she set. When Wolf summoned her, he also summoned another girl who had been a slave and was tied to Sarah, the spoiled brat.

"Wolf knew we had split our resources," Cadence continued. "I'll get to how in a minute. However, he is the one who told Sarah to ramp up her shenanigans. He pulled the power at the house that night. He had told Sarah to take Ava to that house that was being built and he was going to take her from there, but Sam intervened. According to Sam, Sarah stated that Wolf had promised her that she could possess Ava's body and live again, but then reneged on that deal. Sarah is still out there and mad at Wolf."

"Can I interject for a minute?" Andy was the one who asked the question.

"Sure," Cadence said.

"Okay," Andy began. "The overzealous underlings of Wolf during the dorm case happened to be the coroner's assistant and a college board member."

"The board member was Michael Caulfield," Cadence said. "We knew he was off due to what had been going on. But that's a long story that is neither here nor there at this point. That was Naveen's assistant?"

"Yeah," Andy said. "I had gone to Naveen to ask about that symbol you had given me. He had a whole file of murders over the last couple of decades with that symbol on the body. He had compiled a file and sent it over to Rodriguez, but Rodriguez did nothing with it. Now we know why. When I asked him about it, he shut me down. Then, after the Barrington Prison case, I found the file in my top desk drawer. No idea how it got there."

"That's when you brought it to us to make a copy of," Lauren said.

"You were in it, Beth," Aiden said. He figured she had a right to know.

Bethany nodded. "I figured I would be."

"All of this now brings us round to the Scarecrow Farms investigation," Snow said. "This is when I was promoted, and Will joined the team."

"I did bring Ronnie and his sister to Bethany the night of the investigation," Cadence said to Lauren. "That way, they could move on and leave the nightmare of what had happened behind them."

"Thank you," Lauren said. "I'm glad of that."

"At the house, Sam warned you that there was something upstairs that was powerful," Cadence said to Lauren, and Lauren nodded in response. "That being is what vaporized my brother and killed you. But there's more to that story."

"There's more?" Teeny asked the question. She was doing her best to absorb all of this and commit it to memory, but it was a lot of information.

"Yes." Cadence nodded. "Ever since the case at Lexington Hills, we've had someone from the NHD… sorry, Non-Human Division… working with us. They're kind of like the ghost version of the FBI. All along, we knew that a non-human called Shaldoxz was who Wolf was trying to free. At least that was the story. Come to find out that Shaldoxz was free. And while he was non-human, it wasn't what we thought. What we thought was that these murders were sending the energy of blood and pain to Shaldoxz, so he would be strong enough to free himself from his prison. He wasn't in prison. None of that was true. And it all comes back to Scarecrow Farms."

"There were once two non-humans on that piece of land," Will picked up the story now. "One had been there forever. The second was drawn by the pain and blood there, as that parcel of land had been a dumping ground for dead bodies no one wanted found. That one was evil. Feeding off the pain of the area, the second one got strong enough to kick the first one out. The second one had a name. X'Haldzos. The one that got kicked out knew how evil X'Haldzos was. He made his name an anagram of that name, calling himself Shaldoxz. Shaldoxz's true purpose was to funnel blood and pain via a symbol to X'Haldzos to keep him there so that he wouldn't spread his evil anywhere else."

"In order to do that," Cadence said, "Shaldoxz lied. He lied to Wolf about why he needed things done. He lied to us about who he was. We worked with him for months without knowing that Whitfield was Shaldoxz. So now we have Shaldoxz in custody, but X'Haldzos is free. You all saw as it barreled out of the trees, killed Sam, killed Lauren, and then used the portal that the captain opened to go, well, I'm not sure where."

"We do know one place it went," Will said. "Barrington Prison. It killed the remaining spirits there and blew the place up. Like rocks and rubble blew it up."

"Why was Rodriguez opening a portal, anyway?" Andy asked.

"I can give you a general answer. Under the direction of Shaldoxz, he was opening a portal to Barrington Prison," Cadence said. "He and Pruitt were working together to bring the spirits of prisoners over to possess injured bodies. Once possessed, Wolf would sacrifice the bodies, killing two souls. The captain was lied to. Shaldoxz told him that with those murders, he was building an army of spirits. An army he would be able to control to put an end to criminals by force and fear. Now what he was doing there the other night? I have no idea. I don't know if he was trying to do some other sort of she-nanigans because he didn't have another person with him. It was just a rabbit that he killed. But that circle and that portal are almost like the telephone booth from *Bill & Ted* if you know what I mean. Depending on the number you dial, is where you go? Well, in this case, I think depending on the energy or sacrifice you use, your intention with it, that's what you get."

"I think it might be time to find a new job, bro," Aiden said to Andy.

Andy nodded back in response. "No kidding."

"I believe we have brought you all up to speed on what we know," Snow said. "Detective Halleran, thank you for your insight into your captain. I believe it will be useful. There is another reason we are all here." He turned his ice-blue eyes to Aiden, who lifted his eyebrows in surprise. "Aiden, you have been integral to our working relationship. I don't know if this is a side effect of your being in contact with us so often or if it is a natural talent that is blooming late. You're a sensitive."

"Umm, no," Aiden said with a shake of his head. "That was Lauren."

"You proved at the prison that it is you as well," Snow said.

"How?" Aiden was perplexed as to how he had proven this.

"In the solitary confinement cell," Cadence said. "You heard me. It took barely any energy to communicate with you."

"Sensitives and psychics can have spirit guides, as Lauren did," Bethany said.

"I was hoping you would allow me to be yours," Lauren added.

Aiden blinked. "So, you would get to stick with us?"

"As your guide, yes," Lauren said. "I would try to protect you, as Sam did me. I'm told there will be a time for learning how to do so. But I don't see how having a guardian angel who knows you could hurt."

"Would we still get to talk to you?" Derrick asked. "Through the spirit box and all?"

"Yes," Lauren said. "But you can't use it all the time. None of us can pretend that I am not dead."

"I'm not sure how on point you guys are with this whole sensitive thing," Aiden said. "But yeah, I accept."

"Good, that's settled then," Snow said. "I'm hoping we can keep you out of any further deadly investigations or cases. And I am hoping we can bring this X'Haldzos thing to a close soon. We'll all be safer after that."

Aiden nodded, then looked over at Bethany. "Beth, I want you to know..." he faltered, trying to find the words.

"That you're finally moving on?" Bethany prompted. She smiled at him. "Aiden, it's about time. I'm happy for you."

The cell phones of Snow, Will, and Cadence all began to ring at the same time.

"That can't be good," Will said.

"Time for us to go," Cadence said. "Sweet dreams guys."

CHAPTER 5

Explosive

X'Haldzos had the scent of the one he was tracking. Although energies swirled all around him in the bluish-white light of the portal lines, there were no vortexes of power where the scent led. There was, however, a small crack of power. He took hold of the edges of that crack with his taloned fingers and ripped them farther apart.

He crawled up, through the hole he had created in the linoleum floor. Hefting himself fully out of the portal, he looked around. The place was abandoned, that much was obvious. It was weather-worn and decrepit, unlike the place he had just come from. This place looked like it had been grander, once upon a time, with its double staircase up to another floor and rotting wood. The smell he was tracking was faint here, but it was here nonetheless.

Unlike the last place he had traced the scent to, this place was not devoid of spiritual life.

Edith, the monitor of Lexington Hills, appeared in the lobby. She had taken over as the monitor when Ramon left. She had been expecting to see Snow, Riley, or perhaps even Ramon. She certainly was not prepared for the large, black, toad-like creature that was covering where the summoning circle of the chaos entity had been. The old nurse did her best to remain calm in the face of the monstrous thing as all five of its yellow eyes focused on her.

"Where?"

Edith swallowed her fear as the single word echoed in her mind. "Lexington Hills," she replied. She made sure to step back toward the stairs, to keep out of arm's reach of the thing. The talons on the end of its fingers looked dangerous and the creature neither looked nor sounded friendly.

It growled. The sound was both physical and telepathic, loud inside Edith's head and ears. It moved faster than she had expected it to, given its size. The old nurse teleported to the top of the stairs as the creature lunged for where she had been, reaching out with those razor-sharp talons. Edith was glad she had followed her instincts.

X'Haldzos glowered at her from the bottom of the stairs. A menacing chuckle emanated from him. *"Won't save you,"* the demon's voice echoed in her head.

Edith didn't waste a minute. She teleported to Matthew on the second floor. The patient had died during the tuberculosis epidemic in the 1910s. No longer sick in death, he tried to make himself useful around the asylum.

Matthew, his short brown hair matching his light brown eyes, turned and smiled at Edith. The smile quickly faded as he saw the expression on Edith's face.

For her part, Edith didn't wait for a greeting or a question. "Get everyone able to fight ready to do so. Something bad is here."

Matthew didn't ask. The expression on her face told him that there was not a moment to lose. He nodded and teleported out.

As he disappeared from the room, there was an explosion of sound coming from the archway to the second-floor landing of the stairs. Not wanting to teleport into an unknown situation, Edith ran. The banister of the landing had been broken off and pushed into the hallway. The walls were cracked and beginning to fall as the creature tried to shove his mass through the archway. Dust filled the air as the demon forced his way through, breaking the walls as he did so. It looked like he had gotten stuck halfway through. His talons scrabbled against the floor, but he couldn't find any purchase that would let him pull himself through, no matter how much he wriggled and twisted.

He stopped trying and turned his head as much as he could each way, his pus-colored eyes looking every which way. Ruby had been freed of her usual chair by Matthew. He was the only male in the asylum she would tolerate. And Matthew figured no one could possibly be more dangerous than Ruby. She looked at the creature, now stuck in the wall, with the same amount of disgust and contempt she viewed most others with. Ruby knew Edith would have mustered the troops, so to speak. Matthew hadn't returned with anyone yet. Ruby looked at Edith, who shrugged but looked afraid. They didn't really have anything to fight the demon with.

Edith pulled her phone from the pocket of her apron and dialed Cadence's number. She knew Ramon trusted Cadence, as did Ruby. Relief washed through Edith as she heard Cadence answer. "Get here now. We have a big problem." Edith then hung up without giving Cadence time to answer as the creature lashed out toward her with the taloned hand that he had managed to get through the archway. The wood and brick groaned and protested and more cracks spider-webbed out in the walls as the movement loosened the structural integrity of the wall.

Two of the monster's eyes stayed on Edith, while three moved to land on Ruby. Ruby took that to mean it was her turn.

"Who the hell are you, and what the hell do you want?" The cantankerous old woman could always be counted on to meet aggression with aggression.

X'Haldzos flooded Ruby's mind with visions. Visions of blood flowing down a stone from the cracked head of a woman. Images of him using his talons to carefully flay the skin off of Edith and then eat each little strip as she screamed. Pictures of Ruby herself being torn apart, one small piece at a time. And also, images of the one he was searching for and what torture he had in store for them.

Ruby staggered under the visions in her head. The old woman was nothing if not tenacious, however. "You fucker," she spit out the words venomously. "You ain't getting what you want, so stop fucking up my home."

Edith wasn't sure when the fork had gotten into Ruby's hand, but as the old woman leaped forward, it glinted in the light. The creature swung toward Ruby, but Ruby was just as deceptively fast as he was. When she saw his arm move, she teleported onto his head, trying to stab him with the fork. Edith held her breath. Matthew and the others appeared behind her and were stunned by the sight that greeted them. The small, old lady was on top of the huge creature's head as the thing's arm was still in motion.

X'Haldzos saw the woman disappear and felt her feet on his head. He shook his head from side to side violently. Ruby had been trying to stab the demon in one of his ochre-colored eyes. As he shook his head, she toppled, though. The fork stuck into his cheek like a pickaxe into a rock as Ruby fell, but she landed on her feet, teleporting back onto his head with another fork in hand.

The toad-like creature shook his head again, growing weary of this pesky spirit. As the woman started to fall, he grabbed her and squeezed with his hand. More wall cracked. He finally got his other arm through as another part of the wall crumbled to pieces. Ruby grunted in pain as she was squeezed, and she could feel the thing's talons piercing into her. Its once pinned arm now came around as he held Ruby in a grasp she couldn't escape from. The pain prevented her from teleporting.

X'Haldzos let her see his other hand coming toward her, delighting in the fear emanating from the old woman. A singular taloned finger reached out toward Ruby. He made sure he moved slowly, so she could see it coming toward her and fear. He ever so slowly pierced her left arm with the talon. Silver blood began to wet the nightgown the old woman wore. He dragged his talon slowly up, going a little bit deeper as he went. Through the arm, then the left side of her chest, up her neck, to her face. The talon stopped for a moment as X'Haldzos savored the pain and torment of the woman he held. Then his talon, still embedded in her cheek, moved up. He pierced her eyeball and pulled it from her head. Then he tossed her aside like a rag doll.

Edith and another woman moved to Ruby, quickly teleporting her back to her room. As they disappeared, X'Haldzos brought the eyeball on the point of his talon to his mouth. A black tongue, thick and warty, moved between lips that showed razor-sharp teeth as they parted. He licked the eyeball, silver blood dripping from the optic nerve. This was for show, and it got the desired effect. Terror and revulsion filled the room from the handful of spirits Matthew had been able to gather. The demon then popped the eye into his mouth, as if it were an olive on a toothpick.

The spirits began to run at the monster. To protect their home, to avenge Ruby. Edith and the other woman rejoined the group. Edith wondered what was taking Cadence so long. It hadn't been a long time, but for Edith, it felt like forever ago that she had called for help.

As the spirits came at him, X'Haldzos began to puff himself up. He grabbed the closest two, one in each hand, and shoved them in his mouth. He felt his power gathering, and he wanted to feed that power, to punish them for their audacity in trying to fight back against him. The wall crumbled around him at last, finally giving way as his power flared. He grabbed two more spirits and shoved them in his mouth, like a teenager eating potato chips. The sharp teeth in his mouth made audible and quick work of the spirits. He roared and expelled a gas from his mouth and pores that smelled worse than a pile of rotting corpses on a hot summer's day. The smell and the force of the roar pushed the spirits back as the building shook around them. X'Haldzos dropped back down to the lobby as the floor collapsed beneath him. The bricks and wood flew apart, taking out most of the rooms nearest the entryway to the hall and some of the stairs.

As he fell, X'Haldzos lashed out with his hands and was pleased as he felt his talons rip into other spirits. Edith screamed as her left arm was torn from her body. The other taloned hand had found purchase in the core of another spirit's body. He stuffed that one into his mouth in one piece as well. More blood coated his talons, leaving a trail as he made his way back to the portal.

The calls had come from Lexington Hills and from the Observation Bay. Some viewers in the Observation Bay had caught sight of the creature near Ava's house. It had left, but they were alerting Will and Snow. The monitor at Lexington Hills had been calling Cadence.

"On our way," Cadence said, hanging up. She looked at Snow and Will. "Lexington Hills, now," she told them.

They nodded, and all three disappeared from Aiden's bedroom, leaving the four breathers sleeping.

Upon arriving in the lobby of Lexington Hills, their jaws dropped. The lobby was destroyed, just like

Barrington Prison. Bricks and glass had blown out. The back half of the dining hall was visible from the driveway. On what remained of the walls and all over the rubble was the silvery blood of spirits. There was also a trail of spirit blood leading from beneath the balcony of the second floor, toward the circle that had been etched into the floor of the lobby several months ago. Inside the circle was a new crack in the floor that was wide and charred black.

"Oh my God," Cadence said.

Edith arrived in the lobby. There was a rugged stump just above the left elbow where her arm had been, which was tied off tightly with a sheet. Her usually dark hair was matted with silver blood. "This was no God," she said.

"Let me guess," Cadence said. "Looked like a giant toad with five yellow eyes and a bad case of gas."

"You know about it then," Edith said.

"How many were injured?" Snow asked.

"Five were straight up eaten by that thing," Edith said. "Mostly residuals or older spirits. It wounded anyone who tried to fight it. It bellowed, and that's when it blew out the lobby. Then it left. I've got three injured upstairs, and then myself."

Cadence pulled out her phone. She hit a few buttons and put it to her ear. "Ramon, you have to get to Lexington Hills now. It's an emergency." She then nodded and hung up. "He's on his way. Was Ruby hurt?" Cadence had something of a soft spot for the crotchety old woman.

"She's one of the injured, yes," Edith said. "She was the first to try to fight it when it somehow got upstairs. I don't know what it showed her in her head, but she tried to stand her ground and gave out as much venom as it gave her. When the lobby blew, a lot of the upstairs rooms got destroyed."

"I wouldn't expect any less from Ruby," Cade said with a grim smile, glad the old woman was still around to be grumpy about things.

Ramon appeared next to Cadence and looked relieved when she had no obvious wounds. It was then that he noticed the destruction around him. "Oh Dios Mio," he said under his breath, then moved to Edith. "Come upstairs." He took Edith's right hand, and they disappeared.

"I'm going to check on Ruby," Cadence said. "Snow, can you take Will? He hasn't been here yet."

"We'll go upstairs and help Ramon. Let us know if Ruby needs help," Snow replied. Cadence disappeared, and Snow turned to Will. "Don't be offended, Ruby is a patient who died here. She has a distinct dislike for men and gets violent with them. Riley is the only one who Ruby seems to tolerate."

"Gotcha," Will said with a nod.

Cadence appeared in Ruby's room. The hallway outside was damaged as was the first half of her room, including where the door had been. Ruby was standing against the far wall of her room near the window, looking out.

"Ruby?" Cadence said, her voice soft.

Ruby turned, a little wobbly on her feet. Cadence could see why. The left side of her face was a silvery mess. Her left eye was missing, as was the left ear. Ruined flesh dripped blood and revealed some of her teeth through her cheek. Ruby braced herself against the wall and squinted her right eye.

"Libby?" Ruby's voice was hoarse. "That you, girl?"

Cadence had introduced herself to Ruby using a nickname for her middle name. Liberty had turned into Libby. "Yes, Ruby," she said. "Can I try to help you?" She knew she had to be careful with Ruby to not set off a mood.

"Libby, I'm tired, girl. Can you come back another day to visit?" Ruby leaned a little heavier against the wall for support.

Cadence teleported over to where Ruby was, avoiding the giant hole in the floor between them. "Ruby, you need help. You're hurt."

"Bah," Ruby waved Cadence's offered hand away. "I'm just tired. Can't see too well either."

"Ruby," Cadence said, making her voice stern but kind. "You need to come with me. You've been hurt."

Confused, Ruby looked around the room, then lifted a hand to the right side of her face. When the fingers came away bloody, her remaining eye widened in shock. "Libby?" Her voice was shakier and sounded more unsure.

"It's going to be okay, but we need to go out of your room so you can get help," Cadence said in a calm, sure manner. "I'll be right here with you. No one is going to hurt you."

The old woman who usually had such a large, intimidating presence seemed small and broken now. She nodded to Cadence and took her hand. "You'll not leave me?"

"Promise," Cadence said with a nod.

Cade knew where Ramon liked to set up for his medical treatments. At least this time she wasn't the one in need of medical attention. "Now you're going to need to behave," Cade said to Ruby. "You need medical attention and Ramon is the one best qualified to help you. Can you let him do that?"

The animosity for Ramon had run strong in Ruby. After all, she had been the one to kill him in life. She always threw a hissy fit when he entered her room. Cadence didn't want Ruby trying to assault him when he was trying to help her.

"If you say so, Miss Libby," Ruby said with a sigh. "I'm too tired to fight him. Besides, he ain't bothered me in a while."

Cadence didn't tell the old woman that the reason Ramon hadn't bothered her was because he hadn't been at Lexington Hills for a few months. She led Ruby through the halls to the wing that Ramon liked to use. Snow and Will were there in the hall. Both had injured spirits with them. Ramon had to have been behind the closed door there, probably helping Edith. Cadence kept herself between Ruby and the men.

"You're a good girl, Libby," Ruby said.

"Thank you, Ruby," Cade said.

After a moment, the door opened and Ramon blinked, seeing all three of them there with the injured. He looked over each in turn, making sure to keep a safe distance from Ruby. The old woman didn't have any fight left in her, it seemed, as she let Ramon examine her face.

"Alright," Ramon said. "Libby, can you get Ruby comfortable in there?" He gestured to the door to the room across from them. "Snow, Will, take Jim and Matthew to those rooms over there." Ramon pointed to the rooms over to the left. "Stay with them until I get there."

"Abigail wasn't hurt," Snow said. "I asked her to search for anyone else who might need help."

"Thank you," Ramon said. He then waited for Cadence to cross the threshold of the room he had told her to get Ruby into. He kept a couple of feet between himself and Ruby as he followed them in.

Cadence got Ruby settled onto the bed. Ruby was holding tight to Cade's hand as she watched Ramon with wary eyes.

Ramon opened a drawer and pulled some things out. "Ruby," he said, "I'm going to have to sedate you so that I can work on you." He wasn't about to have her start trying to grab medical instruments from his hand and fight him.

"Libby stays," Ruby said. She had the tone of a petulant child, but she wasn't really fighting Ramon, which was a big change.

Ramon smiled and looked over at Cadence. He nodded to Ruby. "Libby can stay."

Mollified, Ruby settled back into the bed and closed her eye. Ramon pulled a syringe from his pocket and injected the contents into Ruby's arm. The old woman relaxed visibly as the medication took hold. Cadence was still holding her hand.

"Snow said this was the work of that demon that got out from Scarecrow Farms last night?" Ramon asked. He had begun applying bandages that were wet with a green liquid to Ruby's face.

"That's what it seems like," Cade answered. "I have no idea why he would come here, though."

"I'm going to have to move Edith and Ruby to the hospital," Ramon said. "They'll be fine, but it's going to take time. Like it did with you and your legs. I'm going to have to warn the staff to be careful with Ruby. I'm hoping to keep her sedated until I can just transfer her back here. I don't want people getting hurt because she feels well enough to get feisty."

"Understandable," Cade said.

Ramon was focused on attending to Ruby, but Cade could sense some tension in him. Maybe it was because he was working with a serious wound. But there was something on his mind that was drawing his lips tight and thin. Something was making his brow furrow. At length, he stood up straight and put his hands on the side of the bed Ruby was sleeping in.

"I'm going to transfer her, and I'll be right back," Ramon said. "Tell Snow and Will I'll be right there."

Cadence let go of Ruby's hand. "Ramon, are you okay?"

"Not really," Ramon said. "But we'll talk about that later. Right now, I need to take care of these people." With that, he disappeared with Ruby and the bed she was on.

Cade sighed and walked out of the room. She stopped outside of the door to the two rooms that Snow and Will were in. "Ramon is taking Ruby to the hospital," she said to them. "He'll be right back."

She frowned and began to pace outside the doors. It didn't take long for Ramon to come back and, without a word to Cadence, he went into Snow's room and shut the door. That was fine with Cadence, she had to think, and pacing was really the best way she could do that.

The roof at the house at the farm had been blown out. It was small compared to the blowout here or at

Barrington, but it had likely been done decades ago when X'Haldzos was weaker, smaller. The creature had left the farm and been somewhere for several hours before it took out Barrington Prison. Another few hours and then it was here.

The common thread seemed to be them. The team. So, was it chasing the breathers? No. It would have gone after the shop or Aiden's place. Was it chasing them? The team had changed, but there was a common thread.

Whitfield.

Whitfield was the one who had been feeding the creature, trying to keep it locked in there. It had barreled its way to the circle at the farm only once the circle had been activated and Whitfield had been inside. It then seemed to be retracing Whitfield's stops. Barrington Prison, Lexington Hills. Was it chasing him? If the creature had left Ava's house unmolested, then it wasn't after Derrick, the only one left alive from that investigation. Everyone else had been there, but their time there had been minimal in comparison. That they knew of. Cade had no real knowledge of whether Whitfield had bothered to be around the house without bothering to tell Sam or not.

"Shit," she muttered. "I need Google."

Snow opened the door and left the room. "Yours is next, Will," he said, calling into the room where Will sat with Matthew. He saw Cadence pacing and arched an eyebrow.

"What are you mulling over?" he asked.

"I think the common thread is Whitfield. I just need some way to search something in order to figure it out," Cadence said, frustration in her voice.

"Is it a location you need to look up?" Given their calls had been locations that had been destroyed, it seemed a logical conclusion.

"Yeah."

"Go to Bonnie," Snow said. "She can look up the Observation Bay person for the place you need."

"You guys good here?" Cadence asked.

"Yes," Snow answered. "Call me or Will with what you find out."

Cadence nodded and disappeared.

Cadence arrived in the waiting room and was surprised to still see Bonnie there. It was getting late.

"How did the meeting go?" Bonnie asked. She hadn't heard about the trouble at Lexington.

"The meeting was fine," she said. "Bonnie, there's trouble, and I need your help. Can you find out who oversees watching the dorm house?"

"Oh no," Bonnie said. She turned to her computer and began typing furiously. "Is Snow okay?"

Cadence couldn't help but smile a little at that. "Yeah, Snow's fine."

"I'm glad," she said, though her body language conveyed more relief than her words did. "Bay 6, station 12," Bonnie said.

"Thank you, Bonnie," Cadence said. She disappeared from the waiting room and appeared at the entry to Observation Bay 6. She made her way into the room, looking at the numbers on the backs of the computers. All of them had small lights on top of them. Most were white and steady. One computer had a red light flashing on the top of it. She knew before looking at the number that it was twelve.

"Where'd the operator for this terminal go?" Cadence asked the person at the next cubicle.

"Supervisor's office," the middle-aged woman answered. "Not sure what happened, but she took off running."

"Where is the supervisor's office?" Cadence asked.

"Straight back," the woman answered.

"Thanks." Cadence glanced at the computer, but the screen had been turned off. With an annoyed sigh, she headed to the supervisor's office. She paused to knock on the door, then entered without waiting for anyone to say that she could come in.

"Hey, who are you? You can't just barge in here," one of the two women, that had to be the supervisor, in the office said.

"I'm Detective Cadence Riley," she said. "Why is terminal twelve off?"

"Because there was an issue with one of the locations it monitors," the tall, thin woman said.

"Let me guess," Cadence said. "College dorm house that was closed due to a massacre a decade ago. Some creature showed up at it, and the building exploded."

Both women registered shock on their faces. "How... how did you know that?" It was the other, smaller woman who asked. She had to have been the operator.

"Because I'm trying to catch that creature," Cade said. "Here, I have an address for you. Can you monitor it? I don't think it's haunted, but I think the creature might go there."

"Mary," the taller woman said. "Take the address and monitor it, please. Detective, we'll need your number so we can contact you with any information we may get."

"Of course," Cade said with a nod. She gave each of the women her number and the home address of her former captain. "There is a man who lives there, so expect him to be around. But if that thing shows up or something happens in that apartment, please call me."

"Yes, Detective," the supervisor said as she nodded.

Cadence nodded in return and then left the office and teleported to her own. No one was there, which she found strange. They should have finished at Lexington by now. She left her office and made her way to Bonnie's reception area. Bonnie was gone, which wasn't all that strange. It was late. Cade knocked on Snow's door and poked her head in. The room was dark. She flipped on the lights and the office was empty.

"So, where the hell are they?" she asked no one. She flipped off the light and closed the door. She had two choices left. The hospital or her apartment. She was tired anyway, as it had been a long couple of days. She opted for her apartment and if they weren't there, she was going to try to grab some sleep before the next disaster occurred.

Appearing in her living room, she found only Ramon. "Hey," she said in greeting.

"Hi," he said in reply. He still seemed a little stiff.

"Are you okay?" Cadence furrowed her brow in concern as she approached him.

"Not really," he said. His body language was stiff, his tone was terse, and he was looking straight ahead at the television, which was off.

"What's wrong?" Cadence asked. He had always been such a supportive presence for her that she was not quite used to him being upset like this.

He pressed his lips together for a moment, trying to think of how best to phrase it. He took Cadence's hand and guided her around the couch so they could sit together. "Cade, I'm worried."

"About what?"

"About you," he said, lifting his blue eyes to peer into her jade eyes.

"I'm fine," she said. That was somewhat of a lie given her emotions, but physically she wasn't hurt.

He gave her a look that said he knew full well that was a lie, but let it go. "This thing that you guys are up against has killed what? Nine or ten spirits today? It's blown out locations as if it were a tornado, and severely injured other spirits. You saw Edith and Ruby."

"I did," Cadence said. "And I saw you help them."

"Not a ton of help. I don't know if Edith will ever get her arm back, and I have no idea if Ruby can regenerate the eye," Ramon said. "Cadence, if something like that happened to you, I don't know what I would do."

"You would do your best to heal me, like you always do," Cadence said.

"Cadence, you aren't hearing me," Ramon said. "I knew being involved with you came with the cost of worrying about you when you were involved in a dangerous case. This one is different. This could be the ultimate death of you."

"I'm sorry, Ramon, but that's the job," Cadence said. "I can't not do it just because it gets a little dicey."

Ramon stood up, shaking his head. "This isn't dicey; it's deadly. I know you like to be cavalier about it, but this is serious, Cadence."

"Are you mad at me?" Cadence hadn't ever seen Ramon like this.

"I'm mad at the situation," Ramon said. "I'm mad that you don't seem to see how much tragedy this could end in. There is no one here that you must prove a point to. No one would think any less of you for showing some common sense and asking to be let out of this case. One, it's your old captain who seems to be the bad guy, at least in part. Two, you just lost your brother. As much as you like to be strong and pretend that you're impervious, I know that it is tearing you apart."

Cadence grew still and Ramon knew he had touched a nerve. "I'm well aware that my brother is gone," Cadence said. Her voice was low, and her teeth were all but clenched together as she spoke. "That wasn't my fault."

"No, Cade, it wasn't," Ramon said. His voice was gentle. "All I'm saying is that this case is beyond your usual kind of dangerous, and you have two very valid reasons to recuse yourself from it."

"Ramon," she said after a moment of thought. "I know you worry about me. I appreciate it, even if it seems like I don't. But I'm not stopping. I'm not getting myself taken off this case. You're going to have to learn to live with that. This is who and what I am. I thought you knew that."

"I do," Ramon said sadly. "I guess I just didn't realize that you were willing to throw yourself off a cliff in order to chase a bad guy."

"Did you not hear how I died?" Cadence remembered fighting the Sommerset Strangler on the fire escape of his building as they were trying to apprehend him and getting tossed off, falling seven stories to her death.

"Cade." Ramon crossed the distance between them and took her hands in his. "Please. I am begging you. This is too dangerous of a case."

"I hear you," Cadence said. "I do. Part of me wishes I could do this for you and make you happy. But no. I'm not leaving Snow and Will alone on this case. I can't. I have to see it through. And not just for them, but for Sam, Lauren, and everyone else whom that demon has hurt. I don't like bullies, human or demonic. And if I have anything to say or do about it, I'm going to make sure it stops."

"God, you can be so damned stubborn!" That was the first time she had heard Ramon yell in anger.

"I'm not the only one in this room like that," Cadence said.

"My stubbornness doesn't run the risk of getting me killed," Ramon said, his voice rising.

"Tell that to the fork Ruby shoved in your neck," Cade said. It was out of her mouth before she had time to think. Throwing his mortal death in his face was not the way she had wanted to go with this argument. Hell, she didn't even want to be arguing. Ramon looked shocked at the fact she had brought up his death.

"I'm sorry," Cade said with a sigh. "I am. I spoke before I thought. It wasn't fair or kind."

"Thank you," Ramon said. He hugged her tightly. "I know I'm being stubborn on this, but I am terrified for you, mi amore."

"I'll be honest, I'm a little terrified, too," Cadence said. "But I'm doing this to try to protect others from ending up like Roland at Barrington Prison, or like Edith and Ruby. Do I have a score to settle with this thing? Absolutely, I'm not going to lie. But what is driving me on this isn't revenge. I need to protect people, Ramon. I need to protect you and Snow and Will and Aiden and everyone else. I swear to you I will be as careful as I can be. Will is working on weapons and defense stuff. Snow is gathering information. We're doing our best to not rush in blind. I can't leave the case because if someone else ends up like Lauren or Sam, I'm going to forever carry that with me. I will feel that if I had been there, it could have been different, that I could have saved them. Sam isn't my fault. Lauren isn't my fault. But if someone else dies because of this thing and I wasn't on the case, I will feel like it is my fault. Can you understand that?"

Ramon sighed and hugged her even tighter to him. "Yeah, I understand that. Your valor is part of what I love about you. The fact that you are a good person. I love you."

"I love you, too," Cadence said.

CHAPTER 6

A Case of the Mondays

The elevator at the police department dinged and stopped with a lurch. As the door opened, Andy stepped off, glad to be out of the box. He usually preferred to take the stairs. However, they had some repairmen updating the safety strips on the edges of the steps. He walked toward the detectives' office, opened the door, and stepped inside.

Keller was at his desk, bent over some paperwork. Meanwhile, Saddiq was sitting on the corner of Keller's desk regaling him with some tale about what happened at a local bar over the weekend. Both greeted Halleran as he walked by them.

"Hey, Halleran," Saddiq said. "Captain was looking for you."

"Yep, sounds like a great start to a Monday," Halleran said. Keller and Saddiq chuckled.

Andy had been expecting this, though. It was going to be tricky. He had to get an appointment with Internal Affairs, and he wanted to be done with that before he approached Rodriguez. He and Aiden had worked together to get a video of just Rodriguez in the circle with whatever he had sacrificed. It did end up showing the ghosts, but more importantly, it showed that he was involved in the death of Lauren Kurtz. IA would probably nail him for not including the captain's presence in his initial report, but that would be a slap on the wrist to what he hoped waited for Rodriguez at the end of this.

Getting to his desk, he saw an orange note on the surface that said, "See me - R."

Yeah, the captain wanted to see him. A glance at the office showed him that Rodriguez's door was closed, and the blinds were closed. *Good.* Andy opened the top drawer of his desk and grabbed the file that he had yet to put back. He slipped it under his jacket and under his arm. He turned and left.

"Yo, forgetting something, man?" Keller asked as Halleran passed by on his way out. Keller pointed to the captain's door. "He needed to see you."

"I have to do something first," Andy replied. "Just do me a favor and if he asks, tell him you didn't see me."

Keller and Saddiq both looked suspicious but agreed.

Andy nodded to his friends and left the office. He headed back to the elevator and up one more floor. He turned and opened the glass doors into the Internal Affairs Division.

"Detective," the man at the desk when Andy walked into the office said. "What can we do you for?"

"I need to speak to someone," Andy said. His heart was in his throat. He knew this had to be done, but there was something about being in the Internal Affairs office that just made him nervous.

"Yep, let me see if anyone is free," the man, whose nameplate on his desk said Neil Perisse, picked up his phone.

"Hey, Nicole, you free for an intake?" Neil paused and nodded. "Okay great, thanks." He then hung up.

"Nicole Powell will be right with you. Have a seat," Neil said.

Andy took a seat and did his best to keep still. He was aware he got fidgety when stressed, and this was the last place he wanted to look nervous. After a few minutes, a woman in her 40s, with silver streaks beginning to run through her brown hair, came over to him.

"Hello detective, I'm Investigator Powell," she offered her hand and Andy rose from the chair to shake it.

"Detective Andrew Halleran," he said in reply.

"Want to come back and tell me what brings you into our ugly side of the building?" Nicole asked with a smile.

"Sure," he answered, returning her smile. He kept the file tightly tucked under his arm as he followed the investigator back into their maze of cubicles. She walked into hers and gestured for him to have a seat in the chair beside the desk. He had to duck to avoid the curtain rod that went across the opening of her cubicle. She then pulled the black curtain closed to offer them some semblance of privacy.

Once they were both seated, she looked at him, offering him a smile. "So, what brings you over here?"

"I need to talk to you about my captain," Andy said, his heart beating fast.

"What about your captain?" Nicole replied, concern showing in the lines of her face.

"He's hidden some things," Andy said. "Mainly that he is a serial killer."

That caused Nicole to sit back in her chair, blinking. "I'm sorry, what?"

Andy took a deep breath and pulled out the file, putting it on her desk. "I was working a case and had talked to the coroner about bodies that had turned up with a specific symbol carved into them. It turns out that there are only a few a year. But it's been going on steadily for a while. The coroner said he brought it to the attention of Captain Rodriguez and had even sent over a file he had been collecting. You can confirm all of this with Naveen. That's the file he sent to Captain Rodriguez. That's the file that Rodriguez sat on because he was the one who was involved in the killings."

Nicole began flipping through the file. Her eyes scanned the pictures, easily picking up the symbol in each one. "How did you come by the file?"

"It was left in my drawer one night," Andy said. "I don't know how it got there, but it was there. I've been mulling it over for a week or so, but then a few nights ago, something happened that confirmed his connection and proved he was involved in another death."

"What evidence do you have of the event that occurred a few nights ago?" the investigator asked.

"Video," Andy said. "Video on a thumb drive taken by witnesses at the event."

"Is this in regard to the event at the Scarecrow Farms property over the weekend?" Nicole closed the file and looked back up at Andy. Apparently, she knew more than he had anticipated. He wasn't sure if that was a good sign or a bad one.

"Yeah, it is," he replied.

"And do you have this thumb drive with the video file with you?" she asked.

"Yeah," he confirmed. "It's a little wild."

"Leave the thumb drive with the video and the file with me," Nicole said. "It's now evidence. I'll open an investigation. Thank you for bringing this to our attention."

Andy rubbed his palms on his pant legs as he nodded. "Yeah, no problem."

"Now, let's go through this again so that we can get your official statement," she said, turning to her computer.

The door was still shut, and the blinds were still closed when Andy returned. Other detectives were in the office now, working on various things. Andy ignored them all and made his way through the office to the captain's door. He knocked on it.

"Come in," came Rodriguez's voice from within.

Andy opened the door, entered, and then closed the door behind him. "You wanted to see me, Captain?"

Rodriguez gestured for Andy to have a seat. The tension in the room was palpable.

"So," Captain Rodriguez began after Andy had taken the seat. "What are we going to do about Friday night?"

"What is there to do?" Andy countered. He didn't want to tip his hand that he had already gone to Internal Affairs. "I saw you there. I saw you kill something, an animal I'm assuming. Riley called you by another name. Wolf. I saw a woman die because of a chain of events you set in motion."

"Or she died due to the chain of events that she and her group set in motion," Rodriguez said. "They were there on an investigation. At least that is why I'm assuming they were there. I wasn't expecting company. That thing, which obviously came from the direction of the house, could have been chasing after them for their presence in its territory."

"Either way, you still killed something," Andy said. "Either way, you have some other identity that you go by."

"Yes, let's discuss that," Rodriguez said. "You didn't seem particularly surprised to see Riley there."

"So?" It wasn't the wittiest reply in Andy's repertoire, but it was all he had at the moment.

"So, I'm curious," Rodriguez said. "How long have you been in contact with her? Or at least known she was around in some fashion."

"Since the dorm incident," Andy replied. He saw no reason to deny his knowledge of Cadence's existence.

"Do you communicate with her on a regular basis?" the captain asked.

"No," Andy said. "Maybe a handful of times since December."

"Was Friday the first time you saw her?"

"Yeah," Andy said. He had seen her on video before. That had been back when Aiden, Lauren, and Derrick had first approached him for help. But as it was video, he didn't really count it.

"You seem to be taking all of this in stride pretty well, detective," Rodriguez said. "But there is something I need you to know."

"Enlighten me," Andy said, shifting in his chair.

"This has all been in the pursuit of justice," Rodriguez said. "We'll be able to have reinforcements like you could never imagine. Think about it. If we controlled something like what we saw the other night and used it to make criminals pay, get them off the streets for good. Things would be better for everyone."

"How do you control something like that?" Andy asked. "Because it looked pretty damn uncontrollable the other night."

"I'm working on that," the captain replied. "That was why I was there, actually. To do something to attempt to control that thing and others like it."

"Basically, what you are saying is that you're not evil, just crazy," Andy said.

"I'm not crazy, and no, I'm not evil either," Rodriguez said.

The usual murmur of voices outside of the office grew louder. Shouts of surprise came from all corners. Andy and Rodriguez were on their feet in an instant. Andy had the safety clasp on his holster undone and his hand on the butt of his gun by the time he opened the door.

The few detectives who remained in the office had their eyes glued to the window of Rodriguez's office. Andy turned and looked. On the glass, written in a red permanent marker that had been dropped to the floor, was "LIAR." It was a child's handwriting, and the "R" was backward.

"Captain," one of the unnerved detectives said, pointing to the open door that Rodriguez and Halleran stood in front of.

Both men turned. The door slammed shut of its own accord. Written in the same red marker across the door was the word "MUDERER." It was in the same childlike handwriting, and both the "D" and the "R" in the word on the door were backward.

Rodriguez could see Sarah, her blonde pin curls perfect as she stood there gloating at him. She stuck her tongue out at him and disappeared. Rodriguez clenched his jaw. Andy looked over at Rodriguez.

"Are we done here?" Andy asked.

"No," Rodriguez replied. He gestured for Andy to get back into his office. He then turned to the detectives in the room. "One of you call a custodian up here to clean that off," he said. He turned and followed Andy back into his office.

They resumed their seats, and each sat just looking at each other for a minute.

"What else did you have to say?" Andy asked after several moments of silence had passed.

"What do you plan to do with the information you learned Friday night?" Rodriguez asked.

"I haven't decided yet," Andy said, lying to his captain while looking him in the eye. "I mean, if I bring up ghosts to anyone, they'd have me in a shrink's office so fast my head would spin. You killed an animal. A woman died in your presence, and you did nothing to help her.

Not even call 911. These are small infractions at best, right? I mean, they're wrong, but it's not like you were holding a smoking gun."

"So, you aren't doing anything then," Rodriguez said.

"No, I said I hadn't decided," Andy said, correcting his captain.

"One more thing," Rodriguez said. "There is a file missing from my locked desk drawer. Do you know anything about it?"

"Considering I have no idea what's in that drawer, no," Andy said. He knew exactly what file Rodriguez was talking about. Internal Affairs currently had it. "What's in the file?"

"It was Riley's personnel file," Rodriguez lied. "If you see it floating around out there, let me know."

"Will do," Andy said.

"Halleran, you're a good detective," the captain said. "I would hate to lose you over a simple misunderstanding."

"A simple misunderstanding?" Andy scoffed. "This isn't a simple misunderstanding. You just said to me that you've been trying to harness spirits to implement some kind of ghostly vigilante justice system. How is that a simple misunderstanding?"

"Because you don't understand the kind of good we could do with it," Captain Rodriguez said. "No more technicalities setting the criminals free to go out and kill again."

"We're cops," Andy said, raising his voice. "We are not judge, jury, and executioners."

"And this could change all of that," Rodriguez said. "If we had command of something that could go through walls and hold a suspect, it would be a game changer.

Think, Halleran. If there had been something like that when we apprehended the Sommerset Strangler, Riley would still be alive. She didn't deserve to die like that, and we both know it. That was a senseless, useless death."

"And you're making things worse," Andy said. "How can you not see that?"

Rodriguez sighed and leaned back in his chair, shaking his head. "I can see we are not going to come to an understanding. At least not yet. I am sorry for that."

Andy rose, shaking his head. "No, what you are after is wrong. And I'm not sure what you have attached to you, but you need to take a minute to sort it out. Things have been happening, like that writing out there, that can't be explained. The guys are talking."

"I'll be taking care of her very soon. Don't worry," Rodriguez said.

Andy shook his head and left his captain's office.

CHAPTER 7

Evolving Theories

"**Y**ou aren't going to believe this," Derrick said as he walked into the New-Age shop.

Aiden looked up from behind the counter as he was ringing out a customer. "What is it, bro?"

Derrick walked over to the counter as Aiden passed the girl her bag of items. She turned and walked out, completely uninterested in whatever it was Derrick had to say. The college kid put the newspaper he had been carrying under his arm on the counter.

The headline read: "Barrington Prison Destroyed!"

"What the hell?" Aiden turned the paper a little to read the article. Derrick rocked back and forth on his feet a little, waiting for Aiden to get to the second part of the story. It took a few minutes before Aiden let out a more emphatic expletive.

"Yeah," Derrick said.

"So, the prison and the old dorm house just exploded," Aiden said, not quite believing it.

"Looks like," Derrick said. "From the inside, with no sign of an actual explosive device. What do we know that does that?"

Aiden vividly recalled the roof of the farmhouse at Scarecrow Farms and the way the second floor had looked: as if something small had exploded that had torn away walls and blown off the roof. "The thing at the farm," Aiden said.

"Bingo," Derrick said. "Now for the scarier part." He pulled his phone out of his back pocket.

"I'm not sure I want to know," Aiden said, a feeling of dread creeping into his core.

"Here." Derrick put his phone down on top of the paper. A local news website was reporting that Lexington Hills, the old, abandoned asylum, seemed to have suffered a similar explosion. There was supposition in the article that it could be connected somehow to the explosions at Barrington and the abandoned dorm.

"Are you kidding me?" Aiden ran a hand through his shaggy brown hair as he stared at the picture of the demolished asylum.

"I wish," Derrick said. "Now what I'm wondering is the scarier thing. Is it chasing us?"

"Chasing us?" Aiden's heart and stomach immediately seemed to switch places.

"Yeah," Derrick said. "I mean, it got Lauren at the farm, then it went back in order. Look at the estimated times of destruction. Barrington was first, then the dorm, then the asylum."

"It might not be chasing us," Aiden said. "It might be chasing Cadence and Snow."

Derrick paused and nodded. "True. I hadn't thought of that. The biggest question is what happens next?"

The spirit chimes by the door began to tinkle together, indicating someone they couldn't see was entering.

"I got the door," Derrick said, moving to lock it and flip the sign to say, "Closed."

Aiden nodded and went to the back office to get the spirit box. The two men met at the back table and sat down, then turned on the spirit box. Static filled the room.

"Who's here with us?" Aiden asked.

"Lauren, Cadence, and Will." It was Lauren's voice that came across the box. Both men felt like smiling and crying at the same time. They missed their friend.

"Welcome back, Lauren," Aiden said, tears in his eyes.

"Thank you," Lauren said. "I'll be around more starting today. They tell me in a week or two I can be around permanently. I'm just training now, learning what I need to do to protect you."

"Speaking of protecting," Cadence said, her voice coming through the static box as she spoke. "I'm sure you guys have seen the news."

"Yeah," Derrick said. "Barrington, the college dorm, and Lexington. It's crazy."

"It's X'Haldzos," Cadence said. Will stood nearby, fiddling with a pouch on his belt. "He is tracing back places we've been."

"Places we've all been," Aiden said. "Your team and us."

"With a couple of exceptions," Cadence said.

"What exceptions?" Derrick was curious.

"The Woods house," Cadence said. "And Ava's house."

"Why are those two places special?" Aiden asked.

"I have a theory," Cadence said. "I'm not sure I'm right, but it's the only thing I can come up with right now. Those are places that Whitfield wasn't involved in much. Whitfield was the non-human entity that X'Haldzos kicked out of the farm."

"You think this thing is after him?" Aiden was trying to connect the dots. The meeting they had in Dreamland had given them all quite a bit of information. He was still working on digesting all of it.

"I'm going to talk to Snow again later," Cadence said. "But I have a feeling there's going to be one more blowout here. If I'm right in my theory, anyway."

"Where?" Derrick asked. "Here?"

"No," Cadence said. "Wolf's home. Anyway, I am leaving Lauren here with you for a while. We're letting you guys break the rules a bit so you can finish working out the earthly things like this shop and where to find papers and stuff."

"We're also working on a way for you to contact us when you need to," Will said, piping up. "It's a difficult thing, but I'm sure I can find a way to make it work. It'll just take a little finessing."

"That would be cool," Derrick said.

"We'll get things settled here," Lauren said. It was directed at Cadence but came through the box, so they all heard it. "I'll be back in a few hours."

Cadence nodded. Lauren had to start making a connection to Aiden, not that she didn't already have one. But it needed to be a psychic connection. And they also had to settle what was going to happen the with shop and such.

Cadence and Will both hugged Lauren, then left.

"Alright," Lauren said, her voice staticky through the box. "Let's talk about what's going to happen with the shop because I think once that gets settled, a lot of weight will be lifted off of Aiden's shoulders."

A knock at the door paused the conversation. Looking over, they saw Teeny. A smile spread on Aiden's face, and he got up to open the door for her. He locked the door once she was in, and they hugged and kissed before heading back to the table. Teeny noted the static-filled room.

"Is someone here?" She gestured to the spirit box on the table as she asked the question.

"Yeah, Lauren's here," Aiden said. "We were just about to talk about what's going to happen with the shop."

"I'm glad you are here, Teeny," Lauren said. "You should be involved in this, too."

"I should?" Teeny was surprised. "I've not been part of this group very long."

"But you are close with Aiden," Lauren said. "Closer than I think either of you know, yet. You should be involved, too. Now, Aiden, what were you thinking about the shop?"

"I was thinking of closing it," Aiden said. "I know you said you were having issues with your customers, given the hours the investigations were taking."

"True," Lauren said. "I've had a thought about all this, though. There is still about a year on the lease. Why not change things up?"

"Change things up how?" Aiden asked.

"Keep part of it a new age shop, but more a supply shop. Crystals, candles, oils, and herbs. Have part of it as a paranormal supply store. Sell spirit boxes, K-2 meters, things like that. And then the back can be for Southern Paranormal Investigations as well as Aiden Perkins Video and Photography."

"You want to divide the store into fourths?" Derrick asked. "How is that going to work?"

"Yeah, I'm not really seeing how that sign is going to come together," Aiden said.

"It is just an idea," Lauren said. "But we do need a dedicated space for the paranormal investigations. And since you have helped me get this place off the ground, I think it's high time you started using it as a base for your business. Sell off all the new-age stuff, I don't care about that. Though I would ask that you keep the spirit chimes just so you know when a spirit has entered the store."

"What about Perkins Photography on the sign, and then just dedicate the back part of the office to Southern Paranormal Investigations?" Teeny suggested.

"That could work," Derrick said with a shrug.

"I've never really thought of having a storefront," Aiden said. "The last thing I want to be stuck doing is photos of kids and families."

"No, you do videos, but you also make photos from stills of the video," Lauren said.

"So maybe Perkins Videography?" Teeny looked at Aiden as she asked the question.

"Eh," Aiden shrugged. "Are you sure you don't want me to keep the store open for you, Lauren?"

"No," Lauren said, her voice decisive. "This was my dream. Not yours, Aiden. You were just gracious enough to help me achieve it. Let me help you achieve yours."

"Man, at this point I'm not even sure what my dreams are," Aiden said.

"Think about it," Lauren said. "I'll be here to help you."

"So will I," Teeny said, reaching over and squeezing his hand.

Cadence and Will materialized in their office. Each went to their desk and took a seat, mulling over what was going on.

"Are you really working on some way for them to contact us if they need us?" Cadence asked after a moment of silence.

"Oh." Will grinned. "Yes, I am. It's not working right yet. I've got to find a frequency that will stay steady and go from them to us, preferably some notification on our phones. It's nowhere near ready. It's just been technical schematics I've been messing with. I'll worry about putting energy into it after this whole mess is done. Right now, my focus has been defense and weaponry."

"Anything new there?" Cadence asked.

"Oh yeah," Will said, in a tone that admonished her for doubting that there would be new developments. "Some personal shields for us, helmets to try to guard against its thoughts, and a few weapons. The weapons are going to have to be carefully directed though. Some of them could be dangerous to us if we're in the blast radius."

"Gotcha," Cadence said with a nod. "Sounds like you've been busy. Just don't overdo the energy. We may have to go at a moment's notice."

"You got it, boss," Will said with a grin and a salute.

A knock sounded on their open door, and Snow was in the door frame. He carried with him the red cube of Whitfield's prison.

"Good afternoon, you two," he said in greeting.

"Hey, Snow," they said in unison.

"Is there any news for me?" Snow set the cube down on Cadence's desk as he asked.

"You know Barrington blew up," Will said.

"Yes," Snow said with a nod.

"And you know Lexington blew up," Cadence added.

"Yes," Snow said, not liking the direction this was heading.

"Well, the dorm house blew out, too," Cadence said. "Same way, all three places."

"It's retracing," Snow said with a nod. "The question is who is it tracing after? We were at all three places, as were our breather friends, as was Whitfield."

"As was Wolf," Cadence added. "So while yes, we do think it is retracing a path, we're not sure who it's going after yet."

"Which is why we asked you to bring Whitfield," Will said. "We thought he might have some insights."

Snow nodded. He pulled a key on a cord from his pocket and held it against the top of the box. Whitfield materialized from the box as if he were being projected from it. Once he was fully there, the box turned white. Whitfield looked around, blinking.

"How long was I in there?" he asked.

"About three days," Snow said.

"That's not long," Whitfield said, looking confused. "What's happened?"

"That's what we're hoping you can tell us," Cadence said. "So far, Barrington Prison, the dorm house, and Lexington Hills Asylum have been blown out. Not up, out. All the spirits at Barrington were slaughtered. Most of the spirits at Lexington Hills were killed or injured. Thankfully, there wasn't anyone left at the dorm to be hurt."

"X'Haldzos," Whitfield said.

"Yepparooni," Will said.

"We want to know your thoughts on this," Cadence said. "Do you think it is following us, following the breathers, following Wolf, or following you? Because it is creating a trail backward through where we have all been."

"The only difference is the two homes," Will said. "The Woods's house and Ava's house. Both were untouched. Although it apparently did pay an unobtrusive visit to Ava's house. It was spotted outside the place by the Observation Bay but didn't go in or cause damage."

"I wasn't involved in the Woods case. And I was barely in on the case with the little girl," Whitfield said, nodding. "Wolf's place?"

"Intact so far," Cadence said.

"Lauren's shop?" Whitfield asked.

"Intact," Will said. "We just came from there."

"I guess we wait then. If it goes after Wolf, we'll know it's either him or me that it's chasing," Whitfield said.

"But you've spent time at the shop, too," Cadence said.

"Yes, but none of us have spent time at Wolf's location," Snow said. "So, if it destroys there, we will know that it is after Whitfield. Otherwise, we're still left guessing."

The phones of all three began buzzing.

"I've got a bad feeling about this," Will said.

"Riley," Cadence said as she answered her phone. Snow and Will answered theirs as well.

"What do you mean?" Cade asked.

"You can't be serious," Snow said.

"No way," Will said, all in unison.

Whitfield watched in silence, wondering what had happened now.

"On our way," they each said, then hung up. Without another word, they left the office with Cadence grabbing Whitfield to teleport him with her.

They arrived at the jail area to see it blown out. There was an arm on the floor, coated in silver blood. Brackett was slumped against a white wall. A silver mark was against the wall above him and trailed down to where he now sat. The cells themselves were blown out. And with a lack of cells, the prisoners were gone.

Cadence let go of Whitfield and pulled out her phone, dialing Ramon. "We need you at the cell block." She then hung up. She knew this was likely to trigger another argument, but it had to be done. Brackett had to be helped. It took only a moment for Ramon to appear there beside her.

He gave Cadence a look but bent down to tend to Brackett without a word.

"So instead of going to Wolf's place or Lauren's, it came here?" Will asked.

"We did make a recent arrest," Snow said. "Pruitt, the former monitor of Barrington Prison."

"It's not after any of the breathers then," Whitfield said, shaking his head. "It was a good theory up until now."

"What do you think, then?" Cadence asked. "Which of us is it after? Because you weren't with us when we came here to interview Pruitt. But Pruitt was from Barrington, which it already targeted."

"It has access to the portals, the conduits," Whitfield said. "It can go wherever it wants. Maybe it did start by chasing the scent of one of us. But this?" He gestured to the broken bits of cells around them. "This is more than just chasing. This thing just let out every spirit, every non-human, everything we deemed too evil to be loose in the world. It's just caused a giant distraction and tried to take itself off our priority list."

"You think it is intelligent enough for that?" Snow asked.

"It was intelligent enough to take over people and drive them to commit terrible crimes," Cadence said, thinking back to Professor Phillips's uncle. "It was intelligent enough to make me back off during the daytime investigation."

"Does it win then?" Will asked. "Do we have to stop chasing it to chase down all of these bad guys?"

"No," Snow said, his tone emphatic. "He does not get taken off our priority list because of this. It moves him up higher. If he can come here and do this kind of damage in here? No. He is at the top of the capture/kill list. Everyone and everything else is below him."

Ramon had moved Brackett to the hospital but had returned to the prison area. "Is there anyone else hurt?"

"Doesn't look like it," Will said. It was easy enough to see through the entirety of the cell block with the cells themselves gone.

Ramon looked at Cadence. "Do you still think you have this under control?"

"I never said I had it under control," Cadence said. "I said I would be able to handle it."

Ramon nodded slowly, then turned quicker than anyone expected and wrapped his hands around Whitfield's throat, pushing the non-human back against the wall.

"Ramon!" Cadence said, her voice raised in alarm.

Will moved to go after Ramon, but Snow put a halting arm in front of the teenager.

"If she gets hurt," Ramon said, his voice a low, threatening growl. "If I must patch her up AGAIN because of you. If she doesn't come home because of you, there will be no place in heaven, hell, or earth that you will be able to hide from me. Do I make myself clear?"

Whitfield squeaked and nodded.

Ramon released his hold on Whitfield, who clutched at his throat. Ramon turned and crossed the few feet to a wide-eyed Cadence. He crooked a finger under her chin and lifted her face. He bent down and kissed her gently. "Handle it," he said. "But come home to me." He then disappeared.

They all stood in stunned silence for a moment. Snow had expected something of an outburst from Ramon directed at Whitfield. However, none of them had expected the doctor to be capable of the aggression he had directed at the non-human. Nor the tenderness he had turned around and shown Cadence in almost the same breath.

"Dude," Will said to Whitfield. "You are so screwed."

Snow moved over to Cadence and stood beside her, facing the opposite way she was. "You're a lucky woman to have someone who loves you so deeply."

"Yeah," Cadence said, nodding. Her voice still sounded stunned, processing what had just happened. "I am."

CHAPTER 8

Panic!

The general mood in the Observation Bay was blind panic. Cadence and Will had gone there after the prison to assess the situation while Snow had taken Whitfield back to his office. Terminal operators were shouting at one another and the tall, skinny woman that Cadence recognized as the supervisor was out of her office and in the thick of it.

"Cross reference the beings with the prison records," she was saying as she caught sight of Cadence and began moving toward her and Will. "Okay," she said, addressing the two of them. "What the hell happened?"

"A non-human just destroyed the cell block downstairs," Cadence said. "It set free every single prisoner down there."

"Shit," the woman said.

"Understatement of the century," Will said.

"And you are?" the supervisor asked, looking down her nose at the teenager.

"This is Detective Will McKenney," Cadence said. "I'm sorry, I'm terrible with names. You are?" She had never bothered to ask the woman's name on her previous visit, but she didn't want to admit that.

"Sherry Goldman," the woman answered.

"Ms. Goldman, do you mind if I address everyone?" Cadence asked.

"Go right ahead," the thin woman replied.

Cadence did a sudden, sharp whistle which succeeded in quieting the panicked workers. "May I have your attention, please?" She already had it, but it seemed the polite thing to say. "There has been a breach downstairs and every prisoner in the entire cell block has been set free. We are working to contain the problem. However, our first order of business is to capture the one that let them all out. I will be sending Ms. Goldman information on that non-human and ask that you all keep an eye out for it. If you see it, let her know immediately.

"I know you all are seeing new spirits and non-humans pop up in places. Please take down the descriptions and the locations. Cross-reference the description with the prison records. Ms. Goldman was correct in that instruction. Let us know if the spirit stays or just moves through. Some of these guys have been locked away for a very long time, so it is important we begin to establish patterns for them. Keep records, I cannot stress that enough. These were the things that we thought we had locked away forever because they were too evil to be allowed to roam around. Recapturing them will be our next priority, so your tracking of them will be of utmost importance in helping us. I or someone from my team will be in contact with Ms. Goldman if there is an update to these instructions. Any questions?"

The operators looked a bit shell-shocked as they all shook their heads. Cadence nodded and turned to Sherry. "You still have my number, right?"

"Yes, Detective," the woman nodded.

"Thank you," Cadence said. "You guys are our eyes and ears right now. Every bit of information you can gather from what you see is going to be important."

"Do you still want us to keep an eye on that one apartment?" Sherry asked.

"Oh, I think at this point that ship has sailed," Cadence said. "We all have much bigger fish to fry."

Sherry turned and went back to doing her best to manage the now somewhat organized chaos of the Observation Bay.

"Good speech, boss," Will said.

"Thanks," Cade said. "I hope it helped. We need every one of them watching over things and feeding us info."

"Agreed," Will said. "So, what's next?"

"Next I think we'd better go check in on our ghost hunters," Cadence said. "They need to know that things just got a hundred times more dangerous."

Will nodded to Cadence and the two of them disappeared.

The chimes next to the door indicating a spirit's entrance jingled as Cadence and Will walked in. Lauren was still there, along with the three breathers. Paperwork was spread out across the table. All of them looked up and over as the chimes tinkled.

Will and Cadence approached the group at the table. Lauren noticed the looks on their faces and was immediately concerned. Aiden felt the change in Lauren's mood. He couldn't explain it yet, but there was already a connection. He reached for the spirit box in the middle of the table and turned it on.

"Hey guys," Aiden said. "What's up?"

"Some serious stuff," Cadence said. "X'Haldzos attacked again. Instead of blowing out a physical building, he attacked on our side."

"Your side?" Derrick asked. "How?"

"We have a place where we keep, well I guess kept, the worst of the worst. Non-human and human, but all evil," Cadence said. "X'Haldzos blew it out. All the cells were blown apart. It ate most of the guards there. One was taken for medical attention. But now every single spirit or non-human that was deemed too dangerous to be on earth anymore is free and roaming around."

"Oh my God," Lauren murmured.

"Yeah, it's thrown a lot of things into chaos," Will said.

"I can imagine," Teeny said.

"X'Haldzos is still our priority," Cadence said. "He needs to be stopped. In the meantime, we have a team working on watching for the escaped prisoners to find where they go. What their habits are, what they do, etcetera. We can determine a priority list from there and warn you guys if there's something mean and local."

"Anything we should do in the meantime?" Aiden asked.

"Or anything I can do?" Lauren asked.

"For right now, just sit tight," Cadence said. "I just wanted to warn you. I don't know what may come in locally, and you may get calls from people seeing increased activity or activity period. If that happens, just be super careful. These things were locked away for a reason. Those spirits aren't going to be a 'let's move you on' situation."

Cadence then turned her attention to Lauren. "Stay close to them. Don't let them do anything stupid."

"Hey!" Derrick and Aiden protested in unison, which made both Teeny and Lauren chuckle.

Ignoring the protestations and chuckles, Cadence continued. "And you need to be careful. You're new. Some things go for newer spirits because they have more life force in them than the older ones. That's why the chaos thing was attacking me at Lexington. That's why you got the video you have of me. Please. Be careful. I don't want what happened to Sam to happen to you."

Lauren nodded to Cadence. "I'll be careful, and I'll see that they are as well."

"I'm gonna see about getting you some things for defense, given the situation," Will said.

"Aren't all guardians going to need increased defensive measures?" Lauren asked.

"Probably," Cadence nodded. "I'm sure there are going to be changes around the office and how things are divided now that a ton of non-human creatures have been let go. But that's for us to worry about. I'm hoping we can take care of X'Haldzos on our end and not even have to involve you in it. You guys have earned a break."

"We've got a lot on our plate right now anyway," Aiden said, gesturing to the papers in front of him. "I don't think we're going to be taking on any new cases for a few weeks."

"Good," Cade said. "Stay low for a while. Just work on your plans and tying up loose ends."

"Will do," Derrick said.

"Oh, Liam will be going home soon," Teeny said. "I forgot to mention it in all this craziness. I have the memory cards from the cameras, though, and he knows Aiden and I will be editing it."

"Good," Cadence said. "Does he remember much?"

"Not that he's said so far," Teeny answered. "He keeps asking me about it. All he remembers is going out there, the glass breaking, then falling. Once he mentioned that he thought he heard me, but I don't know if he heard me when I found him with Detective Halleran or if he might have heard you and confused it for me. But I'm not volunteering the information."

"Thank you," Cadence said. "And please don't. We're already breaking more rules than I can count by giving you guys so much information. The more reined in we can keep it with others, the better. And speaking of Andy, we should probably check in on him. He had to go to work today."

At that moment, Aiden's phone rang. He looked at the caller ID and chuckled as he switched off the spirit box. "Speak of the devil," he said before picking up the line. "Hey, Andy, how's it going?" he greeted.

CHAPTER 9

Pulling the Trigger

Andy Halleran sat in his car in the parking lot of the police station. It was late afternoon, and the sun was beginning to annoy him, but he wasn't making this call from inside the building. He had his cell to his ear, listening to the familiar voice on the other end.

"Bro, are you sure you want me to do this?" Aiden asked.

"Do it," Andy said. "Pull the trigger. I can defend myself on it since I found it randomly placed in a drawer of my desk. Who knows who might've had it before me that could have put it there?"

"You're absolutely positive?" Aiden was stressing his words. He wanted to make sure Andy knew what he was doing. This bell couldn't be un-rung if he changed his mind in fifteen minutes.

"Do it," Andy said, repeating himself. "I'm sure."

"Well, keep a low profile then," Aiden said.

"I'm about to do worse than that," Andy said.

"What do you mean?" Aiden's voice was concerned.

"I'm about to quit," Andy said. "I'm not working with him. Not after knowing what I know."

"Bro, hold on," Aiden said. "You said you opened an IA investigation. He may not be around much longer."

"I know," Andy said. "But I still think it's time for me to move on from this job."

"What are you going to do?" Aiden asked.

"Not sure yet," Andy said. "I have a few ideas. It shouldn't be hard to get a security gig or something."

"Well, you know where I live and work," Aiden said. "Come by if you want to talk."

"Ditto, man," Andy said. "I'm gonna go quit, then go home and watch the news."

"It should be interesting tonight," Aiden said with a chuckle.

"Catch you later, man," Andy said, then hung up.

He got out of his car and began walking to the front doors. He had spent almost a decade working in that precinct. He'd never really thought much about leaving it before. For the last few days, however, it had been on his mind a lot. He knew with his resume, his commendations, he would easily be able to find work somewhere else or even in another field. Given how deep this one secret was allowed to be buried and for how long it was buried, he couldn't in good conscience stay. He smiled and nodded in greeting to the woman at the records window, waiting for the next person to come get their records. He'd seen her for years at that window. He'd seen her hair go from flame red to having white streaks in it. But for all of that, he couldn't remember her name. For some reason that bothered him this time.

He reached the elevator and hit the up button. Keller came around the corner from the break room carrying a bag of chips. Cadence and Will also appeared, though they couldn't be seen by the breathers.

"You look like a man with a lot on your mind," Keller said.

"You look like a man who needs better snack food," Andy said. He was trying to joke it off.

"Everything else I would bother to get was out. The machine needs restocking," Keller said. "So, what's up?"

"That's his excuse every time he gets caught with junk food," Cadence said to Will.

The detectives stepped into the elevator and waited for the doors to close. Cade and Will followed them into the elevator.

Once the doors had slid shut, Andy turned to Keller and shrugged. "You'll hear it, anyway. I'm quitting."

"What the hell for?" Keller asked.

"Oh damn," Cade said. "I never thought he would quit."

"One of those people who is a cop for life?" Will asked.

"I always thought so," Cadence said.

"There's just been a lot lately," Andy said with a shrug.

"I will say you haven't been the same since we lost Riley," Keller said. "But you're a damn good cop. You just need to find your way back to putting your heart into your job again."

"That's the thing, Keller," Andy said. "This job chewed it up and spat it out. I don't have it in me anymore.

Maybe I'll come back. Maybe I find the next great thing. All I know is my gut is telling me it's time to go."

"He has had a tough time, and I'm not just talking about my death," Cadence said. "He was put in danger and almost killed in December. Then the security thing at the prison where Liam got hurt. Then the events at the farm."

"I won't deny there has been something in the air these last couple of weeks," Keller said. "You have my number, right?"

"Yeah," Andy said and nodded.

"Use it," Keller said. "Call me if you need anything."

Andy nodded as the doors opened. Keller preceded him into the Detective Department, holding the door open for him. Andy nodded his thanks and made his way straight for Rodriguez's office. The words written in red marker were still on his door and window. Halleran knocked on the door.

"What the hell happened here?" Cade asked, looking at the writing.

"Looks like a kid's handwriting," Will said.

"Sarah," Cade said. "It has to be. She's still causing Wolf trouble."

"Enter," Rodriguez's voice said from within.

"He can see the dead," Cade said to Will. "I'll go in with Andy. You stay out here. If you see a little girl that looks like she belongs on a southern plantation in the 1800s, give a yell."

Andy opened the door to the office and closed it, moving to stand in front of the desk. Cadence stayed back by the door.

"Halleran," Rodriguez said. "Didn't think I would see you in here so soon." His eyes moved to the door and the corner of his lips twitched up just a tad as he saw Cadence there, too. He knew Halleran likely had no idea he was being followed.

Andy pulled his badge off his belt and laid it down on the captain's desk. He then removed his service weapon, made sure the safety was on, and placed it on Rodriguez's desk as well.

"A little dramatic, don't you think?" the captain asked.

"No, sir," Andy said. "I quit."

"Are you sure you want to do this?" Rodriguez said.

"Yeah," Andy said. "I'm not working with you anymore."

Rodriguez sighed and shook his head. "I'm sorry you can't see the bigger picture, Halleran."

"The bigger picture of you using ghosts to circumvent the law and make us judge, jury, and executioner?" Andy asked, though it was a rhetorical question. "No sir, I see no reality where that is a sane or right plan. I refuse to be a part of you trying to attain it."

"You know she's here, right?" Rodriguez smiled as he said it.

"You aren't funny," Cadence said. She was fairly sure he could hear her.

"Would you like to see your old partner again?" Rodriguez said. "I can make that happen."

Andy stiffened, and the anger pouring out of him was palpable. "If she is here, I wouldn't know. I haven't seen her since the farm. And no, I don't need to see her again."

"That was a bad play, Wolf," Cadence said. She couldn't help the look of smugness that crossed her face. While Andy could still be touchy about her death, he had moved on. That had been a slip she hadn't expected from her old captain.

Rodriguez looked between the ghost of Cadence and the mortal Andy. He knew he could bind Cadence and bestow immeasurable pain on her to keep Andy with him and maneuver him onto his side. But he didn't want to do that. Not to Halleran, and not to Riley. She had been a great cop, and he had been fond of her. The daughter he'd never had.

The captain sighed and gave up his games as he leaned back in his chair. "Fine, I accept your resignation. Go clean out your desk."

Andy nodded and turned to leave, passing through Cadence as he did so. She shuddered, hating that feeling. Rodriguez saw that and laughed. Andy had the door half open and turned at the laugh.

"Something funny about this?" Andy asked.

"No, nothing," Rodriguez said, reaching out to take Andy's weapon and badge off his desk.

Andy nodded and went to his desk. He put his open case files on his desk to be distributed to the other detectives. Other than that, he didn't have much. He grabbed an old plastic bag he once brought in from a gas station for snacks. He tossed a couple of pictures and some pens from his desk into the bag, as well as a book he had been reading during his lunch breaks.

"What's going on?" Saddiq asked, seeing what Andy was doing.

"I quit," Andy said. "That's what's going on."

"What? Why?" Saddiq's jaw had fallen open in surprise.

"I just can't do it anymore, man," Andy said, feeling a bit of relief from the heaviness in his chest. "I'll be in touch. Don't worry."

"I didn't see any little girl," Will said as Cadence exited the office.

"It was worth a shot," Cadence said. "We've got to try to find a way to get her taken care of, too."

"Back to the office, then?" Will asked.

Cadence nodded and they disappeared.

"Are you sure you want to be anonymous?"

Aiden was standing behind the counter of the new-age shop. The file that they had copied for Andy was on the counter between him and the reporter. The reporter was flipping through the pages with wide eyes. The skinny man was looking a little green due to the pictures of corpses, but Aiden could see the eagerness for the story behind the disgust in his dark brown eyes.

"Oh yeah, I'm sure," Aiden said.

"You don't want the credit for being the one to bring down a corrupt cop?" The reporter couldn't believe it.

"I don't need or want that kind of notoriety or hassle," Aiden said. "If you won't keep me anonymous, I'll take the file back."

"No!" the reporter said, his hand tight on the folder. He had no intention of giving up this huge of a story. "I'll keep you anonymous, that's fine. Where did you get the file from to copy it?"

"Not telling," Aiden said. "But at this point, I'm pretty sure you can confirm the allegations with the police department. They already have an Internal Affairs investigation started."

"Really?" The reporter began scribbling notes down on the file jacket.

"Yep," Aiden replied. "You do what you need to do with this. Just keep me out of it. An anonymous source."

"You've got it," the reporter said. He reached over to shake Aiden's hand. "I appreciate the information, Mr. Anonymous."

Aiden nodded and shook his head. Once the reporter was gone, Derrick came out of the back office.

"Are you sure this is a good idea?" Derrick asked as he sat down at the table.

Aiden walked over and sat down as well, feeling both relieved and nervous. "That's what I asked Andy, but he was determined. He said to do it. So, it's done." Aiden shrugged.

"Well, this is going to spark some fireworks," Derrick said. He stretched in the chair, then checked his phone as the device buzzed him with a notification. "Oh man, that's the time? I've got to go. I've got to finish up a paper."

"Take care, bro," Aiden said.

"You gonna be okay here alone?" Derrick asked. Teeny had gone to the hospital to spend time with Liam. Lauren had returned to the afterlife world that the spirits had.

"Yeah," Aiden said with a nod, almost feeling like he would be okay there alone. Almost. "School comes first, remember? Lauren was adamant about that. Don't let her down."

Derrick gave Aiden a little bit of a smile. "I won't let her down. Promise. See you after class tomorrow."

"See you," Aiden said.

Derrick left and Aiden sighed. He ran a hand through his shaggy hair. The sun was sinking into the horizon outside. He grabbed a sheet and began taking an inventory of the candles that were left. He was planning a going-out-of-business sale, and he wanted to make sure he knew how much of what he had, and then would check the records of what the vendor charged to calculate a sale price. He already had a call in to the leasing agent about Lauren's death and his assuming the lease in full.

It was dark by the time his stomach started growling. He finished what he was doing and dropped the papers on the table. He turned off the lights and set the alarm before walking out and locking the door behind him. He turned and made his way down the strip. Some windows were lit in stores that were still open. Others were not, like the accountant's office and dentist's office. They both closed at five. The smell of barbecue grew stronger as he neared Pho-Q.

He opened the door and made his way to the counter. No need to take a table when it was just him. Holly was working the counter, and she gave him a warm smile as she made her way to him.

"Hey, handsome," she said, her voice as warm as her smile. "I'm sorry to hear about Lauren."

"Thanks," Aiden said.

"What can I get for you?" Holly asked. Usually, she flirted with Aiden, but it just didn't seem like the right thing to do at the moment.

"Oh, I'll just take a beef pho and a coke," Aiden said.

"You sure?" Holly asked. "You look like you could use a beer more than a coke."

"Gotta drive home," Aiden said with a shrug. "Thanks, though."

Holly nodded and went off to put in the order. There were televisions above the counter, one at each end. The one near him had the news on. The one at the other end had a football game on. There was a cluster of mostly men at that end of the counter, watching the game and intermittently cheering. Tom came out of the back and made his way over to Aiden.

"Holly got your order in?" Tom asked.

"Yeah." Aiden looked up and paused for a moment. "You're blue now?"

"Yeah," Tom rubbed his newly indigo goatee and ran a hand through the same-colored hair. "I figured I own my own business so why the hell not? I did it a few days ago, but I think you were a little too preoccupied to notice when I came by after what had happened."

"Fair point," Aiden said with a nod.

"Any word on a memorial yet?" Tom asked.

"Waiting to hear back from the funeral home for a date and time," Aiden said. "I'll let you know."

"Well, in the meantime, the memorial outside the shop has been growing," Tom said.

"People have been very generous," Aiden said with a nod and a small smile. "It's good to know she was so loved by people."

"She was," Tom said, nodding. "Have you decided about the shop?"

"Yeah, we still have a year on the lease, so I'm going to change it to a photography studio for myself," Aiden said. "See if I can get more traction having an actual location instead of working out of my apartment."

"That sounds like a solid choice," Tom said. A crash in the kitchen brought whoops and applause from those who heard it, and Tom turned. "Well, that was my sign to get back in the kitchen. Your meal's on me tonight. Take care, man."

"You, too," Aiden said as Holly approached with his drink and his bowl of pho.

"Here you go, hun," she said, setting the things down in front of him.

"Thanks," he said. He caught sight of something on the television. "Hey, Holly, can you turn that up?"

"Sure thing," she said, grabbing the remote from under the counter.

"An anonymous source provided a folder full of pictures of corpses that have the same mark. This serial killer has been operating in our area for several years, and yet no one has heard about it until now," the anchorman said. *"And what could be the reason we haven't heard about the serial killer in our midst? It is alleged that the mastermind behind all these murders is a police captain."*

"Oh my God," Holly said. "Did they arrest the guy?"

Aiden just gestured for her to keep watching. In their vicinity, the area had grown quieter as more people were paying attention to the broadcast.

"Internal Affairs is still investigating this," the anchorman said. *"No arrests have been made yet, but Captain Luis Rodriguez has been placed on administrative leave without pay at this time. Stay tuned to Channel Five News for the most recent updates on this case. And now we're going to turn to Antonio for a look at how the rest of our week looks weather-wise. Antonio?"*

Aiden looked down and began eating his food. People around him were discussing the serial killer case in animated tones. It had begun. It was out of his hands now. The phone in his pocket began vibrating, and he pulled it out, answering it.

"Did you see the news?" Andy's voice came over the line.

"Yeah, I did," Aiden said, his voice somber.

"You don't sound happy," Andy said. "You did a good thing, trust me."

"I just hope it doesn't come back to bite us in the ass," Aiden said.

"Here's hoping," Andy said. "I'll come by the shop tomorrow if that's good."

"Yeah, that's fine," Aiden said. "I'm eating dinner now, then going home to try to get some sleep. I'm exhausted."

"Understood," Andy said. "Hang in there, man. See you tomorrow."

"See ya, bro," Aiden said and then hung up. He finished his pho and when Holly refused to bring him his bill, he tossed the money on the counter as a tip. It was nice of Tom to give him his food on the house, but Holly still had to bring it to him, and he wasn't going to be cheap and not give her a tip. He got into his van and revved the engine up. He had several things to do before the day would be over and he could sleep.

The door to her apartment clicked shut behind her and she stood inside, just looking around. The apartment being empty caused a physical ache in Cade's chest. People had always been with her when she had been home, or she had been busy with work. This was the first time she had been alone in the apartment since Sam had died. It was also the first time she had noticed how the apartment had subtly changed.

The door that had led to Sam's room was gone. It hadn't even been there that long. But now its absence was as painful as his absence in her existence. It was one more reminder that he was no longer there. Cade walked over and touched the wall where it had been. Her chest felt tight, but otherwise, at this moment, she was numb. With her hand on the wall, she pushed, as if the door was just hidden and she could push it open, go into his room, see his things. There was no give. The wall was just a wall without a door.

Cadence crossed over to her couch and sank down into it. She grabbed one of the cushions that she so often threw when she was angry or frustrated. Instead of tossing it, however, she clutched it to her chest. It was almost as if she were trying to push the velvety pillow into the gaping hole she was feeling there.

The room was silent, only the sound of her drawing her scarred feet up onto the couch could be heard. She could have turned on the television to look in on the living. But for now, she was content to acknowledge the pain and the silence. It felt right that she should allow herself a little time to miss her brother.

About half an hour passed in silence as her mind wound through different memories she had with him, both when they were alive and when they were together on this side. Her reverie was interrupted as a thought occurred to her. She moved, setting aside the cushion that she had been snuggling. Cade then held her hands in front of her and closed her eyes.

She knew the picture well. It had been his freshman year and she and their parents had been helping him move into his dorm. Her mom had taken the picture. Sam had been wearing jeans and a Bart Simpson T-shirt. She had been wearing jean shorts and a navy blue tank top, her long hair in two braids. The two were smiling, and they each had an arm around the other's back. The picture had been on prominent display in her apartment until her death. It was one of the pictures that Andy had taken when he had gone to her apartment to collect Darwin.

A few minutes later, Cadence opened her eyes and, in her hands, she held an exact duplicate of that picture, frame and all. A few tears fell from her eyes, splashing on the glass of the frame. But there was also a soft smile on her lips. This felt right. She wiped the fallen tears from the glass and her face, then leaned over and placed the picture on the coffee table.

It was then that she decided that she would recreate the family pictures she had loved so much. Not all right now. Right now, was just for this one picture, it was for Sam. But soon she would have them all back. Just because she was dead didn't mean that she couldn't keep memories of her family.

She pulled her legs back up on the couch and hugged her knees to her chest. Looking at the picture, she smiled. She could almost hear Sam's laughter. It eased the ache in her heart a little.

The door to her apartment opened, and she knew that it was Ramon without ever turning around. She stayed as she was, just hugging her knees to her chest. Things had been a little tense between them lately, and she wasn't sure of his mood just yet. She understood where he was coming from with his worry, but she didn't feel like having another argument tonight.

Ramon was mildly surprised that she didn't turn around at the sound of the door. Cadence was not normally someone who was comfortable keeping her back to a door. Nor was she someone who wouldn't look to see who had just come in. Then again, they shared a connection, so she probably already knew it was him.

He crossed the room and bent over the arm of the couch, slipping his arms around her and placing a soft kiss on the top of her head. He noticed the picture on the coffee table.

"That's new," he said quietly.

"It is," she replied, her voice soft. "I decided that since they took away his room, I would make something else to keep him with me."

"That's wonderful, mi amore," he whispered. He kissed the top of her head one more time before moving around the couch to take a seat beside her. They were quiet together for a moment, both looking at the picture. It was Cadence who broke that silence.

"Do you remember the time that Snow brought me to you because I was out of it? Desolate, I think he called it."

"I do remember that night," Ramon answered with a nod. He slipped an arm around Cadence as she shifted on the couch to be next to him. "I remember being frightened that we might lose you. And then a few nights later, I was scared out of my wits when they brought you in with those burns."

"I seem to do that to you a lot."

"You do, mi amore. Which is why I worry so much about this case you are on."

"I know you worry," she said as she leaned her head on his shoulder. "But that wasn't where I was going with that."

"Oh?" He leaned his head on top of hers, feeling her hair against his cheek.

"Yeah. I was going to say that I'm surprised I haven't gotten that way with this." She gestured to the picture to emphasize that she was talking about the loss of Sam.

"When Snow called to tell me to come to your office, about what had happened, I was worried about it happening. So was he," Ramon replied. "He wanted all of us to be there for you because we weren't sure what kind of emotional state you were going to be in when you came back. But once you were back, I knew you wouldn't fall into desolation again."

"How did you know I would be okay? I didn't even know I would be okay."

"Because you had your anger at first." Ramon gently stroked her hair as he spoke. "And you had your case. You had a mission to stop the thing that ended your brother and brought Lauren over to our side. As much as I hate how dangerous the case is, I know that having something this important to do, to focus on, helps you. Tonight, you created a picture. You aren't throwing pillows or screaming curses at the universe. You're sad and you're quiet, but it seems like you are okay with that. You are accepting your grief instead of fighting against it or letting it swallow you whole."

"I think I am okay with it," she sighed. "I'm not happy, obviously. I miss him. I still feel like I have this huge hole in my being where he was, which probably sounds absurd because I only had him back for a few months."

"It doesn't sound absurd at all, mi amore. He was your brother. He was a good person. And I am so sorry for you that he is once again gone."

Cadence scoffed. "It's okay, but it's not okay. Does that make sense?"

"Si, mi amore. It does make sense."

Cade sighed and snuggled farther into the crook of Ramon's arm. "I love you."

"I love you, too," Ramon whispered. He moved and put a finger under her chin, tilting her head up to his. He then leaned in for a soft, passionate kiss.

CHAPTER 10

More Toys? Oh Boy!

The blank wall of Cadence's and Will's office was now covered corner to corner in an enormous global map. Will sat at his desk with a stack of papers in front of him. The Observation Bay had printed out every sighting of a possible prison escapee for them. Cadence had spent the early morning hours poring through them and putting together the ones that seemed to be the same creature. She had adopted Will's trick of using colored yarn to track the trails and movements of the escaped prisoners. She had always hated that in crime movies and TV shows, but she had to admit it was proving useful.

"Okay," Will said. "Purple goes on the town of Bristol. That one is on the border between Tennessee and Virginia. What did you make purple?"

"Evil God-like creatures," Cadence said.

"Oh," Will said. "Fun. Why Tennessee?"

"Who knows," Cade sighed. "Next?"

A knock sounded on their door, and they turned. Snow stood in the door frame with Whitfield in tow. "I thought perhaps you two might need some help."

Cadence smiled at Snow, glad to see him. "We do, but aren't you snowed under with work, too?" She grinned at the deliberate pun. She loved to irritate him when she could.

Snow rolled his eyes at her pun and shook his head. "I do have a great deal of work, which has increased since the breakout. A talk with Whitfield made me realize something, and I thought it important enough to share."

"Oh?" Cadence said, turning her attention to Snow and Whitfield.

"It's been too quiet," Whitfield said.

"You call this quiet?" Cadence asked, gesturing to the map behind her, full of various colored pushpins and strings.

"I call that a distraction," Whitfield said. "In less than 24 hours, X'Haldzos broke free of the farm, destroyed Barrington Prison, the dorm house at the college, and Lexington Hills before coming here and destroying the prison."

"Great recap," Will said.

Whitfield shook his head in mild frustration. "No, you aren't getting it. He's been quiet. He's building energy. And he knows how to get here."

"You think he's going to attack our whole plane of existence?" Cadence asked.

"I don't know," Whitfield said. "But there is another thing you haven't thought of, or maybe don't know. We also have the only way to the Council here."

The other three grew still. "You think he's going to go after the Council?" Cade asked, looking at Snow.

"We don't know," Snow replied. "It is a valid concern, though. I do believe it when Whitfield says he is building up energy for something big."

Cadence walked to her desk and sat down heavily in her chair. "I think I liked it better when we were hunting Shaldoxz," she said. "No offense," she added, speaking to Whitfield.

"I've been monitoring the portals, when and where they are opening," Snow said.

"You can do that?" Will asked, surprised.

"I can now, yes," Snow said. "That ability came with the promotion, it seems. X'Haldzos's energy is strong when it moves through the portals. Looking back on the records, his movements were easy to track. It's a larger power signature than a normal spirit. Now there have been some other big movements as well, but they haven't been quite the same as X'Haldzos's. Some are bigger, some are smaller. But that one signature is unique."

"You know where he is." Cade stood up from her chair, ready to spring into action.

"Easy tiger," Will said, noting her stance. "We need a plan first."

"Where is he?" Cade asked.

"It looks like he went back to the prison," Snow said. "Now he could have physically moved from the location and be somewhere else since he got there. But his movements, that we've been able to track, lead there."

"He already blew the place up. Why would he go there?" Will asked.

"He's been trying to escape that farmhouse for decades." Whitfield paced as he spoke. "He also knows that we know it was his home for a long time. He's not going to go there if he can help it. From the timeline we have, Barrington was the first place he landed. It's my guess he spent time in the streams themselves, regenerating. He had to recoup some of his energy after jumping and before he could do anything like what he did at the prison. He would see it as a safe place. Specifically, because the portal room is still intact. It's a place for him to rest where he has direct access to a portal he can manipulate. An easy escape route, of sorts."

"Great," Cadence said. "Easy access to go anywhere it wants."

"Pretty much," Whitfield said with a nod.

"Well, that gives us a bit of a leg up," Will said. "We know where it is. We can get some things together and try to bring the fight to it. Kill it if we're lucky."

"Or get killed if you're not," Whitfield said, pointing out the obvious.

"Oh, ye of little faith," Will said with a grin. "I've been working on some things that should come in handy."

"How have you had time?" Cadence asked.

"I make time," Will said with a shrug and a smile.

"Your inventions are unique," Snow said. "But according to your own report, your items had no effect on the demon."

Will recalled hitting X'Haldzos with his "jacks," and the toy-like weapons having no effect on the thing. "Yeah," Will conceded with a nod, "but those were items designed more for spirits than for huge D&D monsters. Over the last day, I've changed up my plans. I've been thinking more along the lines of elephant hunting than squirrel hunting."

"People hunt squirrels?" Whitfield asked in surprise.

"People hunt everything, including each other," Cadence said with a shrug. "Why should squirrels be exempt?"

"She's not wrong," Will said. "Come on. I'll show you guys what I've been working on."

"Come on in," Will said as he opened the door of his apartment for Cadence, Snow, and Whitfield.

The main room of the apartment was a mess. There was a large brown leather sectional that peeked out from beneath bits and bobs of all kinds of wires and springs. A console CRT television was situated on the wall opposite the couch. The clear plastic coffee table in between the couch and TV had a smattering of tools and papers on it. Against the far wall, near the bedroom door, was a drawing desk. On the wall there were posters for *Star Wars*, *Ghostbusters*, *Back to the Future*, and *Alien*.

Cadence smirked slightly as she looked around. "This is very you."

Whitfield was curious as he looked around, and Snow seemed confounded by the mess.

"Thank you," Will said, smiling. "I like it. Sorry about the mess, but eh, you know."

"How do you find anything in this?" Snow asked, gesturing to the room.

"You should see my bedroom. It's way worse," Will said with a chuckle.

"I'm not sure which is worse," Snow said. "The fact that you so readily admit it, or the fact that you seem proud of it."

"Okay, Dad," Cadence said, elbowing Snow. "We're not here to make him clean his room. We're here to see what he has offensive and defensive-wise."

Will was already busying himself by clearing off the couch a bit so the three could sit without breaking anything. Once he had cleared enough of the worn leather, he gestured for them to have a seat. He sat on the floor on the other side of the coffee table, sifting through the various sketches there.

"Okay," Will said. "You guys already know the jacks. I've explained the idea of the marbles to Cadence, but I think for this monster, we need more power than a small glass ball is going to give us."

"Could you explain the idea of your marbles to those of us who weren't there?" Snow requested.

"Right," Will said. "The basic idea was that they were fragile glass balls that would hold a liquid that would be able to have a specific effect on a spirit or non-human. The liquid is specific, so if you use a marble for a spirit on a non-human, it's going to have no effect. The glass breaks upon contact with the being and sprays them with the liquid. It could have a paralyzing effect, a painful effect, or anywhere in between.

"The jacks, which inject instead of spray, were useless against the creature, which tells me the marbles will be, too. So, I thought I would make use of a different kind of toy. It came out after I died, but I always thought it was cool." He put the first sketch down on the empty table.

"A Super Soaker?" Cadence asked.

"Yep," Will said with a smile. "Take the liquid from the marble idea and get a ton of it. Fill the tanks on the water gun, maybe some extra for reloads. Make the liquid for evil non-humans, meant to hurt. This guy isn't playing around, so we can't either."

"Says the man taking his cues for weaponry from a toy catalog," Snow said.

"I am and will always be a Toys 'R' Us kid," Will said. "Don't knock it 'til you try it."

"His stuff has been pretty on point so far," Cadence said.

"For this next one, we're going to need earplugs," Will said, looking at Cadence.

"Are we attacking with loud music or harsh language?" Cadence asked, joking.

"This," Will said, putting the next sketch down with a flourish, "is called a sonic ear. I loved this as a kid. Annoyed my mom with it all the time. The way it works is that it's supposed to let you eavesdrop in on the next room or so. What I'm going to do is weaponize it."

"Weaponize it how?" Whitfield asked.

"This thing loves to roar, right? So, we pull the trigger on this when it starts. It's going to absorb all that noise and send it back at him, amplified." Will grinned as he outlined how it was going to work. "It will send a wall of amplified sound that should stun it for a little bit."

"Nice," Cadence said with an approving nod.

"Oh, we're not done yet," Will said with a grin. "What do you think this is?" He put another drawing down on the table.

"A Koosh ball?" Cadence asked. "Are you serious?"

"Serious as a heart attack." Will nodded.

"How does this … *thing* … have anything to do with defense or offense?" Snow asked.

"Okay, so you see all the little rubbery fingers coming off of the center ball," Will said. "When this hits a non-human, the fingers will extend in an instant, wrapping around the non-hum and entwining with each other. It just ties him up. Might buy us some time for other things."

"Nice," Cadence said again.

"For defense, I have a couple of things that are energy-based," Will said and put another drawing on the table. This drawing had straps in an X going over the chest and back. In the center of the X on each side was an orb. "This baby is a personal shield. Hit the switch, it covers you head to toe. It won't last forever, but it should be able to help you not take damage for a while."

He put another drawing down, this of a set of wide bracelets with the same orbs. "These are smaller shields. Not body length, but you can use them to help deflect any kind of incoming projectile it may send at you. Or deflect its claws."

"This isn't bad stuff," Whitfield said. "What's that?" Whitfield was pointing to a drawing by Will's feet.

"Oh, that won't work," Will said. "It's a Wacky Wally. You know, those sticky octopus toys that crawl down the wall? I was trying to work them so they would explode on contact, and I can, but I think that's on the same scale as the marbles. Too small to work against this one. I'd also thought of those 45 RPM records. Blade the edges so they cut. But they would be probably too difficult or dangerous for us to carry."

"So, how do we get all of this done?" Snow asked.

"That's the trick. We're on limited time and this stuff is going to take energy," Will said. "Is there any way that we can commandeer NHD weapons design or others to help us make these? Or at least make the liquid and canisters so that we can have that to combat the monster."

Snow nodded. "I'll talk to NHD. Can I take these designs?"

"Sure," Will said, nodding. "If they have any questions, they can call me. I would prefer to be involved, to be honest. I know how it is supposed to work and what it is supposed to look like."

"I'll see how many hands I can pull on deck for this and then call you to join them," Snow said.

"That leaves me and Whitfield to try to put out any fires between then and now," Cadence said.

Whitfield looked over at Cadence in surprise. "Me?"

"It's a practical decision, not a personal one," Cadence said, her tone cool. "I haven't forgiven you. Not by a long shot."

Whitfield nodded, accepting her at her word.

"Thank you, Will," Snow said. "This is excellent work on such short notice. And with as divided as your attention must have been."

"Thanks," Will said, beaming with pride as he stood up from the floor. "I'll see if I can come up with anything else. Oh, and if we're keeping Whitfield out of the prison, we may want to take the cube into the field with us. If we can get this thing tied up, we may be able to just zap it into the cube."

Snow nodded. "And after this is all over, I'm going to have NHD working on making more of those cubes. Those are effective little prisons."

"Very effective," Whitfield said with a shudder and a nod.

"Let me make some calls," Snow said. "I'll see you all later."

Snow stood up and he and the others filed out of Will's apartment. Cadence paused on the threshold of the door and looked back at Will.

"Those guys in Development were idiots," Cade said. "You've got a great imagination with unbelievable practical applications."

"Careful there," Will chuckled. "You almost just sounded like you don't mind having me as a partner."

"Jury's still out on that one," Cadence replied with heavy sarcasm in her voice, making it clear that she was joking with him. "I'll see you later."

CHAPTER 11

Company

When the knock sounded on Andy's apartment door, he tensed. Rising from his brown leather couch, he reached for the gun he had in the back waistband of his jeans. He crept toward the door, trying to make as little noise as possible as he clicked the safety off. Andy looked out of the peephole in the door, holding his personal gun in his right hand. When he saw who it was, he clicked the safety back into place. He carefully shoved the gun into the back waistband of his pants and unlocked the door. He then opened it to reveal Aiden on the other side.

Aiden lifted a curious brow at the time it took Andy to answer the door. "I come at a bad time?"

"Nah, man, just being careful," Andy said, gesturing for Aiden to enter. The tall, lanky paranormal investigator with shaggy hair stepped through the doorway and paused just inside. After Aiden was inside, Andy locked his door once again.

"Careful or paranoid?" Aiden asked as he pointed in the general direction of the gun at Andy's back.

"They kind of go hand in hand at this point," Andy replied with a shrug. "Besides, as they say, it's not paranoia if they really are out to get you."

"That's fair," Aiden said, giving a nod.

Andy took a seat on the couch and gestured for Aiden to have a seat as well. "What brings you by?"

Aiden sat down in the well-worn brown leather chair. "Just checking in on you," he answered with a shrug. "You've kind of had a hell of a day."

"Yeah," Andy said with a sigh, idly petting Darwin, who had hopped up onto the couch to seek attention. Darwin had been Cadence's cat when she was alive. After her death, Andy had taken the black fur ball in.

"Which is getting to you more?" Aiden asked. "Quitting the force or the news breaking?"

"Both, I think," Andy said. "Quitting was big enough on its own, but if I'm honest, the reason I'm carrying right now is because of the news. Don't get me wrong, part of me wants to celebrate bringing down a corrupt cop. But I also have a strong suspicion that he has few to no limits and wouldn't hesitate to come after me. I mean, it's not much of a stretch to figure out how the news got the file, since I gave it to Internal Affairs as well."

"Yeah, I think you're right," Aiden said. "It's kind of part of the reason I came by tonight. I didn't want you left alone in case something somewhere went sideways. Hell, I half expected a flood of reporters outside your door."

"Oh, good grief! Don't bring that down upon me! Half the reason we did this anonymously and through you was so none of us ended up with reporters at our doors," Andy said. "Speaking of reporters, or at least people on TV, where's Teeny? You two have been stuck at the hip for the last week or so it seems."

Aiden couldn't help but grin a little. "She's at the hospital. They're releasing Liam tomorrow, so she wanted to spend time with him before he left."

"What's the plan after they release him?" Andy asked.

"Teeny is going to take him to get his meds filled at the pharmacy," Aiden said. "Then she's taking him to the airport and putting him on a plane. A friend of his will pick him up at LAX when he lands, get him home and situated. He's probably going to have to get some home health nurses for a bit, and he is nowhere near done with doctor appointments, but he's going to be okay."

"Given the scene I walked in on at the prison, that's great to hear," Andy said. The image of Liam lying like a broken doll amid all the shattered glass was not an image that would leave his mind soon. Nor was the sound of Cadence's panicked voice coming over the radio to alert him to the danger.

"You look like a man with a lot of thoughts," Aiden commented. "Care to share?"

"Sharing is caring," Andy murmured in reply, then chuckled and shook his head. "Cade always said that, usually right before she stole food or coffee from me." He sighed and shook his head. "Just thinking how life is never going to be the same again. I mean, I knew that when she died. But I had never imagined that any of this was out there. Ghosts, the serial murders. I had thought the captain was a good guy. I just feel like the world turned upside down and I'm scrambling to find my balance and direction."

"I feel you," Aiden said. "I can't even begin to understand how hard it must have been to turn your back on your job. But I've been where you are as far as finding out ghosts are real. Lauren and Dan hired me as a videographer for some of their early expeditions to places to investigate. Dan thought if they started a website and posted videos to it, they could get discovered or something, get rich. I liked the man, but he was always trying to find a quick and easy way to get rich. He never said it, but I think he thought that if he could get them well off, then he would deserve Lauren. Anyways, the first place was a snooze fest. But the second place? We caught shit on video and audio that couldn't be explained. Once I saw that, I was hooked. I had to know more."

"And now you know more than you could ever have imagined," Andy said.

"No kidding," Aiden said, shaking his head. "By the time we did Lexington, we'd been together as a group for almost ten years. I'd seen Lauren and Dan through their divorce, met and lost Bethany. Gained Derrick as a kind of little brother. But that video that we showed you? That floored me. That is the one that pulled the rug out from under me."

"It did the same for me, trust me," Andy said.

"Oh, I know, I saw your face," Aiden said. "But part of me wonders if all of this wasn't all some kind of design."

"What do you mean?" Andy asked, leaning forward a little as Darwin stalked off the couch in search of his food bowl.

"Bear with me here," Aiden said, sitting forward a bit in his chair. "We did the Lexington investigation, which gave us the opportunity to work with Cadence and Snow. Then the dorm thing got us to involve you."

"And save my ass," Andy chimed in.

"Eh, more distracting the bad guy," Aiden demurred with a shrug. "But then, by some weird coincidence, you're the security at the prison. What happened there leads to Teeny joining us. Then Scarecrow Farms, which is when you got the file about the murders, got attacked by a ghost in the basement, and found out your captain is the big boogie man that's been orchestrating all the bad shit that they have been dealing with on the other side."

"So, you're saying this has all been part of some grand plan?" Andy arched a skeptical eyebrow. "That we're destined to work together? To know about the afterlife?"

"Maybe?" Aiden shrugged. "I'm not saying it is a fact. Just something I wonder about. When you start to think about it, it's a hell of a lot of coincidences."

"Well, if there is someone up there thinking this is all fun and games, they need a damned reality check, because it's not," Andy grumbled.

"No kidding," Aiden said with a chuckle.

"Hey if you stay late enough, we can always turn on the news and watch Rodriguez's world burn," Andy said.

"I have a personal stake in celebrating that, so sure." Aiden laughed.

A sudden loud report of a gunshot preceded the door to Andy's apartment flying open by less than a second.

Aiden ducked down in his chair, startled. Meanwhile, Andy went down on one knee in front of the couch but turned so he was facing the door. In a smooth, lightning-fast movement, he had drawn his weapon and clicked the safety off, aiming it at the door.

Captain Rodriguez walked in. He wore jeans, a white sweater, and a black leather jacket. He held his revolver in his right hand, pointing it at the floor, surveying the scene, then frowned as he saw Aiden.

"Didn't realize you would have company," Rodriguez said.

"And that makes blowing the door off of a private residence okay?" Aiden asked in disbelief. In his mind, he was calling out for Lauren, hoping she would return from wherever she was in time to help protect him and Andy from whatever was about to happen.

Rodriguez ignored Aiden. His attention was on Andy, who had not relaxed his weapon. "Are you going to shoot me, Halleran?"

"Considering you just broke into my apartment, I'm strongly considering it," Andy said.

"Dude, the neighbors have probably called the cops by now," Aiden said. He was trying to de-escalate the situation before someone did get shot. Having two guns drawn in the same room he was in made him more than a little nervous.

"I am the cops," Rodriguez said, snapping at Aiden. "I heard a disturbance inside and when there was no answer, I forced the door open to check on the well-being of one of my officers."

"Former officer," Andy said. "I quit, remember? And no one is going to believe that there was no one home and you know it. It's not just my word against yours."

"I wasn't expecting you to have company," Rodriguez growled. "And I'm suspended without pay. Do semantics matter all that much?"

"Yeah, I saw a little something on the six o'clock news about your secret file of corpses," Andy said.

"A secret file that you stole from my office and released to the press," Rodriguez said.

"How on earth did you get to be a captain?" Andy asked. "Your investigative work is shit. I didn't steal the file from your office. I wouldn't even begin to know where to try to find it. Not to mention the fact that the one time I asked you about it, you denied its existence. Therefore, if I didn't have it, I couldn't have given it to the press." Andy lowered his weapon and stood up. Rodriguez had his weapon pointed down and seemed to be more in the mood to talk. The gun seemed to have been just to blow the lock off his door. Something the apartment complex and his neighbors were going to love.

"But you did have it. You gave it to Internal Affairs. You expect me to believe that you just gave it to Internal Affairs and they're the ones that leaked it to the press?" Rodriguez asked.

"I have no idea how it got to the press," Andy lied.

"R-i-g-h-t," Rodriguez said, drawing the word out. "And how it got to IA?"

"Okay, yeah, I might have a hand in that," Andy said.

"Which means you did steal it from my office," Rodriguez said.

"Nope," Andy said, shaking his head. "I found it in my desk. No idea how it got there. The night that the coffee pot flew across your office."

"Sarah," Rodriguez said in a growl.

"Who's Sarah?" Aiden and Andy asked in stereo.

"A bigger pain in my ass than I thought she would be, that's who," Rodriguez answered.

"Speaking of pains in the ass," Aiden said, feeling the bite of the anger he had been trying to stuff down and ignore since Rodriguez entered. "Thanks a ton for running away the other night when my friend was killed because of what you did."

Rodriguez looked at Aiden and narrowed his eyes. "Kid, you are the only unarmed one in the room. Don't be stupid. Let the grown-ups talk."

Aiden drew himself up to his full height as he stood, his anger flaring around him. Rodriguez could see it in his aura, the dark, murky red color licking around the man like flames. He then saw a blueish orb appear near Aiden and he focused his eyes and mind. Lauren came into focus.

Lauren had felt the pull of Aiden's anger. It was like an alarm bell in her head. She reached out as they had taught her to do and began trying to soothe the anger. She could see the danger in the situation and knew Aiden could be a hothead. She didn't want him making things worse. She also pulled out her phone and called Cadence.

Rodriguez smirked a little at seeing the plump form of Lauren's spirit at Aiden's side. It made sense that she would be here. He also noted the accusatory look in her eyes as she looked at Rodriguez, even while she tried to calm her friend. "So," Rodriguez said, turning back to

Andy, "you got lucky and found the fabled missing file. Why not come to me about it?"

"I was trying to decide what I was going to do with it," Andy replied. "I was debating coming to you to talk about it, to see why you were sitting on it. Then Scarecrow Farms happened."

Cadence and Whitfield appeared in the apartment, and both were shocked. Lauren had Aiden, and Cadence hoped she knew enough of her new skills to be able to protect him during this. She then looked at Whitfield.

"I don't trust you with Wolf here," Cade said, shaking her head.

"I'm on your side," Whitfield said. "You have every right not to trust me, but I swear to you that I am on your side."

"This apartment is getting a little crowded," Rodriguez said with a sour look on his face. He had seen Cadence and the one he had known as Shaldoxz teleport in. Sirens could be heard in the distance, the sound growing closer. "And about to be even more crowded, if I had to guess. We'll have to continue this discussion another time." Rodriguez then turned and left.

Andy moved to the door and tried to close it, but the entire doorknob and locking mechanism had been destroyed. "Dammit," Andy growled. "Where am I going to get a new door at this time of night?"

"That was intense," Aiden said, some of the strength lent to him by his anger fading. He sat back down in the chair as if dropped there.

"How is the apartment crowded?" Andy asked as he turned away from the door in anger and disgust.

"Lauren is here," Aiden said. "I can feel her. I can guess she called for backup when she saw you and him with guns."

"At least he can still think things through," Lauren commented to Cadence.

"Always has been quick," Cadence said with a nod.

Two uniformed officers knocked on the door frame of the apartment.

"Come on in," Andy said with a sigh.

"Looks like you have a problem with your door, Detective," one of the officers said.

Andy gave a chuckle that had no humor behind it. "No kidding."

"Detective, can I ask you to put your weapon down?" the other officer asked.

"Do you know them?" Lauren turned to Cadence as the two officers came in.

"I know the one that came in first. He's a great cop," Cadence answered. "The second one I don't know. He looks fresh out of the academy. Especially if a detective with a gun is making him nervous."

"To be fair, he's a former detective," Whitfield piped up. "He quit his job."

"You're talking why?" Cadence asked, turning to Whitfield.

For his part, Whitfield didn't back down. "Because last I checked, I wasn't prevented from doing so. I get that you hate my guts, but you are the one who brought me along."

Cadence sighed and pressed her lips together, reining in whatever smartass comment was dying to fly out of her mouth. Instead, she turned to Lauren. "Are you guys good now?" She gestured to both Lauren and Aiden as she asked the question.

"Yeah, we're good," Lauren nodded.

Cade returned the nod, put a hand on Whitfield's arm, and the two spirits disappeared from Andy's apartment.

"Sure thing, Rosen," Andy said. He held the weapon to the side, facing the ceiling. He clicked the safety into place and then set it down on the coffee table.

"Thank you, Sir," the officer named Rosen said, relaxing visibly. Rosen was on the skinny side with angular features and a sharp nose.

"What happened, Detective?" the other officer asked. Andy knew the other officer as Givens. He was a middle-aged black man who had a wife, four kids, and was a good cop.

"Sir, can you step out into the hall with me?" Rosen asked Aiden.

"Sure, yeah," Aiden said, his voice a little shaky.

Halleran and the other detective paused, letting Rosen get Aiden out into the hall and down from the door a bit. Andy knew the scenario. Get the two witnesses away from each other and then question them. They could then poke holes from there.

"Have a seat, Givens," Andy said. He took a seat on the couch, feeling the adrenaline beginning to fade.

"I'll stand for now. Thank you, Sir," Givens said. The officer did relax his stance, however.

"As you like it," Andy shrugged. "And technically, I'm not a detective anymore. I quit today."

"I heard," Givens said with a sad shake of his head. "It's a damn shame."

"You heard? Damn, that word traveled fast," Andy said.

"Faster when it was attached to what happened with Captain Rodriguez," Givens said. "Do you want to hear how I see it?"

"Sure," Andy said.

"See, I think you gave that file everyone is talking about to IA," Givens said, finally moving to a chair and taking the seat that Aiden had vacated. "I don't know how you got it, and I don't want to know. I don't know if you leaked it to the press or not, and I don't want to know. But I think the captain came here looking for a little face time with you."

"You would be right about that," Andy replied. "He didn't even bother knocking; he just blew the lock off the door."

"You and your friend don't seem wounded," Givens said. He was taking down notes on a pad of paper to be put into a report later.

"No, the only shot fired was the one that took out the door," Andy said. "Other than that, he just talked. He did say that he hadn't expected me to have company. Aiden may just have saved my life."

"And the neighbors who called 911 when they heard the gunshot," Givens said.

"Them too," Andy said with a nod. "Givens, why haven't you applied for detective? You have the brains for it."

"Happy where I'm at right now, Sir," Givens said. "You want a protection detail?"

Andy scoffed and shook his head. "Nah, I'll be fine."

"A locksmith at this time of night is gonna cost you an arm and a leg, Detective," Givens said. "Might want to go to a hotel."

"I would have to find one that takes cats," Andy said. "Not to mention I don't like the idea of leaving the place unattended with an obviously open door. That's like an engraved invitation."

"True," Givens said with a nod. He stood and walked to the door, motioning for Rosen to come back in. "I'll be right back, Detective."

Andy nodded as Rosen and Aiden came back in.

"Is it sad that I'm starting to get used to this?" Aiden asked.

Andy lifted a curious brow. "Get used to what?"

"Being questioned by the police for things I just kind of happened to be around for," Aiden said.

Andy chuckled. "Man, I think it's a job hazard for you at this point."

Aiden looked at Rosen. "Officer, can I use my phone?"

"Sure," Rosen said. He had asked everything he had to ask of Aiden. He knew Givens was getting the paperwork and started to give Andy his report number.

Aiden nodded and hit a couple of buttons, walking toward the windows of the apartment.

"Is it true, Detective?" Rosen asked, leveling his intelligent eyes at Andy.

"Is what true?" Andy asked.

"The file. The captain," Rosen said.

"Yeah," Andy said with a sigh. "It's true."

"Damn," Rosen said. "I'd always thought he was one of the good ones."

"You and me both," Andy said with a grimace.

Givens entered the apartment once more and handed Andy a pamphlet that had the report number and his victim's rights in it.

"I know I don't have to tell you this, but I have to tell you this," Givens said with a slight smile. "You can pick your report up in a couple of days from the records department."

"And if you have any further questions about the incident, you'll be in touch," Andy said with a grin and a nod as he stood up once more. "Yeah, I know the drill."

"For whatever it's worth," Givens said, "we're all hoping you decide to come back."

"Yeah," Rosen said.

"Thanks, guys," Andy said. "Be safe out there."

"He'll be here in about twenty minutes," Aiden said as the cops left.

"Huh? Who will?" Andy asked.

"Locksmith," Aiden said. "He may not be able to help much with the actual door, but he can put a couple of chain locks on or something so that you can avoid getting robbed in the middle of the night."

"Dude, you didn't have to call anyone out," Andy said.

"Oh, it's no problem," Aiden said with a dismissive shrug. "I know the guy. I used to lose my keys all the time. Always called him. When he got married, I did his whole wedding package. We give each other deals when we can."

"Guess I should leave a message for the apartment office that I'm going to need a new door," Andy said with a sigh. He took his gun from the coffee table and put it into the back waistband of his pants once again.

"We still watching the news together?" Aiden asked.

"Sure," Andy said as he dialed his phone, tossing the TV remote to Aiden.

CHAPTER 12

Trouble in the Afterworlds

The white-blue light around him flickered as he sought a way out. He had been tracking the scent through many places. He had found a different variant of it. And now he was following another variant. It was close to the scent of the one he sought. He had gotten close the last time, when he had found that large white room with only two spirits in it. His roar had done more than kill or maim that time. It had set free others of his kind. Different forms, ages, and shapes, but they all had that dark aura of evil.

And so now he sought another place like that. His joy was in fear, destruction, and blood. He thought he could find a place that would have even more of that in store for him. The promise of that is what bought his ultimate prey time to continue to exist.

X'Haldzos burst out of the portal and into an area that was confounding at first. In fact, for a moment, he thought he was still in the conduit because it was so bright there. As his five eyes adjusted, however, he saw an infinite land stretching out before him. There were glass-like domes that contained various environments covering the land. The demon moved toward one of the strange, enclosed biomes.

He moved toward the closest of the domes. Peering within, he could see grass and trees, and even a pond. He could even see a roof nestled among the treetops. The pond was situated near the edge of the dome, and he could see a man fishing there, looking happy as could be.

This elicited a razor-sharp smile from the monster. He knew now where he was, and what these were. He was where the good and pious went to find their version of paradise. Each of these orbs was someone's version of heaven, the Summer Lands, or whatever they called it in their various religions.

He had found the paradise level of the afterworld. Oh, this was going to be fun. They were all laid out there in their bubbles. Easy pickings. When his taloned hand crashed through the bubble of the man fishing, the expression of happiness on the man's face faded and changed to terror. He jumped to his feet; his pole having dropped to the ground in his alarm. He looked around him as he patted himself down, looking for a weapon. His pole, a net, some tackle, and a cooler. He did the only thing he could think of and grabbed his pole, reeling the line back in as quick as he could.

X'Haldzos began moving inside the bubble. Trees broke and fell as he pushed his way through them. All of his yellow eyes were focused on the man as he made his way toward him.

The man had no idea why or how this nightmare of a monster was invading his space. All he knew was that it was here, now. He had no weapons. This was supposed to be his happily ever after. Why would he need a weapon? But just as he had fought in World War II, he would do his best to fight now. No monster was going to take his piece of heaven from him without a fight.

The creature with the rubbery black skin that looked like an oil slick on top of tar crept toward him. The man's rod was now ready, the hook dangling at the end of the line. Breaking the bubble had set off an alarm, he could hear it in the distance. He knew that there would be some form of cavalry on its way. He didn't know if his was the first heaven to be attacked or not. But really, it didn't matter. If he could stop the creature here or delay it long enough for help to get there, it would be worth it. He cast the line, trying to aim the hook for one of the creature's eyes.

X'Haldzos reached out, having anticipated the paltry attack, and caught the hook with his hand. Like with the toy jacks that they had tried to attack him with at the farmhouse, the hook did nothing to him. It did, however, create a line between him and the fisherman. He yanked on the line, but the fisherman dropped the rod right before the demon pulled. The veteran did the next best thing he could think of. He picked up the cooler, which, with the ice and the fish, had some decent weight to it. He hefted it over his head and threw it at the monster.

X'Haldzos let the hook and the line drop from his hand as the cooler hit him in the chest. He was mildly irritated now. He hadn't expected the spirit to be as tenacious as he was. The lazy fisherman wasn't as lazy as he had expected. He reached out in a movement so quick it caught the fisherman off guard and grabbed the spirit of the man in one hand and lifted him up to eye level, which was just about three feet off the ground. X'Haldzos smiled once more, revealing far too many lethal-looking teeth for a mouth that was too wide for its face. Bringing his other hand up, the demon took hold of the man's arm. He pulled, and the arm came off with a satisfying pop-crack-squelch. Silver blood poured from the shoulder area where his arm had been.

The mortal bellowed in pain but did not scream in fear. In fact, other than his initial shock at seeing X'Haldzos, there had been no further terror from the man. The demon frowned as he realized this. He could cause the man pain, but the man was resigned to whatever was coming next. He was grim, determined, and hurting. But he did not fear. He flung the bleeding man away from him, as far as he could, and was at least gratified to hear the crunch of the man's body hitting and crashing through the roof of his home. The spirit could bleed out there if the impact hadn't destroyed him.

X'Haldzos could hear the alarms, but he doubted that anything would be done. And he had a way out if any protective team tried to touch him. He left the fisherman's bubble as it began to dissolve, indicating the spirit was no more. The trees melted away as he left, heading for the next closest dome.

The next bubble was full of clouds at the bottom instead of ground. A white and silver high-spire castle rose from the center of the clouds. Everything there was intricately designed and beautiful. X'Haldzos could recognize that, even if it repulsed him. His repulsion turned to surprise, however, as a white dragon emerged from the clouds and came flying at him as he tore his way into the bubble.

There was a young woman on a parapet of one of the main towers of the castle. She felt fear; X'Haldzos could taste it. Ignoring the dragon, the demon moved toward the woman. Ignoring the dragon proved to be a bad move. Claws tore into his back as the dragon attacked from above and behind. X'Haldzos puffed himself up, the pain he felt adding to his energy as it built. He turned to face the dragon, his own talons now tearing into the arm of the dragon. The dragon screeched as it felt the injury, and it flew back just a little. It recognized the puffing up of the demon. The dragon arched its neck as it took a deep breath and forcefully expelled breath so cold that frost and ice began to form on X'Haldzos's skin.

Movement became painful as ice crackled on his skin. The dragon bobbed in the air, heading down, and ducking a taloned hand as X'Haldzos reached for the flying creature. Coming up, he used his claws again, attempting to open the nightmare creature's throat. X'Haldzos backed up, tromping through the clouds that made up the ground there, narrowly avoiding the attack. He felt something sharp bounce off his back. The ice crackled as he moved just enough to aim two of his mustard-colored eyes at whatever had just hit him.

A winged warrior hovered just outside of the dome and had tossed a spear at him. An angel defending the heavens. The ice began to dissipate from X'Haldzos's skin as the dragon flew near again, his claws now taking a chunk out of the back of the demon's neck. Another spear hit him, bouncing off his back once more.

X'Haldzos gathered his energy and roared. The dome shattered completely, as did three others surrounding this one. The dragon fell through the clouds, the impact of the roar turning him to silver goo as he fell. The castle began to crumble, and the woman screamed as she fell from the fractured parapet. This was one damsel in distress who would not be saved. The two angels that had been attacking from behind were also too close to be much more than a smear of silver from the force of the roar.

The sound of wings flapping in the distance meant that more were coming. X'Haldzos now had a decision to make. He was injured, but only a little. Three more biomes were now fully open to him with prey that was already afraid within. Defenders of the heavens would be arriving soon, and more than likely in force, which meant not only angels, but the legions of devils from the lower reaches as well. All the Afterworld would come to defend itself now. He could leave now and avoid any further injury. He knew the way here now and could come back any time unless they figured out some way to bar his re-entry.

He was hungry after his roar, though. And there were some tasty meals nearby. The threat of the annoyance of the angels and devils attacking him currently paled in comparison to his hunger. He moved for the first open paradise and began to cut a swath through the afterworld, leaving his trail in the silver blood of spirits. When the first of the combined forces of Heaven and Hell reached him, he turned and began fighting through them to make his way back to the portal. He had destroyed twenty different paradises before they had managed to come in force, not just sending a handful of angels or devils at a time to try to handle him. While the thrill of having this smorgasbord to chew through exhilarated him, he was full. He was also beginning to tire, and he knew if they were coming at him this strongly, he would have to fight his way back. It wasn't that he didn't love a good fight. He just didn't like fights that weren't in his favor.

As he neared the portal, the fight changed. Around the portal were three entities with bright gold auras. Gods. They were trying to block his escape as their servants tried to kill him. One of them was a man with the head of a lion wielding a bow and a quiver of arrows. Another was an Asian man in green robes with a crescent blade sword that was also green, the hilt of which looked like an ornate Asian dragon. The third was a mountain of a man in loose brown shorts, no shirt, and very detailed war paint and tattoos. That one wielded a spear.

Apedemak, the lion-headed one, growled a warning. Guan Gong, the man in green robes, nodded, as if he understood the growl, and readied himself in a stance, his blade in front of him. Tumatauenga, the Māori god of war, hefted his spear above his shoulder.

X'Haldzos began to gather his power, what he had left of it. He had never imagined that the gods would make an appearance. The legions of Heaven and Hell realms, sure. But the gods? He hadn't realized that his incursion here would get them this riled up.

The god with the three lion heads, Apedemak, made the first move. With his bow, he launched an arrow at X'Haldzos. He snarled word and the tip of the arrow exploded into flame. X'Haldzos changed his trajectory a bit and the flaming arrow that would have hit him in the head thumped into the ground of one of the biomes he had destroyed.

While Apedemak readied another arrow, both Guan Gong and Tumatauenga stepped forward. Guan had his sword ready. Tumatauenga held his spear forward but spoke.

"Stop, evil creature," Tumatauenga ordered, his voice rough and deep. "You will not defile this place and escape."

"Back," was X'Haldzos's only reply, and it echoed through the minds of everyone in the vicinity. The volume of it brought normal spirits to their knees. The flights of some angels and devils changed as they were brought lower or sent off track by the voice. Some even fell to the ground.

"We will not allow your actions to go unpunished," Guan said, his Asian accent thick.

Apedemak let another arrow loose, this time adding no magic to it. He didn't want anything to distract the large, black toad-like creature from speaking with the other two. They had its attention. Apedemak wanted it kept there.

X'Haldzos caught the motion of the fired arrow, however. He watched it with one eye while the other four were trained on the two speaking gods. Once he saw where it was likely to land, he moved to his right a bit. This time, he was a little too slow, and the arrow grazed his hind leg. Unlike the spears and swords of the angels and devils that had bounced off him like thrown pebbles, annoying and pesky, but harmless, this hurt. Like the dragon's bite, this did damage.

X'Haldzos snarled in pain as the edge of the arrowhead sliced through the thick black skin of his left hind leg. He used this pain to his advantage, however, and added the pain to the energy he was bringing together. He would flatten these three gods as he had flattened the paradise bubbles behind him. That was when another pain made him howl and look down.

Guan Gong had taken the opportunity to swing his sword across X'Haldzos's throat. It cut him, but not deeply. Blood began to ooze from the cut, slow and thick, like molasses in the cold. Guan was grim, unhappy that his blow had not been a mortal one. The stench of the blood coming from the cuts in the leg and throat began driving some of the legions back. It was one of sour vinegar, hot tar, and rotting meat, all at once.

Guan stepped back, gagging at the smell, and brought up the neck of his robes to cover his nose. Tumatauenga seemed unphased. He lunged forward, spear aimed up, going for one of the creature's eyes. X'Haldzos lurched to the left and ducked his head. The spear went through his cheek and into his mouth. Having missed his mark, Tumatauenga began heaving himself up, trying to use his spear as a lever to scale the creature. But while the pain that had blossomed in X'Haldzos's face was sharp, his teeth were sharper.

X'Haldzos bit down on the wooden shaft of the spear, his teeth cracking the wood and making short work of any leverage the Māori god thought he might have. Tumatauenga fell, landing on his rump.

X'Haldzos had had enough. Enough of putting up with their paltry attacks. Enough of putting up with them thinking they could stop him. Gods or not, he was not going to be brought down by anyone or anything. Not if he could help it. He puffed himself up. Yells from angels and devils warned the three gods to back off. Some of them knew what was coming and had seen their comrades fall to this attack.

As he gathered his breath and his power, he lashed out with a taloned hand. He caught Tumatauenga as the god rose to his feet, slashing him across his painted belly, covering the black ink with golden blood. The same slashing movement continued, tearing into the green robes of Guan Gong. Apedemak was already moving back and was spared the attack.

X'Haldzos roared, sending his will and his power out with the roar. A smell somehow viler than the scent of the creature's blood accompanied a yellowish cloud that billowed from the creature's mouth as he roared. The force of it flattened everything within 30 yards in any direction from X'Haldzos. Angels, devils, and gods alike were thrown back violently to land in the shattered heavens of spirits. Many spirits didn't survive the force of the shattering of their paradise. Some did.

As X'Haldzos stepped onto the portal, he caught the scent. Not the one he was tracking, but similar. Too much like it to be anything but a relative.

One end of the paradise was shattered. The Māori god had been thrown through the shattered opening at the closer end of the sphere. The spirit of a man, dressed in a highly decorated military uniform, was helping the god. That's all X'Haldzos could make out before the energy of the portal took him away from the battlefield he had created and back to the safety of his lair.

Cadence woke to her phone not buzzing, not ringing, but making a kind of shrill, ear-splitting tone that reminded her of the fire alarm at the police station. She jumped, startled, and grabbed the phone. The entirety of the screen was flashing red and white.

"What the hell…" Cadence mumbled as she tried different ways to silence the noise. At length, she elected to stuff it under her pillow for a moment as she dressed. There was a knock on the door of her bedroom.

"Come in," she said, yelling over the noise of the phone as she pulled it out from under her pillow. Snow entered the room, and she showed her phone to him. "Make it stop!" she shouted over the alarm.

Snow took the phone, and angling to show her, swiped a checkmark on the screen. The silence that followed the alarm shutting off seemed almost as loud as the alarm itself.

"My apologies," Snow said. "I never thought to show you that because it so rarely happens."

"What the hell was it?" Cadence was still shaken. Waking to a wailing alarm tended to do that.

"An alarm that goes out to all of us when something has gone wrong," Snow said. "It comes from higher up in the chain of command. It lets us know that something terrible is going on and that a higher-up representative will inform us about it."

A knock sounded on Cadence's front door, and she shouted for whoever was there to come in. Will and Whitfield came in together. Whitfield looked disheveled as usual, and Will looked like he had been sleeping in his clothes.

"You guys got the alarm, right?" Will's eyes were huge, and he looked spooked.

"Yeah," Cadence said with a nod. "I'm just not sure what we do next."

"Get some paper and pens for us all," Snow said. "If you don't mind us waiting for the announcement here, that is. They'll have someone do a kind of press conference on the television about whatever this is. We may need to take notes."

"Sure," Cade said and went to a closet near her front door. She opened it and from a drawer inside, she pulled out four legal pads and four pens. She began handing them out, but Will grabbed the pens and shook his head.

"Just because it's the end of the world doesn't mean you can't have a little fun," Will said. He took the pens and went back to the closet. He opened the drawer again and smiled. He dumped the four black ink pens back into the drawer and pulled out four pens of different colors. After closing the drawer and the closet, he made his way over to the group and handed a red pen to Cadence, a black pen to Snow, a green pen to Whitfield, and kept the bright blue one for himself.

"You are so weird," Cadence said with a shake of her head as she tried to hide a smile.

Snow took his pen without comment and sat down on Cadence's couch. He uncapped the pen and wrote the date in the top corner of the page and then titled the paper "Alarm Report." He then paused, sniffing for a moment. He bent down and sniffed the page, then the pen.

"Is that … licorice?" Snow asked.

"Yeah!" Will was happy that Snow had realized that it was a scented pen.

"Why?" Snow turned in his seat to face Will as he asked this.

"Why not? Duh!" Will shook his head and made his way around the couch to sit on the floor by the armchair.

"You took the energy to give us scented ink pens?" Cadence couldn't believe it. She had loved the stupid things as a kid, even into her young teenage years, but hadn't really thought about them much since.

"Sometimes, it's the little things," Will said with a shrug.

"Watermelon?" Whitfield was sniffing his green pen, trying to identify the scent.

"Yep," Will said, grinning. "Cade, I figured you were a strawberry girl."

"It's creepy that you figured that out," Cadence said, moving to take a seat on her couch. Whitfield took a seat in the armchair. "So, what's yours then, blue boy?"

"Blueberry, all the way," Will said and took a deep sniff of his uncapped pen.

The television turned on of its own accord, which cut short the discussion of scented pens. The location was one Cadence had never seen before. A gossamer-like rainbow drape filled the screen behind a marble podium.

A woman walked onto the stage and stood behind the podium. She had long, thick, brown hair that was pinned away from her face but left to fall down her back in curls. She wore a white Grecian toga-style dress that matched her large, white, feathered wings. Her brown eyes and beautiful face were the picture of solemnity.

"Hello," the woman said, her voice melodic. "For those who may not know, I am Iris, a messenger for the gods. I know you all have questions, and I hope to be able to answer them in time, but for now, there will be information and instructions given out." She paused and took a breath before continuing.

"In the last hour, there was an assault on the afterworld. A non-human entity entered the afterworld via a portal and proceeded to wreak havoc and destruction there for a short time. Off-council deities were able to beat the creature back but not destroy it. This marks the first assault on the afterworld in recorded history. Many spirits were lost and many of the deities involved in defending the afterworld were injured by the creature.

"The council has been made aware that a special forces team has already been created in response to this threat. Orders will be going out to the appropriate NHD offices to assist this team in their efforts to destroy or imprison this entity. The appropriate observation bays for the geographical area the creature is believed to be hiding in have been alerted and will be mobilized to keep a hyper-vigilant watch on the area. Other bays may be used in this effort as well.

"The new medical facility is becoming over-tasked, so we are asking for people who had medical experience in life to volunteer their knowledge and service there, if they would be so willing.

"We are currently taking a tally of the spirits that were removed from their afterworld with such violence. If you have a loved one on that list, you will be made aware soon. The various deities of war have been mobilized to defend the afterworld and the high heavens. Various guardian beasts have been released to patrol as well. For that reason, the intake of spirits to their afterworlds will cease for the time being. Extra space is being made for the expected accumulation of waylaid spirits."

Iris paused for a moment to let everyone have a little time to digest what she had just said. "We will mourn when the threat is gone. Let us instead now concentrate on doing all we can to take care of this danger and heal our wounded. These are the words from the gods."

The television turned itself off and the scratching of Snow's pen on his paper was the only sound in the room for the time being. The other three had been so dumbfounded by what had occurred that the thought of taking notes had fled their minds.

"The afterworlds?" Cadence turned to Snow. "Was she talking about heaven and hell?"

"Yes," Snow said. "You've seen how Bethany guides people to determine what fate they are moving on to based on their values, religion, and actions and behaviors in life. Each one goes to their own version of heaven or hell. It's like a lot of small bubbles that seem vast if you are in them. At least that's how it was once described to me."

"How would X'Haldzos even attack that?" Will asked.

"I have a feeling we will have to go see what happened," Snow said. "Survey the damage ourselves."

"At least we know we have a window," Whitfield said with a sigh. "He always seems to have downtime between attacks.

"Maybe we should go on the offensive then," Cadence said. "We've been told he is hanging out around the portal area at the prison. We go in loaded for bear and maybe we can end this now."

"Or we go in loaded for bear and find out that fighting him is like fighting a whole den of bears," Whitfield said. "I'm sorry Cadence, I'm not letting you get hurt. And I'm not gonna lie. I like you, but it's also because I am now terrified of your boyfriend if anything happens to you."

"We can't rush in," Snow said. "Ramon and his threats aside, there are just too many unknowns in that kind of action. I know you like to jump into action first and think about it later, but this is the wrong time for that kind of recklessness. This thing took on deities. Gods. And it hurt them. Let me say it again for good measure. It … injured … gods. No matter how good Will's designs are, we have no actual idea of their efficacy against this creature."

Snow paused as his phone began to ring. "Snow," he said as he answered. He blinked and a look of shock crossed his face. "Yes, I'm here with them now." He paused as the person on the other side spoke. "Of course, we'll be right there." He then hung up his phone, still looking stunned.

"Who was it?" Cadence prompted him for an answer, as she wasn't used to him looking floored like this.

"We have an audience with those trying to shore up defenses in the higher heavens," Snow said.

"What?" Cadence asked.

"Like Ares or someone?" Will was on his feet in an instant.

"Ares, Hachiman, Indra, Tyr, a few others I'm sure," Snow said, rising to his feet.

"Me too?" Whitfield was unsure of his place with the team.

"You harbor more knowledge about this creature than we do," Snow said. "So yes, you too."

Near the front door of her apartment, a glowing circle appeared on Cadence's floor. Snow nodded toward it and gestured for everyone to go there. "That would be our portal to the heavens."

They made their way across the apartment and, one by one, they stepped into the circle.

Cadence, Snow, Will, and Whitfield appeared in a large, circular room. In the center of the room was a wide, round table of gold-veined marble. Smooth, round columns rose to the ceiling and held swooping arcs of curtains in crimson and black. The floor and ceiling were made of the same marble as the table. Red and black velvet benches surrounded the table. There was an ornate red door on the far side of the room. The walls between the columns had paintings, ornately framed in gold, of various gods that represented war, combat, or strife. To say the room was opulent would be a disservice to the room, as it was so much more.

The extravagant red door opened, and three gods filed into the room. A tall, dark-haired man with a full mustache and beard was the first to enter the room. He wore a Grecian toga, which did little to hide his muscular form, and golden sandals with straps that laced to his knees. On his head was a golden helmet with a thick red bristle at the top.

The next man to enter the room had well-tanned skin and four arms. He wore only chunky gold beaded necklaces and pants with an intricate design of deep red and gold but was otherwise barefoot and topless. A golden crown that reminded Cadence of a three-tiered birthday cake rested atop his head.

The third person to enter was a raven-haired woman with sapphire-like eyes and a black crow perched on her shoulder. She wore a gauzy sleeveless black dress, belted at the waist with a simple blood-red cord of rope. She was pale, and it seemed as though there were long-healed battle scars on her arms.

Snow bowed toward the man carrying the helmet. "Ares," he said in greeting, recognizing the god from his youth studying religions and myths.

"Thoth said you were quick," Ares said with a pleased nod. "Please, all of you, be seated. These are my colleagues: Indra of the Hindu and Badb of the Celts." He indicated the four-armed man was Indra and the woman was Badb.

"I am Osmund Snow," Snow said, introducing himself as they all walked to take seats on the benches around the table. "This is Cadence Riley. The young man is Will McKenny, and the other is Whitfield."

"A non-human in a human guise," Badb said, sounding amused. "This is a strange group."

Whitfield didn't seem startled to be called out so fast about what he was. These were, after all, gods.

Ares wasted no time beginning the meeting. "How much time do we have before the next attack?"

"We don't know," Snow answered.

"We have noticed that as the attacks have become bigger and bolder, there seems to be more recoup time needed for X'Haldzos," Will said.

"We also have tracked his resting place to the remains of Barrington Prison," Cadence said. "We were discussing the options of going on the offensive when we got the call to come here."

"That wouldn't be a wise decision," Badb said, the crow on her shoulder giving a squawk. "Beings more powerful than you were injured, or worse, in the last attack this creature wrought on us."

"Will has designed some tools that might prove useful in the fight," Whitfield said.

"Useful tools do not make an assault a wise decision," Indra said, folding two of his four arms in front of his chest.

Ares rose from his seat with a sigh. "While I can appreciate the desire to be direct and bring the war to this creature, it's not something I can sanction."

Cadence slid her gaze sideways to Snow and wondered, *Since when do we need any sanction from Ares?* Snow made the most negligible motion of his finger for her to stay silent.

"The creature is, after all, sleeping," Indra continued, as Ares began to walk in a circle around the room.

"It's not like anyone here would be known for causing sleep or confusion among their enemies either," Badb said. She gave a false innocent look, which told Cadence that confusing enemies is precisely what Badb was known for.

"However," Ares said. "There is an opportunity for misdirection and distraction. If, perchance, some stronger beings were to go on the attack. If they were to find this creature in its new lair. There might be an opportunity for some clever spirits to take advantage of this distraction to destroy or imprison the non-human."

"But, as Ares said, this is something we could never sanction," Indra said.

"Thoth has made it clear that we are not allowed to put weaker beings into danger," Badb said.

"And while no offense is meant, you four are weaker beings," Indra said.

Ares circled back around to his bench and sat once more. "For as brave and clever as you are, the path is clear. We shall be planning to attack within the hour." Ares leveled his gaze at Will. "Have you enough tools to help support an attack should they be requested?"

"I have enough, your Warfulness," Will said.

Ares looked amused at the title Will had given him. "And you, Osmund Snow. As one who stands half in their world and half in ours, would you be prepared should it come down to us having to call on you as an only somewhat less powerful being?"

"I am ready and willing to assist howsoever you should have need of me," Snow said, sounding quite British and formal.

"Child of my islands," Badb said, addressing Cadence. "I cannot ask for your help. That much has been made clear, yes?"

"Yes," Cadence said, bowing her head to Badb. "But I would willingly give it all the same. This must come to an end."

Badb gave a pleased nod.

Indra looked over at Whitfield. "You look like you have something to add."

Whitfield nodded and stood. "I wanted you all to know, as I have told them, that I take full responsibility for this. It was my trying to trap X'Haldzos where he was that led to his strength. My feeding him led to him getting bigger and stronger. Once this is over, I submit to your judgment."

"Ares," Badb said. "This one is non-human. As a technicality, he is not a lesser powered spirit, nor is he a lesser powered deity."

"Agreed," Indra said.

Ares stroked his chin between his thumb and forefinger for a moment as he thought. "You will come with us, non-human. There are final plans to be laid out and your knowledge will be useful."

Whitfield regretted speaking up, but he nodded, accepting their decision. He did want to help fix what he had caused. Being part of the forward attack hadn't been his desire, though.

"There is one request we would make," Snow interjected before anyone could make a move to end the meeting, which seemed where things were going.

"And what would this request be, demigod?" Indra asked, an eyebrow lifted in curiosity.

"To survey the damage in the afterworlds," Snow replied. "In each previous attack, we have been able to survey the field of attack. That has given us a gauge of how strong the creature has gotten between each attack. The scope of damage and power used also gives us a rough estimate of how long he will take to recover from the attack, giving us an estimated window of time in which to operate to attempt to anticipate him. Prior to this, we didn't know where he was going. But if he's found a way into the afterworld, with countless souls defenseless and waiting to be devoured? I would doubt he's going to leave it with just one attack. Especially as he was able to injure the gods that so quickly assembled to defeat him."

Ares paused and thought, steepling his fingers in front of his lips as he did so.

"It is possible to give them time to do this and to let the non-human go with them," Indra suggested, his eyes on Ares. "The non-human could then return to us and bring back the information so we may better plan the attack."

"I would go with them," Badb volunteered. "To see the damage firsthand, and to bring back the errant non-human." Her lips crooked into an uneven smile as she added, "That way we are obeying the letter of the law Thoth himself set out. The lesser beings are not without our presence in a field in which they may face danger during this time."

Ares lifted an eyebrow. "Indeed," he murmured. He took a deep breath in through his nose and straightened his back. "As you wish. Badb, you will accompany our strange little quartet to the afterworlds. Show them the scope of the attack and the damage that was wrought. Then return with the non-human and information. The attack shall commence one hour from your return from the afterworlds."

Badb bowed her head to Ares. "My mission is known to me."

The three gods rose from the table. Indra gestured toward where the spirits had entered, and a gentle glow began to illuminate the room behind where they sat.

"Thank you for your counsel," Ares said. "I regret that we are unable to avail ourselves of your help. Aside from the information that the non-human will bring back with him, of course."

Badb left the other two deities to join Will, Cadence, Whitfield, and Snow as they walked back to the glowing circle. The motley crew of five stepped into the portal and the golden light surrounded them. When it dissipated, they found themselves in the afterworlds.

They were near the bluish portal that X'Haldzos had come through. Around them was a wide swath of emptiness. It was like standing on hard, bare ground that was shrouded in thick fog. They could see twinkling through the fog in some areas, remnants of a broken heaven looking like shattered glass.

"Come," Badb said, "I will show you his path."

She led them to the area that had been the fisherman's heaven. "This was the first one. The spirit fought back, but there was little he could do. The second heaven, your demon found a bit more frustrating."

She led them through the fog; the phantom sounds of a moving river were still there, even if the river wasn't. At some steps, Cadence felt like there was tall grass tangling around her feet, but looking down, it was just fog.

"What was challenging about this one?" Whitfield asked.

"It was the paradise of a young woman who loved to dream. Her paradise was a mythical castle in the clouds, guarded by a dragon that was her friend. The dragon was able to fight and hurt X'Haldzos."

"A creation of a spirit in paradise was actually able to hurt it?" Whitfield sounded stunned.

"Aye," Badb answered with a solemn nod. "That dragon is what gave alarm to the gods and the legions both."

"Legions?" Cade asked.

"Yes, daughter," Badb answered. "What you would think of as the Legions of Hell."

"Wouldn't they side with X'Haldzos? I mean, if they're from Hell?"

Badb laughed, a sound that managed to be both indulgent and terrorizing at the same time. "The Legions guard Hell, as you call it. They see that the evil spirits are punished according to their crimes and keep the place secure. A much lesser-known fact is that they aren't the demons most think them to be nowadays. Just different forms of gods and angels."

They had retraced X'Haldzos's path to the site where he had fought the three gods. There were still golden shimmers of blood here and there, showing where the gods had been injured. But there were also oily black patches as well, evidence of X'Haldzos's injuries.

"Who was here?" Snow inquired.

"Apedemak of Nubia, Guan Gong of China, and Tumatauenga of the Māori," Badb answered. "Apedemak managed to come through the battle relatively unscathed, but both Guan Gong and Tumatauenga were injured by the creature before his powerful roar threw everyone back far enough for him to make good his escape."

"How did X'Haldzos injure the two?" Whitfield asked.

"A taloned attack sliced through both of them in one fell swoop," Badb replied. She then entwined her arm with Cadence's. "Guan and Apedemak landed close together over there," she said, using her other hand to point to the right, indicating a still half-standing bubble of paradise. "You three go investigate there while I take she of my isles to go see where the great Māori warrior god landed."

Will, Snow, and Whitfield exchanged curious glances, but none of them was about to gainsay the goddess. Cadence looked perplexed as well, but didn't sense any danger from Badb although she was keenly aware that she was arm-in-arm with a goddess of war and death. She nodded to the guys that it was okay and turned to follow along wherever Badb was leading.

"The roar was great, and from what I hear, not only did it do great damage, but it smelled quite foul," Badb commented.

"Yeah, we call it his 'mustard gas attack,'" Cadence said as she walked with Badb. "Not because it is mustard gas, but it reeks, and when he uses it, it comes out in this cloud of yellow."

"So, he is large, tough-skinned, sharp-taloned, and has the use of both sonic and breath weapons," Badb summarized.

"In a nutshell," Cadence nodded.

"And it took your brother."

Cadence stopped sharply and looked at Badb as the goddess said that.

"You feign confusion, but I felt the rage and blood-lust rolling off of you as soon as I entered the war room," Badb said. "You are a child of my kind, so I have a connection. I have brought you here for several reasons, child."

"And those are?" Cadence asked, feeling herself close off, and begin to straddle the line of her defense/fight mode. It was only a subtle change in how she held her posture, the stance of her legs. But Badb noticed.

"Relax, child," the goddess laughed. "I mean you no harm. I brought you here to talk with you plainly. Though I am sure you caught on to the general deception and double meanings being tossed around in the war room, I wish to be plain. And I do want to show you where Tumatauenga landed. It will be of interest to you. But we must speak first."

"Okay," Cadence said, relaxing her stance once more.

"One who fights from a place of anger, from a place of bloodlust, is easily unbalanced. I would not want you to be caught off balance when fighting such a being as powerful as this."

"So you're saying the quiet part out loud now," Cade said in a matter-of-fact manner. "We are going to be included in this fight."

"Thoth's words were as we said," Badb shrugged, releasing Cadence's arm. "And just as doubled-sided as the words we spoke in the war room. The intention is for you all to be included in our plans. Your non-human friend will be the go-between for us. But I need you to go in ready for battle. That means being neutral and not consumed with vengeance for your brother. To that end, I have brought you here."

"To where the Māori god landed from battle?" Cadence was confused. "How is that going to help me not want vengeance?"

"The one who helped the Māori until other help could arrive," Badb said, gesturing to the broken opening of the paradise bubble. "I will wait for you here."

Cadence stepped into the opening, not sure why Badb was bringing her there. The fog that had been thick on the ground changed to snow, and she found her footsteps crunching as she made her way in.

That would be good snowman snow, she thought to herself. She made her way along the path through the trees and stopped. Her mouth hung open in awe.

Before her was a house she remembered from her childhood. A large, Tudor-style house with a huge kitchen and a bay window in the family room. She was coming from the left side of the house, and she could see the Christmas lights all over the house and in the windows, including the little electric candles they had in each window when she was a child. The azalea bushes that hid the front sidewalk as it arched to the right to meet the driveway were covered in lights as well. When spring came, those hedges would be full of flowers. Between the sidewalk and the curb was a pine tree, as tall as the house itself. Like the rest of the house, it was doused in twinkling lights. For ornaments, it had pinecones strung up on it with green and red yarn. Those cones had been rolled in peanut butter and covered with birdseed.

She was home.

The garage door to the right of the house began making noise as the opener began hoisting the door up.

"I'll be in before dinner's done," a male voice that made her heart sing said. "I just want to shovel some of this snow." Cadence found her feet crunching through the snow even faster, running toward the sound of her father's voice. She skidded to a halt as he came around the corner of the garage to the driveway. He had a shovel alright, but it was hoisted up to defend himself. He stopped his swing short as it dawned on him that his daughter was in front of him.

"Cade," he dropped the shovel and brought her into a fierce hug. "What are you doing here?"

"Did you see the message from Iris?" She had no idea if her family would have gotten the message here in a paradise home.

"I saw it, yes." He nodded as he implied that her mother hadn't. When she had seen him briefly after her own mortal death, he had implied at that time that her mom was in a heaven that kept her unaware of what was really going on.

"You know that special team they mentioned?" she winced as she said it, not sure how her father would take the news. He had gone nuclear when he had found out she intended to join the police.

"I had a feeling you would somehow be involved in that." He looked unhappy, but not angry.

"Um, Dad, there is one thing I have to tell you." She looked down at her feet in the snow, unable to bring herself to meet his eyes as she said what she had to.

"What is it, Cade?" He knew when she acted like this that it was something serious, and something he wouldn't like. He assumed it was something about her being involved with the team.

"Sam's gone," she said quickly, ripping the metaphorical band-aid off as tears felt cold on her cheeks. "That thing that was attacking here? It killed him. Like, for good, killed him. He doesn't exist anymore."

Her father did the unexpected and wrapped her up in a hug again. "I'm so sorry, sweetie."

Cade was stunned enough that her tears stopped. "No, Dad, it's my fault. He wouldn't have been there if he and I hadn't hooked back up. If he hadn't followed in my footsteps to help other people."

"Your brother was always going to help other people, Cadence," her father said, his deep voice gentle. "He was going to be a teacher. He protected his dorm mates and girlfriend and died doing it. He then tried to help you and your friends. He followed his path. You are following yours. I'm sorry for you that his path ended. I know you and he loved each other very much." He then paused, looking over to where the shattered end of the heavenly bubble was. "And had I known that about the demon when the Māori had landed here, I would have followed the son of a bitch and killed him or died trying. Just like I know you want to."

"Mom's gonna hate me for this," Cadence said.

"Your mother is fine," her father replied. "You remember this place, right?"

"Yeah." She nodded, looking around with a smile. "I was seven when we moved here. Sam was five. We got to live here for five years. Our longest time in any house. Military brats don't often get to put down roots like that."

"Your mother's version of heaven is here. Christmastime. You're eight and Sam is six. You're both here. We watch movies, make cookies, decorate, even go to town sometimes."

"I showed that town to Ramon on our first date," Cadence said with a smile. "Told him some of our traditions."

"Ramon?" Sternness crept back into her father's voice and it made her smile. It was the same tone he had used any time she had brought up the name of a boy she liked.

"You'll have to meet him if you can," she said. "Between you and me, I think he's the one."

Her father straightened himself up to his full height and lifted an eyebrow. "I'll just have to see about that." He then smiled and put a hand on her shoulder. "But know this, princess. You are not at fault for your brother. He was happy you two had found each other again. And he was happy he was being of help. And know how very proud I am of you. Be careful. I love you. And warn this Ramon of yours that he and I are going to have to meet. Soon."

Cadence smiled and lifted herself on her tiptoes to kiss her dad on his cheek. "I love you, Dad."

"Go on," he urged. "I've got to get back in and you've got a demon to stop." He bent down and kissed her on the cheek. He took a long look at her, then picked up his shovel, turned, and went back into the garage. Machinery whirred once more as the garage door came down.

Cadence turned and followed the path back to where Badb waited.

"You are steadier now," Badb said. It was a statement, not a question.

"Yes," Cadence nodded.

"Good, because there is one more thing you need to know." She stepped aside and gestured to the three approaching men who were accompanied by a nine-foot-tall, horned, leathery-winged member of the legion.

"What news?" Badb asked.

"We're going to have a longer window between attacks," Whitfield says. "I'd estimate 12 to 14 hours. He used a lot of energy."

"But his coming here blew our theory out of the water," Will said with a frown.

"And what theory was that?" Badb tilted her head, curious.

"That it was following someone," Snow said. "The places it had previously attacked were all places that had the same circle of people attached to them. But this isn't a place any of us have been."

Badb then turned her gray gaze to Cadence and Cade froze as she understood. "No, but someone here has been around one of us. He's been chasing me."

Badb nodded and smiled, glad that Cadence now understood. She made a gesture with one hand.

There was a sound like the squawking of a crow, and the three human spirits found themselves back in Will's and Cadence's office.

"That was weird," Will said.

"Yet informative," Snow added.

"I guess we have our official plan," Cadence said. "We prepare for war."

CHAPTER 13

Death and Insanity

Aiden, Teeny, Derrick, and Andy filed into the shop, and Aiden locked the door behind them as the spirit chimes tinkled together. The men were in black suits and ties, Teeny in a black dress. Without a word, Derrick went to the coffeemaker to begin the process of brewing. The other three flopped into chairs.

Lauren was with them; the chimes had alerted them to that, and Aiden was glad. Even though she was gone, she wasn't truly gone. At least for him.

"These are becoming too regular an occurrence for me," Andy said.

"Funerals?" It was Teeny who asked the question.

"Yeah," Andy answered.

"Hey, Derrick, grab the box from back there, will ya?" Aiden asked as he began to smell the coffee as it dripped down into the pot.

"On it," Derrick said. He grabbed the spirit box and brought it to the table, letting the coffee brew. He flicked the switch and static filled the room.

"That was the strangest experience I have ever had," Lauren's voice said as it came through the box. "I never thought I would be attending my own funeral."

"Was it okay?" Aiden asked.

"It was beautiful," Lauren said through the static. "I never imagined so many would come. And I know you worked hard on the eulogy."

Aiden scoffed. "That's cheating. You only know that because you've been around me."

"I thought Tom said some great stuff," Derrick said, setting cups of coffee in front of Aiden and Teeny. He disappeared for a moment back to the office, then reappeared with two more cups. He placed one in front of Andy and then sat down.

"He did," Andy said.

"Enough talk of the funeral," Lauren said. "It's over. Hopefully, now we can all start moving forward."

"It's weird, it almost feels like life has been paused for a while," Derrick said.

"Yeah," Aiden said with a nod. "In a way. And I've been so angry at everyone else that it didn't pause for, you know? I just want to scream at them. How can you be moving and doing things and acting like this wonderful person isn't gone? But I know in other ways it must keep moving on." He looked around the shop with its shelves half empty. Sale signs were posted here and there. To him, it felt sacrilegious to be closing Lauren's shop. But he knew he had to. She had been right. It was her dream, not his. So now it was time to make a try for his dream.

Teeny checked her phone as she took it from her purse. "Oh, Liam texted. He's landed in California and sends his best. He said he's sorry he missed the funeral."

"At least he got back home okay," Andy said.

"As banged up as he was, I'm still surprised he got released from the hospital this soon," Derrick said.

"No kidding," Aiden said, sipping his coffee. He moved to pull out the green, felt, four-leaf clover that he used as a signal for when Cadence was there, but realized that with the spirit box on he didn't need to.

"Are you okay?" Teeny said, noting the motion.

"Yeah," Aiden said. "I just feel weird. I mean, no offense, Lauren, but I'm glad that all of that is over with. But then I feel guilty for feeling that way. It's a constant yo-yo."

"It will pass," Lauren said. "And there's no need for you to feel guilty. I went through this with Dan, remember? I know how you feel. With this over, you can finally focus on moving forward, and that's nothing to feel bad about."

"It kind of feels nice right now," Derrick said, staring into his coffee. "Lauren is still our den mother."

Aiden chuckled a little at that. "I guess she is."

There was a knock on the glass door, and they looked up. Tom and Chris from Pho-Q down the strip mall were at the door with large bags. Aiden got up and unlocked the door, letting them in.

"You may or may not be hungry, but we figured you might as well have some food," Tom said.

"It's easier to remember to eat when the food is already in front of you," Chris said.

"Wow, thanks," Derrick said.

"That's really sweet of you guys," Teeny said.

"Lauren was a nice lady," Tom said with a shrug. He set down his bags of food on the glass counter and ran a hand through his silvery hair. "You guys are kind of cool, too, but don't let it go to your heads."

Aiden chuckled. "We'll try Tom, we'll try."

"Well, we figure you're probably done with seeing people today, so we'll get out of your hair," Chris said. It was a funny comment coming from Chris, as he had his head shaved to almost bald.

"Thanks, man, we appreciate it," Aiden said, shaking hands with both Tom and Chris.

"No problem. Enjoy," Tom said. He and Chris turned and exited the shop, heading back down the strip mall to their restaurant.

It didn't take long for the smell of barbecue to overpower the smell of coffee. That's when all four of them realized that they were hungry. It just hadn't registered yet.

"You know, I hate to admit this, but I've never eaten there," Andy said.

"Bro, you can't beat this stuff," Aiden said as he began unpacking the bags and laying things out. The containers were all labeled. They had sent over almost everything on their menu that they knew Aiden and Derrick liked.

"Here," Aiden said, passing a covered bowl over to Andy. "This is the pork pho. It's amazeballs."

"So, this is barbecue soup?" Andy asked, looking a little skeptical.

"Just try it," Teeny said. "I was skittish about it too in the beginning, but it's really good."

They grabbed some food and took it back to the table. Silence reigned as the four dug into their food with gusto. Even Andy, after the first bite, was hooked. Lauren just hung around, letting them eat, letting them get used to the new dynamic. She could see the bonds between them as she watched them. The rosy bond of new love between Aiden and Teeny. The strong brotherly bond between Aiden and Derrick, and the strong bond of friendship between Andy and Aiden. It all centered around Aiden; he was now the center of the group. The heart. The gravity in their world. She could see the holes in Aiden and Derrick, where the bonds to her had been. In time, those would close and be replaced with new bonds.

A ringing phone broke the silence. Andy pulled his phone out of his jacket and looked at the caller ID.

"I don't think I want to answer that," Andy said. The caller ID said, "Captain R."

"What does he want now?" Aiden asked.

"Who knows?" Andy said. "I haven't seen or heard from him since the night he blew down my door."

"He blew down your door?" Derrick was shocked.

"Just like the big bad wolf," Teeny said. Aiden had told her about what had happened.

"That's what he calls himself, anyway," Andy said with a shrug. "So, I guess it fits." An alert buzzed on Andy's phone, letting him know he had a voicemail message. "Let's see what he wants."

Andy pushed the button and put it on speaker as he put in the clearance code for his voicemail.

"Halleran," Rodriguez's voice came through the phone speaker. "We need to get a few things clear between us. No audience this time. Meet me at ten tonight at the circle on the property of the farm. Alone. Cliché, I know, but still. Alone."

"God, could he twirl his mustache anymore?" Teeny asked with a roll of her eyes.

"Twirl his mustache?" Derrick asked.

"He's playing the villain," Teeny explained.

"Oh," Derrick said with a nod of understanding.

"The thing is, he didn't use to be a villain," Andy said. "Well, I guess he was," Andy amended, thinking about the thick file of corpses that were due to his command or handiwork. "I just never saw him in that light until Scarecrow Farms."

"It's funny what people can hide from others," Lauren said through the static, the spirit box still on. "Or even themselves."

"True," Aiden said with a nod.

"I guess we're gearing up later then?" Derrick asked.

"Gearing up for what?" Andy asked.

"There is no way we are letting you walk into that trap without backup, bro," Aiden said.

"You aren't cops," Andy said. "And these tools aren't going to help against him," he added with a gesture to the spirit box.

"We have cameras," Teeny said with a shrug.

"And audio recorders," Derrick said, nodding.

"We can go early, put some recorders down in inconspicuous places," Aiden said. "Then we videotape you from the tree line. That way, if things go sideways, you have evidence."

"I mean, that has to be why he wants you alone," Teeny said. "No witnesses, no evidence."

"Bulletproof vest, man," Derrick said. "Might wanna wear one."

"I quit, I don't just have them lying around," Andy said. But then a thought occurred to him and an eyebrow picked up. "Or maybe I have a better idea."

Andy picked up his phone and dialed a number. After a moment, he smiled. "Keller, it's Halleran." He paused as Keller said something. "Yeah, you too, man. Listen, I need a favor."

Keller knocked on the glass door of the New-Age shop. He spared a glance at the pile of flowers, stuffed animals, crystals, and candles to his left. He could see Halleran through the glass with a trio of others. One of those others, a tall man with shaggy hair, was coming to open the door.

"Hi, I'm Aiden," the man said as he opened the door. "Come on in." Aiden stepped aside, holding the door open, and Keller walked in.

Andy rose and walked over, meeting Keller halfway through the store, and shook his hand. "Thanks for coming out, man."

"Welcome," Keller nodded. He then looked around the store. "Two questions. One, what are you doing here? And two, what am I doing here?"

"Why don't you have a seat?" Andy said, gesturing to the table. They had brought out the extra chair from the back office, so there was room for five.

"That's an ominous beginning," Keller grumbled. He moved to the table and took a seat as Andy and Aiden joined him.

"First, before I answer your questions, introductions." Andy took a deep breath and gestured to each person as he introduced them. "You met Aiden at the door. The woman beside him is Teeny, and then there's Derrick on the other side of you. Guys, this is Detective Anthony Keller."

They all greeted the steel-haired man with nods and murmured hellos, somewhat intimidated by the hard glare from his brown eyes.

"Hi." Keller nodded. "You can call me Detective Keller. Now what the hell is going on, Halleran? You quit, then the captain gets outed as a killer and ousted. He'll probably be arrested soon. Now you call me to come here. These have been the weirdest few days, and I just want to get off the ride. You gonna explain some of this shit now?"

Andy could tell Keller wasn't in the friendliest of moods. "I'll explain. Calm down. But at the end of this, I'm going to ask for a huge favor, okay?"

Keller lifted a skeptical eyebrow. "Just get to talking. We'll see about a favor at the end of it."

Andy nodded. "I'm sure you've suspected that I'm the one who turned in the file on Rodriguez to IA."

"Yeah, I'm not an idiot," Keller said.

"Didn't think you were, just making sure you knew for a fact it was me. I didn't steal the file like Rodriguez thinks. You know all the weird stuff that's been happening in the office? That was one of the weird things. I had asked about that file and been told it didn't exist. Then one day it turns up in my desk drawer."

"Are you the one who turned it over to the press, too?" Keller asked.

"That would be me," Aiden said, entering the conversation.

"But I asked him to do it," Andy said.

"That way it wasn't tied to you because you had turned the file into IA." Keller sighed and rubbed his careworn face with his hands. "So, some of this is starting to make sense. When did you even learn about that file to ask about it if it was so secret?"

"Naveen."

"The coroner?" Keller couldn't keep the surprise from his voice. "How the hell did that conversation come about?"

"I was doing some research on a case," Andy answered, choosing his words carefully. "I asked about corpses with a specific mark on them. Naveen told me he had noticed it years ago and had started keeping a file on it, sending all the info to Rodriguez. He said he was surprised we hadn't caught the killer yet but was impressed we'd managed to keep a serial killer out of the news."

"When was this?" Keller was curious.

"Back in December, when I got clobbered at that college dorm house," Andy answered.

"I recall some of you guys being involved in that, too." He remembered the story and recalled giving Andy good-natured hell for needing civvies to come to his rescue. He had thought it odd that Andy was even at that dorm house, to begin with. He knew the history. He knew Riley's brother had been there. At first, he had thought it was some weird way to carry Riley's torch.

But when the whole thing about Caulfield came out, he ditched that idea.

"I thought it might have been Caulfield who was in on that," Andy said with a sigh. "I had no idea at that point that the captain was involved. And yes, they were there. I'm sure you read the reports. They saw someone hauling my unconscious self into the house."

"How did you guys know this lunkhead, anyway?" Keller turned to Aiden and Derrick as he asked the question. He knew a woman had been with them at the time, too, but he knew that the woman at the table wasn't the same woman. He had read about her fate in the papers.

"I knew Cadence," Aiden said, lying only a little. "I recognized Andy as the dude was hauling him out of the trunk of the car."

Keller nodded a little. "So, are you gonna be running this New-Age crystal place now that you've quit the force?" It was a joke; he knew Andy would do no such thing. But he had to try to make a joke, or he felt his head would explode as timelines and bits of information snapped together in his head.

Andy knew Keller was processing things, so he returned the friendly gesture. "Yeah, you know, I was thinking paint this place pink and purple, all the candles and herbs, it would be a chick magnet, right?"

"Brother, you don't need this shop to be a chick magnet. I know how many girls you've dated." He was going to say he knew how many notches were on the bedpost but changed it at the last second due to being in mixed company. "So, what is this favor you want?"

In reply, Andy played the voicemail from Rodriguez that he had saved on his phone. Keller listened and his natural scowl grew deeper. As the message ended, Keller looked at Andy.

"You know it's a trap, right?" Keller couldn't believe the captain would even think that Andy would fall for something like this. "Obviously you're not going."

"I know it's a trap," Andy replied, nodding. "But I am going."

"You can't be serious!" Keller got up out of his chair and loomed over Andy. "This is ridiculous. He's already shot off your damned door. Yeah, word about that got around the precinct fast. You know the man is armed. Why would you just go out there?"

"That's the favor. I'm hoping you'll help me," Andy said. He gestured for Keller to take a seat, knowing this was the make-it-or-break-it moment. If Keller sat, Andy would get his favor. If Keller walked, Andy would have to make other plans.

"You're crazy, you know that, right?" Keller gave a long, resigned sigh and sat back down. "Fucking insane, all of you." He looked at Aiden. "You're seriously okay with him planning to do this?"

"That all depends on if you help or not," Aiden said.

Keller looked at the table and adjusted the gold wedding band on his left hand. "Screw it. In for a penny, in for a pound. What do you need?"

The night was cold and cloudy as Andy parked his car on the side of the road. The road ran parallel to the piece of farmland that had the circle in it. He could see Rodriguez's car a few feet away. This was why they hadn't seen him pass by the house that night. He had come through that way. The field was obscured for the most part by a thin line of trees and brush between it and the road.

"Here we go," Andy said, muttering to himself. He double-checked the gun he had holstered at his side. The winter coat he was wearing was long enough to hide it from plain view. He had a bad feeling it was going to come down to a gunfight. He didn't want that. No good cop ever really did.

He disliked that Rodriguez had gotten there first. Who knew what kind of trap he had been able to set up. Last time he hadn't even known other people were there. That had just been a coincidence of enormous and tragic proportions. Andy took a deep breath and sighed, opening his car door. His shoes crunched on the cold, stiff grass and dry leaves as he made his way through the trees. The flashlight on his phone helped light the way and allowed him to check for any traps that may have been laid.

It only took a couple of minutes for him to emerge in the field. He could see the dark form of Rodriguez in the circle of stones. There was no shimmering blue shield like there had been, so there had been no obvious magic yet.

That I know of, Andy reminded himself. *Ghosts are one thing. This whole magic crap is a different can of worms.*

"Halleran," Rodriguez said, greeting Andy as the younger man approached the circle.

"Captain," Andy replied.

"I'm surprised you still are calling me that," Rodriguez said.

"Old habits die hard," Andy said with a shrug. "Would you prefer I call you Wolf?"

"So, you did hear Riley call me that," Rodriguez said.

"I've heard a lot of stuff," Andy said. "From Riley, from you, from others. All of it seems to amount to you being out of your mind." As they talked, Andy was careful to stay outside of the stone circle.

"What you think doesn't matter," the old captain said with a shrug. "It's obvious that you won't see eye to eye with me on this topic. But that doesn't matter."

"It doesn't matter?" Andy scoffed. "You seemed dead set on trying to get me to see eye to eye with you before on all of this. An army of ghosts to help you keep the peace. An army of ghosts to help the police strike fear into the hearts of evildoers. It all seems a little too comic book-y for me."

"You just don't have the imagination required to see the bigger picture," Rodriguez said. "It's getting worse out there, Halleran, and you know. You've seen it. Criminals are far more emboldened than they used to be. If we had a force of phantoms at our command, the Sommerset Strangler would have been rendered immobile and Riley would still be with us. Did you ever think of that?"

"I've thought about a lot in the last few months," Andy said. "Riley and I shared a lot of philosophies in life. One of them being that when your number was up, your number was up. If he hadn't gotten her, something else would have."

"Well then, I guess this time it's your number that's up," Rodriguez said.

"Jesus, could you be more of a walking cliché?" Andy was frustrated at the rehashing of all of this. He knew it was going to come to a fight, be it fists or guns. He just wanted to get to that part and have it over already.

"Considering I don't have a mustache or black top hat; I suppose that answer is yes. I could be more of a walking cliché," Rodriguez said.

Andy rolled his eyes. "You're stalling. Why?"

"Because I don't want it to come to this, Halleran," Rodriguez said, looking as frustrated as Andy felt. "You're a good cop and a good man. I don't want things to go this way."

"You don't want to kill me," Andy said. "Great, so don't."

"I don't want to enslave you," Rodriguez corrected.

"Well, considering I'm not about to set foot into that damned circle, I doubt that's an issue," Andy said.

Rodriguez chuckled and shook his head. "Who says I need the circle to enslave you?"

That was when it started, and time slowed down for Andy, as it always did.

Rodriguez reached for the gun holstered at his hip. At the first hint of that motion, Andy's hand moved to his own holster, hidden under the flap of his jacket. Breath came out in puffs of steam from both men. Their guns pulled free at the same time, and they leveled them at each other.

Rodriguez's mouth was moving, saying some kind of incantation as his finger squeezed the trigger. Andy's finger did the same. The bullets fired from their chambers, flashes and sharp noises breaking the dark silence of the winter night. Rodriguez's bullet went low, aiming for the thigh to take Andy down without killing him yet, knowing the man was probably wearing a vest beneath his clothes. Andy's bullet went high, hitting Rodriguez square between the eyes. Both men dropped simultane-ously, one silent, the other yelling in pain and surprise that the shot had been so low.

Andy clasped his leg, his jeans darkening with blood. He let go of his gun, letting it lie in the grass as his hands worked to free his belt from around his waist. Little puffs of air came from his mouth as he swore in every color of the rainbow and a few different languages.

He heard footsteps running toward him from the tree line separating this field from the field with the main farmhouse. Sirens could be heard in the distance.

"I've got it, bro," Aiden said, his own hands a little shaky as he grabbed the belt and used it as a tourniquet on Andy's leg. Derrick went over to make sure Wolf was down and not just pretending. The hole in the former police captain's forehead convinced him that the man was not going to get back up.

"We called 911, they are on the way," Teeny said.

"Thanks," Andy said through gritted teeth.

A flashlight could be seen making its way through the thin line of trees by the road. "Shit, did he have backup?" Aiden asked, panicking in the moment. He didn't want another life-or-death situation coming to a head.

"No," Andy said. "I did, remember?"

Keller came jogging up into the field and looked over the scene. "Jesus," he said in a whisper.

Derrick was busy grabbing the two small GoPro cameras they had set underneath the stone outcrop-pings to get video of what happened. He then grabbed the audio recorders as well.

"Not Jesus," Andy said, his breathing a little fast due to pain. "No matter what he thought."

"Oh," Keller said, seeing Derrick. "Those aren't necessary."

"What?" Derrick wasn't sure he had heard the cop correctly as he tried to hide the cameras and recorders, in case he wasn't supposed to have them.

"Wired," Andy said, his teeth clenched.

"I wasn't letting him borrow a vest without being able to get evidence," the large cop said. "I wired him up with sound and a fiberoptic camera. I'm shocked Rodriguez didn't figure that out."

"Did he seem like he was in his right mind to you?" Aiden asked.

"Nope," Keller said, squatting down next to Andy. "Ambulance should be here soon," he said as the sirens got louder. "You hang in there for me, okay?" He then pulled up Andy's sweater, revealing the wiring. He began the process of unhooking it all.

Andy clenched his fists in pain around the frosty grass as Keller worked. Red and white lights flashed, and the siren was so close it was screaming before it cut off. Keller got the last of the wire set up off Andy and pulled his sweater back down over the vest. "Don't let 'em keep it," he told Andy.

Aiden looked over at Derrick. "Take Teeny back to the shop. I'll call you guys. I'm gonna go with him."

Derrick nodded, and he and Teeny began to make their way back through the trees.

"This will be a little messy," Keller said, as the EMTs made their way into the field. "But the video and audio were clear. It was self-defense."

Self-defense or not, Andy felt like crying. This was the first time he had taken a life. He had fired his weapon in the line of duty before, sure. But he usually aimed at the person's center mass, as he had been taught in the academy. To incapacitate the criminal, not to kill. But Andy also knew that if he hadn't killed Rodriguez on the first shot that Rodriguez would have been pulling some magic crap out of his ass. He knew that he had saved his own life, that he had done what he had to do. But knowing it and feeling it were two different things. And right now, the weight of taking a life was as painful as the gunshot in his thigh.

Wolf materialized beside his body, stunned for a moment. Laughter nearby brought his attention to the girl. Her blonde curls bounced as she laughed and pointed at Wolf.

"Sarah," he growled.

"He killed you good," she said in her southern drawl. "It's like you din't even know what hit ya!"

Rodriguez looked back over and saw his body lying on the ground, the bullet hole between his eyes. Keller was running into the field and was careful to avoid the spray of blood, bone, and brains on the ground. Halleran had taken the kill shot. Rodriguez knew it was probable that the man had a vest on underneath his coat, so he had aimed low. He had intended to take Halleran to the ground and give him one last chance. He hadn't expected Andy to go for the kill.

"Shit," Rodriguez said.

Sarah was still laughing. She moved forward and poked him. "That's what ya git fer lyin' to me, you stinkin' liar."

Rodriguez reached out a hand, his reactions fast for one so newly dead. His hand wrapped around the little girl's throat. Her blue eyes, which had been full of glee and malice, went wide in surprise.

"This is your doing, isn't it?" Rodriguez asked. He could hear Andy and Keller's voices, but it didn't matter what they were saying. Not anymore. "You got the file out of my office, didn't you?"

"I told you I'd pay you back for lyin' to me," Sarah said, her voice strained by the pressure on her throat. Defiance lit her eyes, despite her current predicament. "Now you're as dead as me and with no way back, either." The child then stuck her tongue out at Rodriguez. After all, he was a ghost, the same as her now. What could he do?

What she didn't count on was Rodriguez's knowledge of the afterlife.

Rodriguez began muttering something under his breath, something Sarah couldn't make out. The hand around her throat began to faintly glow. Once again, her eyes widened.

"Open your mouth, Sarah," Wolf said, once more growling.

Defiance and pain gleamed in her eyes as she made a stubborn face. Her brow was furrowed, and her lips pressed tight. In the distance, sirens could be heard. Wolf increased the pressure on her throat. It was gradual, but as she kept her mouth shut, he increased the pressure until she gave in and opened her mouth. However, in doing so, she took the opportunity to stick her tongue out at him again.

It didn't matter.

Wolf let go of her throat only to seize the lower half of her mouth with that hand. His other hand was also glowing. He gripped the top half of her mouth with that hand. The little girl screamed as Wolf held her mouth open. She tried to close her mouth to bite him, but he was pulling the top and the bottom apart. She could feel her jaws pop open, and tears fell from her eyes as she screamed.

With a roar of strength, Wolf ripped the top half of her head from the bottom, silvery blood splattering all over him and on the stones of the outer circle they were near. He then gripped one of her arms and pulled, tearing the appendage off as easily as the wing off a fly. He didn't care about the metallic liquid covering him. This child had been a thorn in his side for weeks. She was the ultimate reason he was here, dead. She was the one who led to him being publicly ruined.

The fact that he had been the one to summon her to do his bidding didn't enter his mind. He was rage, pure and simple. Her spirit body dissolved as the man who had promised her life once more killed her for good. Wolf, alone, remained; the lone spirit in the field, covered in the spirit blood of the little girl.

He turned away from the silver-covered ground and the ground covered in mortal gore. He walked past Halleran and Keller as the ambulance arrived on the street just past the thin line of trees separating the road from the field, continuing to march through the thicker line of trees toward the homestead of Scarecrow Farms.

He knew enough to not stay where he had died. His spirit would be picked up. There was no way he was going to be subjected to the afterworld or to being put into service in some way. He was going to remain free. And he was going to see to it that *they* would pay. It would take time and planning. But he had all the time in the world now.

He just needed to regroup and get his head straight.

CHAPTER 14

An Echo of Family Past

The bells indicating that a living person had entered the shop chimed. Aiden was at the register, cashing out a sale. Teeny was helping a young woman back in the herb section, and Derrick was at the round table with his laptop out. As the other two were busy, Derrick was the first person to see the woman and recognize her as trouble. Lauren, her spirit always close to Aiden, saw her second.

"Oh no," Lauren said to no one in particular.

The woman was stunning at first glance. Curves in all the right places and none of the wrong ones. Thick, curly, black hair spilled over her shoulders. Her well-manicured nails were painted black; the ring finger of each had a tear-shaped crystal embedded into the polish.

She wore a black dress which accentuated her physical assets. Black high heels helped show off toned legs. She wore large, dark sunglasses and a black pill-box hat that had a short black lace veil on the front.

Aiden sent the customer off with her bag of purchased goods and looked at the woman. Something about her seemed somewhat familiar. "Hi, can I help you?"

"Yes," she said, pulling a black handkerchief embroidered with silver out of her black clutch purse. "Where will the funeral be, and at what time?"

"Uh, I'm sorry. Lauren's funeral was yesterday," Aiden said.

"What?" The woman's tone changed from grief to annoyance on a hairpin.

"Her funeral was yesterday," Aiden repeated. He noticed out of the corner of his eyes that Derrick was coming over to him, while Teeny and her customer had both stopped to watch.

"How dare you hold her funeral without me there!"

"And you are?" Derrick asked, having no idea who she was. But, with the attitude change, Aide had realized who the woman was.

"Valerie, don't do this," Lauren groaned.

"I am her sister," the woman replied. "Valerie Lowenstein."

"Why did you think the funeral was today?" Derrick asked.

"It's a Sunday. Isn't that when you usually hold a funeral?"

"Funerals, like births and deaths, can happen any day of the week, Valerie. You should remember that, as your own father's funeral was on a Wednesday," Aiden spoke up. He recalled the stories Lauren would tell about her sister. The two hadn't really spoken in years. Lauren had been considered the black sheep of the family. She had followed her dreams and married for love. Valerie was the golden child who had married a doctor, a plastic surgeon, no less. She was also the chief operating officer of a Fortune 500 company. She was vain, self-centered, and a royal bitch, according to Lauren.

Valerie made a face like she had smelled something awful. "Well, how was I to know? It's not like you called me."

"It's not like you called here to find out either," Aiden countered. "Most of her customers and friends did. They managed to make it out yesterday, more than I thought would. But here you are, head to toe in black and ready for a funeral you missed. Have a good flight home, Valerie."

"Whatever, just give me the keys to her house, and I'll be on my way." She held out her hand expectantly.

"I'm sorry. What was that?" Aiden couldn't believe what he had heard.

Valerie sighed and spoke slowly and exaggeratedly, as one might to someone who was deaf or whom they thought was stupid. She repeated word for word her demand for the house keys.

"Why on earth would we give you the house keys?" Derrick asked. He half debated pulling out his phone to record the interaction, a "Karen" in the wild. But he wouldn't disrespect Lauren like that. He hadn't even known she had a sister before now, but given this, he could see why she didn't talk about her.

Valerie pulled the sunglasses down on the bridge of her nose, looked Derrick over disapprovingly, then pushed them back up. "Hush, child, the grown-ups are talking."

Lauren could see the annoyance in Aiden growing, beginning to embark on anger. She knew she should be trying to calm him, trying to keep him even. But dammit, Valerie deserved this for coming here. And especially for talking to Derrick like that.

"Okay, look," Aiden said, his voice dipping lower in range, as it usually did when he was getting angry. "Here's what's going to happen. You have 5 seconds to get out of this store before I call the police and have you trespassed from this building. You are going to go home, and never spare your sister another thought, because I know good and well you never did while she was alive."

Valerie scoffed. "Oh, come on, a bit dramatic don't you think? I'm her sister. Her home, car, hell, maybe even this store, are mine now. So maybe I should call the police and have **you** trespassed."

Aiden looked for one second like his anger was going to boil over, but then a smile spread across his face, and he leaned back against the back counter. "Sure, why don't you go ahead and do that? Let's see how this works for you."

His smile gave her pause, but only for a moment. With a sigh, she pulled her cell phone out of her high-end clutch and dialed 911. "Yes," she said as they answered and gave the address of where she was. "I need someone here immediately. There's a man here who won't leave and is stealing from me." She paused as the dispatcher worked and answered her. "Thank you." Valerie hung up, looking smug.

Aiden looked at Derrick. "Go into the back office, would you? Get the envelope we got the other day."

Lauren couldn't help but smile. Her sister was definitely not going to expect how this was about to play out. For his part, Aiden just stayed standing against the back counter, his arms crossed over his chest, a light smile playing across his face. Teeny and her customer had both taken seats at the round table to watch, both feeling like they needed popcorn.

Derrick came back from the back office with a large manilla envelope and went behind the counter to stand with Aiden.

"Are you finally seeing reason?" Valerie asked. "Are you going to give me what's mine?" She reached over for the envelope and Derrick swiftly put it behind his back where she couldn't reach it.

"This is not yours, lady," Derrick said.

A squad car pulled up, lights and sirens going. The officers got out and entered the store. Valerie wasted no time.

"Oh officers, thank God you're here. These two have stolen from me and refuse to leave my store. And after the death of my sister." She paused, dabbing her eyes beneath the sunglasses as if she were crying. "It's just all too much."

One of the cops lifted an eyebrow. "Um, Aiden, what's going on?"

"This is Lauren's sister, Valerie," Aiden said.

"Pleasure to meet you, ma'am. Your sister was a kind woman. We're all sorry for your loss," the other officer said.

"Trust me, Brewer," Aiden said, "she is nothing like her sister."

"I can't believe this," Valerie said. "I want these two escorted out of my store, and if they try to resist, I want them arrested."

"You're store ma'am?" Brewer asked. "This store is a leased piece of realty. The owner owns the entire strip here."

"Then the lease would pass to me. I am her only living relative," Valerie declared, quite sure of herself.

"Except your sister wasn't the only one on the lease, Valerie," Aiden said. "I'm on it, too. I helped her get this place. So, with her passing, I am now the sole lessee on the paperwork."

"So, ma'am, you can't have them trespassed," Brewer explained. "Aiden here is still in charge of this store."

"And I would like her trespassed," Aiden said.

"Hey, Brewer," the other officer said. "Listen to this." Both officers stepped back and listened to their radios close to their ears, and turned them down. Lauren could hear it and was torn between being appalled and cheering.

"Ma'am, were you at 3826 Wildwood Lane yesterday?"

"That's Lauren's house," Derrick said.

"Were you there, ma'am?" Brewer reiterated.

"Of course I was there. It was my sister's home. I'm entitled to it. Unless you're somehow magically on the paperwork there, too?" Valerie asked with venom in her voice toward Aiden.

"And did you try to break into the property, ma'am?"

"I did not try to break in. I was looking for the spare key," Valerie huffed. "It wasn't on top of the door frame; it wasn't underneath the welcome mat. Not in or under any of the planters on the front porch. I thought maybe one of the rocks would be a fake one with a hide-a-key place, but I couldn't find it."

"Brewer, how did you know she was there?"

"A neighbor made a report of a woman matching her description trying to break into the house," Brewer said with a glance at Valerie. "Except she didn't stop with just looking for a spare key. The neighbor called us when she started trying the doors and windows."

"Yes, yes, the nosey neighbor came out and said he had called the police. Old man obviously didn't have enough to do." Val sighed in annoyance.

Aiden slid the envelope from behind Derrick and moved over to the side of the counter that was away from Valerie. "Officer Brewer, you might be interested in seeing this."

As Brewer approached, Aiden opened the large manilla envelope and pulled out the papers contained within. One set of papers began with the heading *Last Will and Testament*. Brewer took it and began scanning over the wording. "Right," he said at length. "We'll take it from here."

"Are you finally going to get him to give over my keys?" Valerie asked.

"No ma'am, but you are being trespassed from this store, and you are going to be arrested for attempted burglary of a dwelling," Brewer answered, taking his cuffs off his belt.

"You have got to be kidding me," Valerie said, putting her handkerchief and her phone away in her purse.

"No ma'am. Second-degree felonies aren't a joke," the other officer said.

"And for the record, Lauren Kurtz left everything to Aiden and Derrick. You were not mentioned in the will at all," Brewer added.

Valerie looked at Aiden, apoplectic in anger. Aiden gave her a small smile and a wave. "And yes, officers, I will be pressing charges for the attempted burglary."

Part of Lauren felt victorious, finally seeing her sanctimonious bitch of a sister go down for her shenanigans. Part of her felt bad for feeling good about it. It was her only sibling, after all. But then again, her found family here meant more to her than Valerie ever had. The woman had been conniving and manipulative all of Lauren's life, being that Valerie was the older sibling. That was why she had made the decision years ago to erase her sister from her life.

"Thanks, guys," Aiden said.

Valerie was struggling against the other officer as he tried to escort her out. "You can't treat me like this," she howled. "I'm a COO. I make more in a month than you do in a year!" Seeing that they weren't going to stop, she dropped to the floor. "You are not arresting me. Get me out of these handcuffs. I'll have your badges for this!"

"Ma'am, get up, or we will be adding resisting arrest to your line of charges," the other officer said.

"And if you don't get up, we'll just carry you out of here," Brewer said with a shrug.

"You can't treat me like this," Valerie said, letting her body be dead weight as she fought against being arrested.

"Alright, Haverstead, you get her arms," Brewer said. The other officer nodded and grabbed Valerie under her arms. Brewer reached down and grabbed her legs around her knees. Derrick hurried from around the counter to hold the door open for the officers with a grin as Aiden began putting away the paperwork. He wasn't thrilled about having Lauren's sister arrested, but he also wasn't going to set a precedent of letting her come in here and treat them like that, either. Hopefully, she would never come back once she was released and went home.

The officers got her loaded into the car and waved goodbye to Aiden and Derrick.

Teeny looked at the gentleman she had been helping with the herbs. "I'm sorry. I completely forgot where we were at with your order."

"That's okay," he answered with a chuckle. "I did, too."

CHAPTER 15

A Time for War

Mostly, just broken brick and glass remained in the central part of the prison. The sky above the carcass of the building was appropriately black. Clouds covered the night sky, imprisoning the light from the stars and the moon. The shroud of darkness allowed X'Haldzos some safety from being seen. His strength was beginning to return as he slept inside the room containing the portal. He had been spared this room from his destruction because of its usefulness.

A crow flew into the skeletal remains of the prison. It cawed twice and then flew off again. From the trees behind the prison, a thick, soupy fog began to roll quickly in, as if it were a fog with purpose. Before long, it enshrouded the execution building, then the yard, then the prison itself. It seeped into the cells that remained and under the cracks of doors and in between bars. It was the kind of fog that feels wet in your lungs when you breathe.

X'Haldzos stirred a little in his sleep, then settled down once more, slipping into an even deeper slumber.

A circle emitting a golden glow appeared on the floor of the central prison area. Ares, Badb, and Indra appeared. All three were armored and ready for battle.

Ares wore his helm with the crimson bristle on top. His scarlet cape seemed to almost glow red in the fog. His normally golden armor seemed to glint red. He had a sword sheathed on his hip, and a spear in his hand.

Indra's clothing hadn't changed, but he was carrying weapons in three of his four hands. One hand carried his most well-known weapon, the Vajra. It would occasionally crackle with electricity. He also carried a vicious-looking hook and a sword.

Badb wore what appeared to be steel cuirass armor that glinted silver in the light of the portal. It bore an engraving of a crow on the stomach. The goddess carried no weapons. She didn't have to. She would carry her magic into battle, and it was enough. Even without her sisters, she was confident that the three of them would have no need of assistance.

"The non-human said the demon has made its lair this way," Indra said, pointing in the direction of the prison's rec room.

"It's there," Badb said with a nod as she absently stroked the feathers of her crow. "It's sleeping." Her crow took off from its perch on her shoulder to fly down the hallway engulfed in the fog.

The three gods moved down the hall, the fog parting for them. Despite their armor, their movements were silent. The benefit of being divine. The crow was on the floor in front of the rec room, hopping around, waiting for them. When they neared, it flew back up to perch on Badb's shoulder.

"You weren't going to start this without us, were you?" Cadence said in a whisper.

"You were told not to be involved," Ares said. He looked Cadence and Will up and down, unable to believe what he was seeing. They had no armor, just some straps with a glowing orb in the center over their chests and orbs on their wrists. They carried what looked like guns attached to some sort of tanks they wore on each hip. Their belts had pouches. Ares was sure he didn't want to know what ridiculousness was in them. They did not look prepared for battle.

"No, we were told that you couldn't ask for our help," Will said. "At least, if I understood the insinuations correctly."

Indra smiled as his Vajra crackled. "Of course. Since you are here offering your help, it would be rude to not avail ourselves of such a tool."

Badb gave Cadence a light smile and nod of greeting, though she was of Ares's mind that the spirits were not prepared for the battle ahead. They looked more like court jesters with their colors and trinkets. She hoped the child of her isles would fare well in the battle ahead.

For Cadence's part, she still didn't like this place. Demon or no demon, destroyed or intact, it just had a very nasty feel to it. She was aware, however, that this was no time to be spooked.

"We will let you know when to enter the fray," Ares said. "Let us take the first volleys of whatever it may throw at an attacker." Without waiting for an answer from Cadence or Will, he turned and kicked open the door. The power of his kick took the door off its hinges. It flew across the room until it hit the side of X'Haldzos's sleeping form.

X'Haldzos stirred in his sleep once more, but this time he did not fall back into slumber. He struggled to wake, knowing something was wrong. He could see the fog swirling around him. But where was he? Why was he here? The floor was too hard and too cold to be his usual home, the farmhouse.

A white-blue color of lightning lit the fog, and pain blossomed on his side as a thunderous crash followed the strike. Indra had used his Vajra and unleashed a thunderbolt and lightning strike, a Bhaudhara. Meanwhile, Badb's fog of confusion was working well on the creature.

Was there a thunderstorm? Had lightning just hit him through the hole in the roof he had caused at the farmhouse? X'Haldzos was still confused, trying to piece together where he was and what was happening. He felt no rain, so how could it be a thunderstorm? His yellow, catlike eyes looked all around, trying to find something familiar to latch on to. But all around him was a thick, swirling fog.

An arc of red light descended through the fog, and a large spear pierced one of his eyes. X'Haldzos howled in pain, letting out a belch of gas as he did. The foul smell drove Ares back, gagging, unable to dislodge his spear from the demon's eye.

The fog began to dissipate as Badb gathered her power. As the fog abated, the confusion abated. X'Haldzos now remembered where he was. He remembered getting free of the farmhouse, and his search to make the defiant one pay. With his four remaining eyes, X'Haldzos could now see the three attacking him. He thought of using his roar to destroy the room, thus killing the human-like creatures attacking him. They had the same auras about them as the ones who had tried to drive him from the afterworld. He knew them for gods. The other gods he had handled in the afterworlds hadn't been too impressive. He'd been able to injure them or get them out of the way of his escape easily. Not that it hadn't cost him some flesh, because it had, but it was nothing that wouldn't heal.

Indra put his Vajra to use, letting out another Bhaudhara, lightning hitting the creature on the back. X'Haldzos felt the pain of the lightning, especially where it hit the claw marks left by the dragon. The deafening rumble of thunder made him vibrate to his core. But none of it was as bad as the pain in his now ruined eye. He would make sure they would be destroyed slowly and in exquisite pain for that.

The ceiling of the room began to glow red, and both Indra and Ares stepped back. They knew all too well what was coming. Badb was famous for her rain of fire.

Raindrops of flame slowly began to drop from the ceiling, picking up speed until they became a torrential downpour. X'Haldzos bellowed as he felt his thick, rubbery skin burning. His scabs from the previous battle burned away, and the fire seared even farther into his thick flesh. The first few layers of his skin crisped until they fell off like pieces of old paint from an ancient wall.

X'Haldzos turned and filled his throat, then belched. Yellowish fog filled the room and drove all three gods back to the doorway.

"Duck," Cadence said to the three gods in the doorway. Without question, they did as they were told, and Cadence threw the Koosh Ball. Just as Will had said, the tendrils of the ball immediately began to wrap around the large form of X'Haldzos as it hit. The trouble was that X'Haldzos was so large that the restraining bands looked like they would be too little to keep the thing restrained for long.

"Not helpful," Ares said, assessing the situation as the restraining bands slowly broke.

"Yeah, well, he was a bit smaller the last time we saw him," Will said in retort.

Meanwhile, X'Haldzos sniffed the air. All he had to do was move a little or breathe deeply to snap the bands of whatever it was they had tried to bind him with. But in so doing, he caught the scent. The scent of the one he had been searching for. The one he wanted to destroy for being so bold as to stand against him, walk away, and then return despite his presence. The woman had been uneasy upon her return. Who wouldn't be? He was not the only evil at the farmhouse, just the worst.

X'Haldzos shuffled slightly, turning toward the door that he had been sideways to, toward the scent he wanted to snuff out of existence. As he moved, the spear bobbed in his eye, still sticking out, unretrieved by Ares. He growled in pain and tried to swipe the thing away, but his arms weren't long enough to reach. And he had grown far too large to bend down to make up for their lack of length.

"I smell you," X'Haldzos thought to the minds of everyone there: the three gods and the two mortal spirits. *"No escape tonight. Mine."*

The volume of his intrusion into their minds drove the mortal spirits to their knees, their hands clapping uselessly over their ears. The gods were shaken, too, unsteady for a moment on their feet. But they were more accustomed to telepathy, sometimes at that volume. Therefore, their recovery was far quicker than that of Cadence and Will.

"Go for the eyes," Cadence said from the floor. She had been watching as the last of the restraints popped off and had seen him try to swipe the spear out of his eye. "That seems to be what is bugging him the most." She would not address the fact that he had just made it very plain that she was his target. She glanced at Will, who was looking at her with concern.

"Don't go getting soft on me, kid," she said as she began to pick herself up off the floor. "I am not letting that asshole have any say on how I end my story."

Will grinned and nodded, getting up as well. As he did, the gods moved back in, Indra in the lead, his Vajra crackling, his other weapons at the ready.

A black, tar-like arm swiped out at a speed they had not thought the creature capable of, and a talon slashed at the legs of Indra, who was closest. The claw cut through the man's Achilles tendons and with a yelp of pain, the four-armed god went down. The god's blood flowed from the sliced skin on the backs of his ankles.

"Badb, can you do another fog?" Cadence asked. She had a fanny pack she was already pulling around to her front. Ramon had made her take it, despite her protestations that fanny packs had gone out in the eighties. Of course, Will had thought it looked cool.

Badb shot Cadence a look that all but screamed that she was not accustomed to taking tactical advice from a mortal, but she did as she was asked. The fog materialized through the center of the room, rolling outward.

Cadence got on the floor and began to army-crawl across the debris-littered floor toward where Indra had fallen. Her hands felt around on the floor, getting a few slices from stone and glass along the way as she searched for the fallen god. As she had assumed it would, the fog affected her as well, which is why she had been repeating the mantra of "Find Indra" in her head since she started crawling in.

The fog had encased X'Haldzos instantly. He grew lethargic and confused. Why was he angry? Why did he hurt so badly? He couldn't remember what had happened to his eye, either. Had he gotten a bone in it by accident? He could hear and feel someone in pain near him, and his mouth began to salivate. He was hungry. But he was tired, too, and it was only one lone person. He heard shuffling around him on the floor. Stupid wildlife. They weren't good for food or amusement. The confusing effects of the fog, or at least their depth, had lessened a bit due to the focus his pain provided him. He could also smell something close. Something that he knew he wanted to hurt. He reached out and swiped with a taloned finger that still dripped gold blood from wounding Indra. He connected with nothing, however.

Cadence found one of Indra's arms and grasped it tightly. The god flinched for a moment, then relaxed, gripping her arm back with that hand and another. Cadence began to back up, dragging the wounded Indra with her. When they got close enough, Ares lent his strength, grabbing Cadence by the waist, and hauling her and Indra out of the room.

Badb wasted no time while the others were busy, creating another rain firestorm from the now scorched ceiling above X'Haldzos. Once more, the demon screamed in pain as his thick skin bubbled and burned and his previous wounds deepened.

Cadence got Indra out of the doorway and against the wall nearby. Unzipping the fanny pack, she found a roll of gauze and a needle and thread. "This may help for a time," she said. "But I'm not going to lie, it's going to suck. And you'll need to be seen at the medical facility."

"I am not unused to pain," Indra said, bracing himself. "Continue."

Cadence said a small prayer to all the gods that she was about to do this right. She had basic medical training as an officer, but something like this that required stitches to stop the bleeding and would require more to mend the internal damage? Not something you encounter in the field without calling paramedics.

Cadence began with the needle and thread, stitching together the torn skin. "This isn't going to look pretty," she said. "I've not had much practice at stitches." She could hear X'Haldzos roaring from pain and smelled the smoke as the fire rained down on him.

"You didn't heal your fellow warriors on the battlefield?" Indra asked through gritted teeth.

"I'm not a warrior, I'm a cop," Cadence said, trying to explain as she stitched. "It's a different kind of war, and if one of us gets hurt, we usually call for healers. Paramedics, we call them."

"You are wrong," Indra said. "You are a warrior. Or at least you have the heart of one. Thoth chooses his people carefully."

In the rec room, the creature began rearing back for one of his gassy roars as the firestorm died. Ares, prepared, moved to deepen the slice on the creature's throat in an attempt to rob him of that weapon. Then Will jumped in front with his sonic ear pointed at X'Haldzos. Ares looked a little put out at having his attack interrupted by Will's presence and managed to stop the arc of the sword a mere two inches from Will's shoulder.

"It is unwise to stand in between a warrior and his target," Ares said in a frustrated growl.

"I trusted you not to hit me," Will said. "Trust me." He then hit a black button on the side of the sonic ear.

X'Haldzos let loose his roar, the foul stench of his gaseous breath filling the room. Will gagged but hit the blue trigger button on the sonic ear.

The sound that emitted from the innocuous-looking megaphone was like a tyrannosaurus roar in a small enclosure, magnified by ten. Ares dropped his sword and clasped his hands to his ears, as did Badb, and all of them were driven back by both the stench and the sound. Will was dry heaving, tears pouring down his face as if he had just cut up a hundred onions.

"Whatever that was, I'm glad we missed it," Indra said as Cadence was wrapping gauze around his ankles.

"I think that was Will's sonic ear," Cadence said. She then pulled her cell phone out. "Whitfield, Indra to medical please."

She hung up, pocketed the phone, and twisted the fanny pack so that it rested on her backside, just below the tanks of liquid she carried. Whitfield appeared in a flash, grabbed Indra, and disappeared again. Cadence just hoped that Whitfield was done betraying them. All she needed was to lose a god on her watch. She had stabilized the wounds as best she could, on the off chance that Whitfield didn't take him to the medical facility. But if he did, she was sure she would hear about her sloppy stitchwork from Ramon later. And she would take the teasing and be glad to be there for it.

When she entered the room again, Will was hanging by the door. He had stopped gagging, and he was wiping his eyes. He looked like he had been pepper sprayed, though. Badb was in between them and Ares was using his sword to parry a strike from X'Haldzos's talon. His sword was true and not only did he parry the attack, he managed to cut off two of the four taloned fingers.

That was when X'Haldzos realized it was not going as well for him as he had envisioned. He wanted the mortal spirit of the female. But the desire for her pain was making him too desperate to win. His fight with the gods previously had made him perhaps a little too cocky. He turned, doing his best to ignore whatever the gods and mortals might do to him, and focus on the portal.

"We cannot let him escape," Badb said, her voice strained.

"No shit," Cadence almost said. Instead, her brain-to-mouth filter engaged in time and she said, "We've got it. Just give it everything you have."

The ceiling began to glow red again and both Will and Cadence unhitched their Super-Soaker-like guns, pointing them at X'Haldzos. Ares hurried around one side of the creature, doing his best to stay clear of the glowing embers of the ceiling and the aim of whatever it was the two mortal spirits had. The fiery rain began to fall for a third time in the room, beginning to bring with it bits of the ceiling beams as they were now getting burned through instead of just scorched. Pushing their triggers, the liquid from the large water guns unleashed and began seeping into the burst blisters of X'Haldzos's overcooked skin. Cadence moved a little, aiming her stream at the creature's eyes, two of which immediately began to melt as if they had turned into raw eggs, dripping down the demon's black face.

A roar of defiance and pain burst forth from X'Haldzos, a sound that was reaction only, not an attack. A talon of his uninjured hand reached for the portal to activate it, but several charred beams fell from the crumbling ceiling on top of the sigil-covered stone. Cadence nodded to Will as she clicked on the second tank on her gun, moving around to the other side of X'Haldzos's face, determined to get the rest of his eyes. Will hit a number on his speed dial. The other person didn't even say hello.

"Now!" Will yelled into his phone.

Cadence let the spray fly, and another pained bellow ripped from the creature as the last of his eyes melted. X'Haldzos then took a few stunned steps back as Whitfield rose from the portal stone, through the blackened and ashy beams, bearing a spear specially made by Will in hand. It had what looked like large jack points all over the metallic spear tip, which was four feet long. The other two feet were the wood handle.

Will and Cadence pressed their attack with the concoction in their water tanks. Badb let her rain fire fall but kept the area concentrated on just over the demon itself. Ares began artfully slicing at the uninjured hand. Whitfield drove the spear up, through X'Haldzos's chin and into his brain. Each point on the spear released toxins and poisons that had been specifically designed for X'Haldzos by Will.

The angry and pained roars of the creature became whimpers, and its thrashing slowed. Ares continued to filet the creature's limbs to pieces. Badb let her fire continue to fall, and Cadence and Will let the spray continue until it was used up.

The gore that remained of X'Haldzos did not move. It did not make a sound. The red from the ceiling died and dark moved into the rec room once more, lit only by the glowing portal Whitfield stood on, and the embers of the ceiling as they cooled. Will and Cadence hit their flashlights, and all five in the room began a slow circle around what was left of the demon. Satisfied that it had been ended, once and for all, the morbid dance around the carcass ended and they all looked at each other.

"Indra?" Badb asked.

"Alive, in the medical facility," Cadence said. Whitfield nodded to Cadence that he had done what was asked and dropped Indra off where he had been told to.

"You have our thanks for that," Ares said.

"Thank you all for helping me finally put an end to that damned thing," Whitfield said. "I would say I couldn't have done it without you, but I think the last couple of centuries have been evidence of that."

"Indeed," Badb said.

"Do we need to do anything to dispose of this?" Cadence asked, gesturing to the still-sizzling thing.

"It will dissolve in an hour or so to just a shadow on the floor," Ares said. "X'Haldzos is gone. He cannot be summoned back."

"That's a relief," Whitfield said.

"Are we really sure about that?" Will looked between them all as he asked the question. "I mean, they say that all the time in comic books, but we all know no one stays dead in the comics. And horror flicks? Cadence, help me out. How many Jason and Michael flicks have there been?"

"Except this is no poet's fiction," Ares said. "Though I will grant you it was a hero's journey for some. But no. The thing is dead and gone. He will be naught but a shadow on the stone soon enough."

"Time to go then," Cadence said, gesturing Whitfield over to her and Will.

Whitfield made his way over to them, giving the smoking corpse a last kick in parting as he went. He then looked at Badb and Ares. "Do you want us to take you to Indra?"

"We will check in on him later," Badb said.

"We have to check in with the others first," Ares said.

Cadence, Will, and Whitfield nodded. They disappeared from the ruins of Barrington Prison.

The ghost hospital, as Cadence liked to call it, was hopping. It was the most frantic and busy she had ever seen the place. There were nurses and doctors moving with expediency from one room to another or all out teleporting to other wards. Cadence, Will, and Whitfield all appeared in a corridor and were almost run over by a harried-looking nurse.

Cadence was bowled over from behind, but arms caught her and held her tight. "When I saw Indra, I was worried," came Ramon's voice from behind her.

Cadence couldn't help but smile at the familiar feeling of his arms wrapped around her and the sound of his voice in her ear. Will gave a bit of an embarrassed smile and backed off with Whitfield.

"Why don't you check on Indra," Will said. "I'll take Whitfield, and we'll go back and report to Snow."

"Wait," Ramon said. He looked both Will and Whitfield over with scrutiny. "Any injuries to either of you?"

"No," Whitfield said, now terrified of the scratches he had seen on Cadence when he picked up Indra. Ramon's threat was still very present in his mind.

"Nope," Will said as well.

Ramon then turned to Cadence. "And you, Detective Riley?"

"Just a few scratches," she said, showing him her hands. "Nothing band-aids and Neosporin won't cure. Well, if I was mortal."

"Did you beat it?" Ramon's eyes looked between the three of them intently, and Whitfield was uncomfortable under the usually mild doctor's gaze.

"We did!" Cadence couldn't help but grin as she said it. It had been the biggest, baddest foe she had ever taken on, dead or alive. And now she had survived to tell the tale of its carcass disintegrating in the prison rec room.

Ramon walked over to Will and Whitfield. He clasped hands with both. Whitfield shrank for a moment, afraid that the good doctor was going to follow through on his threat now that he had seen the cuts on Cade's hands. As he became aware of Ramon's intentions, though, he took the hand offered him and shook it. Ramon was sure to squeeze his hand particularly tight though and was gratified at the slight wince Whitfield gave.

"Go to Snow," Ramon said with a nod. "He has paced a bald track into his carpet by now, I'm sure."

Will and Whitfield nodded and disappeared from the hallway, much to an oncoming doctor's relief.

"Let's get these hands bandaged," Ramon said.

"It looks like you guys have bigger fish to fry than a few scrapes and cuts," Cadence said.

"If they are your scrapes and cuts, I have nothing more important to take care of," Ramon said.

As unromantic at heart as Cadence was, that line made even her melt. "Did you like, step out of a romance novel or something?" she asked. "You always know what to say or do."

"I'm from a different time, remember?" Ramon said with a smile. "Romanticism was not shunned in place of cynicism at that time."

"Ouch," Cadence said with a laugh. "Feeling a little called out here now, Doc. How is Indra?"

"Lucky," Ramon said, leading Cadence into an exam room.

"Lucky? Were his wounds that bad?" she asked.

"Not like you mean," Ramon said. "I meant he is lucky that gods don't scar. That suture job was awful. I need to teach you to do it properly."

Cadence laughed. "Hey, I told you upfront I was no good at being a doc. Or a nurse, or much else medical. Maybe a school nurse. Maybe. On a good day."

Ramon sat her in the chair in the exam room and laughed. "Don't knock school nurses," he said as he began to wash her hands as gently as he could, taking tweezers to remove embedded detritus.

"Are you kidding me? I am not in any way knocking them," Cadence said. "They patched me up a hell of a lot when I was a kid."

"I can imagine," Ramon said with a chuckle. "So, what comes next for you, mi amore?"

"Report to Snow," Cadence said with a sigh. "A ton of paperwork. Another get-together with the breathers is probably in order as well."

"About that," Ramon said.

"Oh no," Cadence said, noting his demeanor change. "What's happened?"

"This came across the line a few hours ago," Ramon said. "Right as you and Will left for the prison." He handed her a piece of paper.

She took it with the hand he wasn't currently bandaging and read it through twice. "Is this a joke?"

"I've not heard it refuted yet," Ramon said.

"Captain Rodriguez is dead? At Andy's hands?" Cadence couldn't hide her disbelief at this development.

"And the captain's spirit is missing," Ramon said. "It never came through processing."

"I would ask how that is possible, but after dealing with Irene Woods, I know it can happen," Cadence said.

"Exactly," Ramon said. "They sent people out to find him, but none of them were successful."

"I'll have to check in on what happened with that, too," Cadence said, wincing as Ramon moved on to cleaning out her other hand.

"To return to your initial question, Indra will be fine. He just needs rest and to heal," Ramon said. "And all joking about your sewing skills aside, you did the right thing. He needed immediate attention. You stopped the crucial emergency and then had Whitfield get him to help. That was good."

"Glad I could help," Cadence said. "Up until that point, I felt like a seventh wheel. We weren't really doing much up until then. It was mostly him, Babd, and Ares."

"You don't give yourself enough credit," Ramon said. "I'm sure Snow will, though. Go on, you're released. Get some rest soon though. The paperwork and other meetings can wait until tomorrow. I'll see you at home. Oh, and Ruby has been asking for you. I don't know if you want to see her now or perhaps tomorrow, but she has been asking."

"How is she doing?" Cadence asked as her forehead furrowed with concern.

"She has a female doctor, and I gave strict orders for no males in her room. She has been a better patient than she ever was for me," Ramon chuckled.

"Well, I mean, she killed you," Cadence reminded him, not that he needed the reminder. "Her being a better-behaved patient is kind of a low bar. I'll go now. I can spare a few minutes."

He leaned in and gave her a soft kiss, his fingers holding her chin between them for a moment. Without releasing her, and with his lips still touching hers, he inhaled. As if he were tasting and smelling her all at once to prove to himself that she was still there.

"Go," he whispered, drawing away from her.

"Well, after that I kinda don't want to," Cadence said.

Ramon laughed and shook his head. "I'll see you at home, mi amore. She's in room 20."

With that assurance, Cadence left the room. She walked down the hallway, dodging nurses and doctors as they moved. *At least now, things here might begin to settle down.* She hoped so, at least.

She found the room easily and peeked in. Ruby looked small in the bed as she slept. She had bandages covering the left side of her face, torso, and her left arm ended in a stump a few inches below her shoulder. Cadence frowned. Ruby could be a pain in the ass, sure. But she was still, oddly, a friend.

Cadence knocked on the open door and Ruby turned, opening her good eye. She squinted at the Cade, then smiled. "Libby!" Ruby greeted her.

"Can I come in, Miss Ruby?" the detective asked.

"Get your ass in here, girl, and let me look at you," the old woman ordered.

Cadence laughed a little and went to Ruby's bedside. "How are you doing? I've been worried."

"You were worried?" Ruby's voice was hoarse as she scoffed. "I stood toe to toe with that son of a bitch, and he had to tear me damn near in two to get me to back down. Worried, pah."

Cadence tried to suppress her grin but failed. "I'm impressed. I know what it took to take him out. You did very well."

"He was looking for you, Libby," Ruby confided. "You gotta be caref—Wait, he's dead? Gone?"

"Yes," Cade nodded. "It took my team and three gods to do it. But we got him."

Ruby's whole frame sagged in relief. "Oh good. The bastard got into my head. He showed me awful things he wanted to do to you. You're a good girl, Libby. I didn't want him getting to you."

Cade smiled at her comfortingly, then leaned down and kissed Ruby on the cheek. "I'm glad you're safe. What are you going to do now? Lexington Hills was half destroyed by that attack."

"I've been talkin' to someone who says they know you. Looks like an angel or some kinda porcelain doll that woman."

Cade knew exactly who Ruby was talking about. "You've been talking to Bethany?"

"Yeah, that's her name," Ruby nodded.

"About what?" Cadence had a good idea about what, given Bethany's job, but she wanted to hear it from Ruby herself.

"Movin' on. Doing something other than hanging around a crumbling building." Ruby looked at Cadence, and Cadence could see the pain and exhaustion plain on her face. "I ain't much for how I wound up," she added, lifting the stump of her left arm and hissing in pain.

"So, are you thinking of heaven? Or reincarnation?"

"Not sure yet," Ruby answered. "I need to see what my options are. I did, however, make amends with Ramon."

Cadence blinked in surprise. "What?!"

Ruby waved her right hand, dismissing the reaction. "I've had time to think about things I've done. Mistakes made. Now don't get me wrong, I'm still gonna give people hell if they deserve it. But he didn't. I know that now."

Cadence smiled. "Good, that makes me happy."

"It should, since I hear you're shackin' up with him," Ruby said, giving Cade a look of disapproval. "You're too good for him." She nodded as if to emphasize the point. "Even if you lied to me."

"I did what?"

"Oh, don't play coy with me, Miss Detective Cadence Riley." Ruby looked like she might be miffed, but then shook her head. "Bethany explained to me why you did it, though. Can't say I blame you. I would have screamed out your name if I'd thought about it. It was a smart thing to do. Where'd you get the name Libby from, anyway?"

"My middle name is Liberty. Libby is a nickname for that. I went through a phase in middle school where I decided I hated my first name, and my father said to go by my middle name then. I didn't like Liberty either, but I did like Libby. So, for 6th and 7th grade, that's what I went by."

"Sounds like a thing a kid that age might do," Ruby nodded. "I'll make sure I see you before I go anywhere." Ruby paused, then looked Cadence square in the eye. "Countless times you have put yourself on the line for us. Gotten hurt. Bad. Lost people. Most of the damn morons in this life don't know what you've done to help save their asses. But I do. Thank you."

"Thank you," Cadence said, after swallowing the immediate urge to say she hadn't done much. "Now get some rest, Miss Ruby."

"Oh my God, dude, you should have seen it!" Will exclaimed. "She gets down and army crawls under the fog to save Indra, and as she is crawling back, the demon is slashing out trying to find them and Ares just grabs her by the waist and hauls them both out of there before it can get them."

Cadence opened the door to Snow's office after hanging about outside just long enough to hear Will's tale of Indra's rescue.

"It wasn't all that dramatic," Cadence said as she closed the door behind her. "You're exaggerating a bit."

"Am not!" Will protested. "You were in it; you didn't see it."

A chill crept up her spine. If it was as Will said, she and Indra had been closer to further harm than she had thought. It was a good thing Ramon didn't know about that part yet.

Snow moved across the room and hugged Cadence close. "I'm glad you're safe," he said.

"Thanks," Cadence said. "And don't let Will fool you. I was not the hero of the day. Most of his inventions were right on the mark. The Koosh ball would have worked, but the creature had gotten larger than expected."

"That's somewhat terrifying," Snow said.

"Yes, it is," a deep voice said from the doorway. Thoth wore his Croft suit, which was just him in normal clothes instead of ancient Egyptian garb. "Which is why I gave express orders for you two not to be involved in any battle against it."

"Ares, Badb, and Indra did make that clear, Sir," Snow said.

Cadence looked between the Snow and Croft. "Are you both serious right now? I would have thought in the last several months that the two of you would have figured out that expressly ordering me not to do something means that I am going to do it."

Will coughed behind his hand to hide his grin at her comment.

Croft grinned. "Why do you think I gave Ares that order and told him to tell you I had given it? But that made it your choice. I wasn't ordering you into battle. I didn't feel comfortable doing that. There was too much danger involved."

"Like there hasn't been all along?" Cadence asked.

"True," Croft said with a begrudging nod. "But the three of you have risen to the occasion more than once, exceeding expectations."

"Thank you, Sir," Will mumbled.

"Indeed, thank you," Snow said.

"Don't thank me just yet. You all are likely to become victims of your own success." Croft's tone was serious as he spoke. "Don't forget, we have a very large population of evil beings on the loose now, thanks to X'Haldzos. And several of the gods are aware of you now by name. That could be good, or perhaps not. It all is going to depend on how things go."

"What things?" Cade asked.

"Recapture of those once imprisoned," Croft said as he moved to a chair and took a seat. "You are the head of the special task force, Riley, the face of it. All eyes will be on you to see what happens next."

"Great," Cade sighed. "Can't wait." She looked around the room and paused. "Where is Whitfield?" Cadence asked, realizing that she hadn't seen the man who had made the killing blow in here.

Snow pointed to his desk and the red cube on it.

"You know he made the final blow, right?" Will said, echoing Cadence's thoughts.

"While that is admirable, he still has to pay for actions that lead to innumerable deaths," Snow said. "One good deed is not enough to erase everything he has so misguidedly done for so long. So, until another prison is built, he will remain in that holding cell."

"I'll make more of those for you," Will said.

"No," Croft said. "Give your designs to Research and Development. They will create them. We will need more than just what you alone can produce until we can get the prison rebuilt. And those smaller models are better than the cells we had, so adjustments to the whole prison are going to be made."

"And while Whitfield may be its first occupant, what about all of those who escaped when X'Haldzos let them all loose?" It was Cadence who asked the question. "Are we destroying or recapturing?"

"Whatever the situation deems necessary," Croft said in a matter-of-fact tone. "Recapture if you can, but if you need to destroy a thing for others' safety, then do it. I trust your judgment on the acceptable use of force. There will be changes coming though, you know that, right? Take tonight off, then regroup with your breathers tomorrow."

"Speaking of breathers and people who need to populate our little ghost prison cells," Cadence began.

"Ah, so you heard about Wolf then?" Snow said.

"Yeah," Cadence said with a nod. "I kinda can't believe Andy actually killed him."

"He did, but he was wounded in the process," Snow said, then held up a hand to forestall her next words. "He is in the hospital, but he is stable. I've checked."

"But we have lost Wolf's spirit," Croft said.

"Great," Will said. "Another bad guy out there to cause trouble for us."

"And one who knows how we work, thanks to Whitfield," Cadence said with a sigh.

"That, my friends, is a problem for another day," Croft said. "Go home, get the rest you so richly deserve. The big hurdle is past, but that's not to say there aren't more coming up."

Cadence and Will nodded and rose as Croft left. "We'll see you tomorrow, Snow."

"Good work, Will," Snow said, shaking the teenager's hand. "I'll see you tomorrow."

Will teleported home, the smile still on his face, though he was beginning to feel the effects of all the energy he had spent.

Snow then hugged Cadence again. "You have no idea how relieved I am that you are safe."

"You and Ramon both," Cadence said.

"His interest is of a different vein than mine," Snow said with a smile. "He is glad his paramour is safe. I am glad my daughter is safe."

Cadence's nose stung for a moment as she found herself suddenly fighting back tears. "Snow, I…" but she trailed off.

"I mean it, Cadence," Snow said. "I had daughters, but never got the chance to know them as adults. I can only hope that they had at least one-tenth of your spirit and fight. Your parents and brother are proud of you. I know that. And please know that I am, too."

It was her turn to hug him, and she did so tightly. "Not many girls are lucky enough to have two great dads, but I can count myself among those few."

"Thank you," he said, his voice soft. "Now go home, get rest. I want those bandages off your hands as soon as possible. You have no idea of the mountain of paperwork you are in for."

"You do realize that's not exactly an incentive, right?" she asked with a laugh.

He just laughed and shooed her off.

Cadence teleported home.

CHAPTER 15

Playing Catch Up

IV bags hung on the pole next to Andy's hospital bed. The machine above his head and to the left beeped out the readings of his heart rate, his oxygen levels, and his blood pressure. Andy was sleeping, his peace half-induced by the pain medication he had been given.

Will and Cadence appeared in the hospital room, and Cadence frowned.

"He means a lot to you, huh?" Will meant it to be a rhetorical question.

"Yeah," Cade said. "He does. We met at the academy. We've been best friends since then. He was my partner before I died."

"Sorry he got hurt," Will said.

"Not your fault," Cadence said, shaking her head. "It's our captain's fault. At least Andy got him."

"Well, killed him," Will said, amending Cade's statement. "We're the ones who are going to have to get him."

"True," Cadence said with a sigh. "Give me a minute."

"Sure thing," Will said, wandering over to look out of the hospital room window, which afforded him a lovely view of the roof of the ER and a parking lot.

Cadence touched Andy's hand and closed her eyes. In moments, she was in his dream. "Dream" wasn't really the right term for it, though. She was in a dark area, and Andy was with her. He was wrapped head to toe in thick fuzzy blankets, with only his face peeking out. He was in a recliner and on the far wall, a fuzzy playback of his last meeting with Wolf was playing on repeat.

"Andy," Cadence said and put a hand on where she thought his arm would be. She knew enough to know that the darkness of the room, the swaddling in fuzzy blankets, even the bad resolution of the "movie" as it played, were all effects of the pain medication he had been given.

Andy turned his head a little and smiled sleepily when he saw her. "Hey you," he greeted. "How's tricks?"

"I should be asking you that," Cadence laughed softly. "You're the one who faced down our old boss." She looked at the screen for a moment and caught the final few moments, both men with their guns drawn and aimed. The simultaneous firing of the weapons. Both men going down, one injured, one dead.

"It was a good kill, right?" Andy looked at her from within his blankets, panic plain on his face.

Cade nodded to him. "It was. You made the right call." She wasn't about to let him know that their side had dropped the ball and been unable to collect him before he escaped.

"Keller knew," Andy babbled. "Keller knew. He heard the message. He agreed to help. I wasn't out there alone and unmonitored."

"Shhh," Cadence tried to calm him. "It's going to be okay. You're going to be okay. You're going to heal up from this and be fine."

"Can I confess something to you, Cade?"

"Of course, doofus, we're friends," Cade chuckled.

"The only thing I was truly afraid of out there was that I wouldn't ever see you again. That he would find a way to kill me and seal my soul away somehow. Make me into some kind of slave to him. And a very small part of me was hoping he would kill me so we could be together again. Riley and Halleran, back in action together, you know?"

Cadence pressed her lips together for a moment, trying to think of how best to phrase her response. "Andy, when it's your time to come over to this side, I'll be right there throwing you a welcome party. But now isn't your time. You can help me out best by being here and being you. And you were right in your assumptions. Rodriguez very likely would have had something ready to enslave you to him. That's why he went for the knee wound, to incapacitate you. Hopefully, you won't be on my side of things until after your grandkids have grown up."

Andy scoffed at that idea and somehow worked his hand free of the blankets to grab her hand. Cade noticed blood seeping through the blanket where his knee was.

The pain meds were wearing off. A quick glance at the screen confirmed it. The screen was closer and in sharper focus. Cade gave his hand a squeeze.

"Stay with the group if you can," Cade suggested. "You can do a lot of good with them."

"What about you?"

"What about me?" She furrowed her brow, not understanding what he was asking.

"I never get to ask how you are." Andy shrugged. The blankets had become loose, and he could make the gesture now. "It's always problem after problem, but never a catch-up."

"I'm okay," Cade said. "Not great, but I'm dealing with Sam's death better than I did when he died the first time. I've got a great support system. And so do you. It's time for me to go now," Cade ended gently. She squeezed his hand one more time, then let it go. She walked to the back of the room and left his dream.

Cadence opened her eyes and let go of Andy's physical hand. Will caught the motion and moved over to her. "Everything cool?"

"Yeah, his meds are wearing off, though," Cade replied.

"Not much we can do about that," Will shrugged.

"Nope," Cade agreed. "Thanks for indulging me. I know this isn't the top of our priority list right now."

"I get that you needed to come and see him to set your head straight," Will said, rolling his eyes. "Jeez, you know, sometimes you're like talking to my mom. She was always apologizing for crap that wasn't her fault."

"I didn't apologize, I said thanks." Cade thwapped him on the arm.

"So, back to the office?" Will asked.

The door to the hospital room opened and Aiden walked in with Derrick and Teeny. Lauren was close behind them but made her way over to Cadence and Will as Teeny and Derrick took a seat in chairs while Aiden leaned against the windowsill.

"How did it go?" Lauren asked. "Did you manage to get that thing?"

"It was a little hairy at times," Cadence said. "But the thing has been killed for good."

"And Whitfield?"

"The first occupant of the new prison," Will said.

"I'm glad you guys are safe," Lauren said. "Do you have any insight into this beyond what Aiden knows?" She tilted her head toward Andy as she spoke.

"Nothing fantastic," Cadence said. "The captain knew enough of the afterlife to hightail his spirit out of there once he realized he was dead. We're currently looking for him."

"On top of all of the escaped prisoners you have," Lauren said, shaking her head.

"Yep," Cadence said with a nod. "I have spoken to Andy in his dream, mainly to check up on him. I didn't tell him we lost Rodriguez's spirit. Call me a coward, but it kind of felt like kicking him while he was down." She opened her mouth to say something else, but the door to the hospital room opened.

"Dr. Michaels," Teeny greeted the bespectacled man in the white coat.

The doctor blinked in surprise. "I had forgotten you know the detective. But he was the one who helped get you and your friend here after his accident."

"Yeah, he was," Teeny replied with a nod.

A groan came from the bed, and everyone turned their attention to Andy as he woke up.

"I love being the center of attention," Andy said, trying to wisecrack. His voice cracked, and he went into a coughing fit at the end of his sentence. Derrick grabbed the Styrofoam cup on the bed tray with its spoon and half-melted ice. He spooned up a couple of ice chips and let Andy have them.

Dr. Michaels took the opportunity of everyone's silence to speak. "Detective, I need to talk to you about your condition. Do you want me to clear the room?"

Andy shook his head. "They can hear whatever you say. They have my permission to know. I'd end up telling them, anyway."

The doctor nodded, running a hand over his receding hairline. "You've had surgery on your leg to remove the bullet and repair the vascular and muscle damage. If things go well, you should be able to get out of here in a couple of days. You'll need an assistive device to walk, either crutches or a walker, for a while. You will have to go to physical therapy to rebuild muscle strength. I do need to examine your leg, sir."

Andy tossed back the covers from his injured leg, not really caring what anyone saw. He just wanted to get this over with so that the doc would leave, and he could talk to his friends. He knew they had to compare notes.

His leg was wrapped from below his knee to almost his crotch area. In the middle of all that area was a small area about the size of a quarter of blood.

"The blood is normal. In fact, that should be all of it you'll see. We'll keep an eye on the bandage and if it starts looking like more blood is seeping into the bandage, we'll remove the bandage to assess what's causing it." The doctor took a moment and pulled a black Sharpie from the pocket of the white coat he was wearing over his green scrubs. He gently circled the area around the blood, effectively giving a visual perimeter the nurses could check against when they checked on him.

Andy winced and gave a small hiss of pain.

"On a scale of 1 to 10, what's your pain level at?" the doctor asked.

"An eight, I guess? It's worse than it was a couple of minutes ago, and then that circle you drew made it hurt even more."

Everyone else in the room, human and spirit alike, stayed quiet while Andy and his doctor talked.

Dr. Michaels nodded. "I'll have the nurse bring you some pain medication." He then turned to the others in the room. "You can visit with him, but the pain medicine is going to make him very sleepy. It's best to let him rest."

"No problem, Doctor. We just wanted to check in on him," Teeny assured the man.

"I'll leave you to it and go speak with the nurse. I'll see you tomorrow, Detective."

"I quit the force," Andy said. "Just call me Andy."

Andy grabbed his cane from the passenger seat of his car and slowly got out of his car. He winced a little at the pain but straightened to standing easily enough. It was the initial jolt of weight bearing that caused the pain and it was getting better the more he did it. His time in the hospital had lasted a week, as they wanted time to get him set up with rehabilitation and physical therapy. He had done crutches for two weeks and then was thankfully downgraded to using a cane. The physical therapist had said his progress was due to being in such good shape before the incident. Andy, however, was convinced that he was just determined to get the hell off the crutches. He had already been on the cane for one week, which meant it had been a month since the shooting.

The strip mall was still very much like it had always been, except for a new sign over what had been the new-age shop. The sign now read "Southern Paranormal Researchers" and had an image of a ghost in a magnifying glass. The bell over the door chimed as Andy limped his way in with his cane.

The items in the new-age shop had mostly been cleared away, except for the spirit chimes in the front window. Candles had given way to K-2 and Mel Meters. The herbs had gone, and in their place were various Ovilus devices, audio recorders, and SB Ghost boxes. Crystals remained, though in smaller supply and selection, and added to them were REM pods, light grid systems, and various cameras.

The round table in the back area was still there, as were the chairs. The store was a monument to the old adage: "The more life changes, the more it stays the same." A smile spread across Andy's face.

"Lucy, I'm home," he called out. A group of customers was with Aiden as he was explaining the differences between some of the merchandise. He looked up and gestured for Andy to have a seat at the table. Andy was still getting used to Aiden's new look. Gone was the shaggy hair. He'd shaved it all off and grown a goatee. It was a look that was growing on Andy.

Andy chuckled and limped to the table. Having just come from physical therapy, he was sore, so the limp was showing, despite the cane. He looked around the shop, surprised to find Aiden on his own. Just as the thought crossed his mind, Teeny came into sight outside. She had apparently just gone down the strip mall to Pho-Q to get lunch. The bells chimed as she came back in with two large bags from the eatery, and the scent was as immediate as it was mouthwatering.

"Hey!" she greeted Andy as she set the bags down on the table. "If it isn't my favorite ex-cop."

He had gotten used to that greeting from her. It was still an uncomfortable title, but he hadn't been able to come to terms with the thought of going back to that line of work, either. Right now, he was living off his savings, what little money he had inherited from Cadence, and his boyish charm and good looks. With everything that had happened, he had become something of a local celebrity, even though that had been the last thing he wanted to happen. He was a hero for exposing a deadly corrupt cop and had even been hailed a hero for killing that same corrupt cop once all the evidence and eyewitness statements had exonerated him. He'd had meetings with the mayor and the governor. He'd been invited to be on the news and on local talk shows, both on TV and radio, which he'd turned down. He wasn't about to try to make money from Rodriguez's death. Rodriguez may not have had a spouse or children, but he had parents and siblings somewhere. Andy wasn't about to put them through any more pain than they were already going through.

"I don't suppose you have anything in there for me, do you?" Andy asked as she started emptying the bags.

"It physically hurts when you doubt me," Teeny teased. She set a to-go bowl in front of him.

"You're an angel," Andy sighed, inhaling deeply as he took the cover off his bowl. "Where's Derrick?"

"He had a midterm today," Teeny answered.

Aiden moved with the four people to the register as he balanced a few boxes in his arms. He was eager to finish up the sale as he was hungry, too. He rang out the group, which was comprised of a group of friends starting their own ghost-hunting group. As he bagged their purchases, they peppered him with questions about good places to start.

"Do your research," Aiden said with a shrug. "You live here, so you have to know at least some of the local ghost stories, right?"

"Yeah, but Lexington Hills and Barrington Prison are little more than rubble now," one of the group complained.

"There's that Scarecrow Farms place," one of the guys suggested but then was immediately shot dirty looks by the rest of his friends. "Shit, right, sorry."

"Don't be sorry," Aiden said. "But don't go there. It's private property, and it's due to be torn down any day now. Take it slow. I know for a fact that the college campus has some ghost stories, and the old theater downtown."

"Okay, cool, thanks," the man paying for all the items said. They grabbed their purchases and left.

Aiden sat down with a sigh and eagerly opened his bowl.

"You okay?" Teeny asked, rubbing Aiden's arm.

"Yeah," Aiden said after swallowing his first bite of food. "Seeing them reminded me of how we started out, you know? Dan, Lauren, me, and Bethany. Then Derrick. We were babes in the woods and had no idea how deep and dark the forest was going to get."

Aiden felt a cold touch on his shoulder and a calmness overtook him. Lauren was there.

"How much longer 'til Derrick graduates?" Andy asked, his obvious change of topic appreciated by both Aiden and Teeny.

"Only a couple more months," Aiden said. "In May."

"What are the plans then?" Andy looked between Teeny and Aiden. It dawned on him that he had tied himself to them, to the group. It was no longer the three of them, Teeny, Aiden, and Derrick. It was the four of them, including him. He wasn't sure when over the last month that had happened, but he was now aware that it had.

"I'm really not sure, bro," Aiden shrugged.

"One hell of a party for Derrick, that's for sure," Teeny said. "Liam said he'd come back out, too."

"I know Derrick's family is coming to town for the ceremony," Aiden said. "Derrick has been talking about that. He does and doesn't want them to visit."

"I can understand that," Andy nodded.

"Other than that, we're getting this shop off the ground. And maybe once a certain someone decides to stop pretending to be an old man, we'll get back to our real work." Aiden smirked a bit before Teeny hit him on his arm.

"He's recovering from being shot. Don't be a dick," she fussed at Aiden.

"Yes, dear," he said with a grin and took a spoonful from his bowl.

Andy laughed. "Please, Teeny, he's just jealous that once I'm done with PT, he won't be able to keep up with me."

The three laughed in unison, and Lauren smiled at the camaraderie. She knew that this was a moment of calm before the storm of what was to come.

The office that Cadence and Will shared was completely different. Gone was almost everything resembling a normal office, including the shape. The office was circular now and seemed very futuristic. Will had taken some of the downtime they had been given to binge-watch anything and everything with futuristic tech overtones. Things were changing every day as research and development finished one schematic after another for them.

The observation bays that they oversaw were segmented by region of the globe. The walls of their office were some form of material that was like sunglasses that changed in the dark to normal glass. They could be made clear or opaque at will, so Will and Cade could see a certain section of bays if needed. Eventually, they would be pared down to just being in one region, but a great many spirits needed to be trained. Croft and Snow were weeding through applicants, both new spirits and older ones.

Cadence sat at her shiny black desk, looking at the global map that was digitally spread on the circular wall. There were multiple glowing spots of various colors on the map. The brighter the glow, the bigger the escaped bad guy. At least that was how Will had explained it. Cade shook her head in dismay.

"Where do we even start with all of this?" she gestured to the map. "Do we just throw darts at it and go after whatever we hit?"

"We're still sifting through reports," a woman said from the couch against the wall. Her name was Michelle, and she was their assistant.

"What's the holdup?" Will asked. He had his feet casually kicked up on his desk and was tossing his rubber ball up in the air and catching it, as was his habit.

"Well, there is a difference of opinion as to how the threats should be given priority," Michelle replied, her blue eyes looking at Will from her freckled face. "Some think it needs to be based on what they did to get there, others think a power level scale needs to be made."

"Is this where we joke about the power level being over 9000?" Cade asked. Neither of them got the joke, but Sam would have laughed.

"What do you think it should be based on?" Will asked Michelle.

"Given the way you two work, and what I know of you? I think it should be based on the immediate threat to humans. If some old monster destroyed a village back in the 1100s and has gone back to haunt his old ruin of a castle, that's not an immediate threat. The maniacal ghost of someone going back to haunt their old mansion that has a nice family residing in it would take priority for you guys. At least that's what I think." Michelle gave a shrug and shifted the files in her lap.

"And that's why you're an awesome assistant," Will said.

"Exactly." Cadence nodded. "We need them prioritized by immediate threat to the living, then sub-prioritized in those categories by power. One evil ghost vs one evil non-human, both a threat to the living; the non-human is going to come first because it can cause more damage."

"Got it," Michelle said as she made notes. "I'll go back to them with that. Hopefully, I can have a working list for you soon."

"Each person in the bay should be responsible for one of the escapees. I don't want them splitting their time between multiple. We need to be clear on where they are, their habits, their powers, everything."

"I don't know if we have enough operators for that, Detective Riley," Michelle responded.

"Double them up until we have enough," Cadence said. "I know we're going to have a bumpy ride for a while until we can get enough staff, or we can whittle the evil population back down again."

"Snow's working on it," Will said with a shrug. "He won't leave us hanging."

"I know," Cadence said with a smile. "This is just a lot of responsibility. And Wolf is still out there, too."

"Cadence," Will said as he dropped his feet and looked over at her, his expression serious. "It's going to be okay. We're gonna get him. And all of them," he added, pointing to the map.

A red light went off in the office, beginning to strobe.

"Shit," Cadence muttered. "Michelle..."

"I've got the marching orders," Michelle said calmly as she stood up. "We'll get the list together for you."

Will had brought up a data screen in between him and Cadence as she looked down at the spirit read out on her desktop. "Why on earth are we getting an alarm for a mid-level poltergeist?"

"Because it feeds on fear and pain and is currently haunting a preschool?" Will replied.

"Yeah, that would do it," Cade sighed as she rose.

"Yep." Will headed to the lockers that had been installed between couches around the perimeter of the room. He grabbed a white cube made by research and development from his schematic. He grabbed another and tossed it to Cadence. She held it and moved to the map, where the red light was blinking.

"Ready?" she asked as Will joined her.

"Hit it," he replied with a nod. Cadence reached up and touched the blinking red light.

Dead Woods

The pale crescent moon was clear above the trees, but the man running through the woods was immune to the tranquility of the night sky. His feet pounded the ground as he ran, paying little heed to branches that whipped his face, leaving small trails of blood on his sweaty skin. He ran to a tree and stopped, putting his hand on the trunk to balance himself as he tried to both catch his breath and listen.

His heart was pounding in his ears, both from the running and from fear. In a fight-or-flight situation, he had discovered which one he was. A crash of underbrush, heard over the bass drum in his ears, caught his attention. No more time to catch his breath.

He pushed off the tree and continued to run. He knew if he could reach the bottom of the trail, he could find safety. There would be a road. There would be a bar. That was this hill, right? Or was it the next? He prayed it was this one. He wasn't sure he could survive another hill.

The people at the bar had told him that going out there alone was ill-advised. He had been too cavalier about it. He had been out there many times over the years. He thought he knew it like the back of his hand. He had thought their warnings were out of an overabundance of caution. Perhaps they had seen too many newcomers get hurt. But he was no newcomer.

A snarl brought his thoughts very much to the present. Was it closer? He had no idea what it was he was running from; he had only caught the shadow. The large, foul-smelling, furious-sounding shadow. In that moment, everything left his brain. There were no more survivalist skills, no more hunting skills, no more common sense. All that was left was the overpowering need to run. And run he did, leaving everything back at the campsite, including his flashlight.

He took a chance to look behind him, trying to ascertain how close the shadow was. It turned out that trying to look behind him while running downhill was more of a threat to him. His foot slipped on the bloody gore of some nocturnal animal's kill. With a shout of surprise, he fell as his leg slipped out from under him and he began to roll downhill.

He was no longer sure if the crashing sound was him or whatever was chasing him. His hands struck out, trying to find roots, vines, any way of stopping his accelerating descent. His efforts became more desperate as it registered that he was rolling straight toward a massive tree trunk.

His fingers clawed at the ground. He tried to get some kind of purchase on the ground with his feet, but he was going too fast and was now too dizzy to get any kind of meaningful grasp on the ground enough to slow him. He hit the tree trunk with the side of his head and the world swam in stars before he passed out.

The shadow loomed over his prone body.

AUTHOR BIO

Growing up in a haunted house and having a father who loved horror set the stage for Amanda's creative life. This Urban Fantasy author has been writing since her teen years, blending horror, fantasy, and the paranormal. Amanda balances a day job, her writing, her family, and helping her husband run a board game group and YouTube channel, Tabletop Misfits. Local to Southwest Florida and a total geek, you can often find her at conventions, either as a vendor or an attendee.

More Books by Amanda

Waking Up Dead
Dead Vessel
The Dead Show
Dead Revelations
Dead Carnage
Dead Woods

BOOK CLUB QUESTIONS

1. After reading the first book in this series, how did you predict the series was going to end? Were you right?

2. Did you realize that X'Haldzos was chasing a character before the characters themselves did? Who did you think he was chasing?

3. Do you like the author's decision to have Lauren continue to be a part of Aiden's and Derrick's lives? Why or why not?

4. There are three large open threads leading from this novel. 1) The escape of all the evil from the ghostly prison. 2) The "Missing God" case of Zeus being MIA. 3) Captain Rodriguez, aka Wolf, being missing in the afterlife. Which do you want the author to tackle first?

5. On the flip side of the above question, which of the three threads do you think will be left as a "final battle" of the series?

6. What do you think Wolf is going to do now that he is free of corporeal bonds?

7. What has been the most surprising event, in your opinion, throughout the series so far?

8. If you met the author in person, what would you yell at them about regarding the story? Compliment them on?

9. What do you think is going to happen in the series as it continues, knowing the three major threads that are hanging?

10. So far, the series has had some true stories of the paranormal that the author herself has lived through. What do you think was the truth sprinkled in the fiction?

More books from 4 Horsemen Publications

Fantasy, SciFi, & Paranormal Romance

Beau Lake
The Beast Beside Me
The Beast Within Me
Taming the Beast: Novella
The Beast After Me
Charming the Beast
The Beast Like Me

Chelsea Burton Dunn
By Moonlight
Moonbound
Bloodthirsty

D. Lambert
Rydan
Celebrant
Northlander
Esparan
King
Traitor
His Last Name

J.M. Paquette
Klauden's Ring
Solyn's Body
The Inbetween
Hannah's Heart
Call Me Forth
Invite Me In
Keep Me Close
Heart of Stone

Kait Disney-Leugers
Antique Magic
Blood Magic
Heart Magic

Lyra R. Saenz
Prelude
Sonata
Scherzo
Falsetto in the Woods: Novella
The Devil's Trill
Ragtime Swing
Midnight Cumbia
Sea Song De La Corsaire

Paige Lavoie
I'm in Love with Mothman
I'm Engaged to Mothman
Dear Galaxy

Robert J. Lewis
Shadow Guardian and the Three Bears
Shadow Guardian and the Big Bad Wolf
Shadow Guardian and the Boys
That Went Woof

T.S. Simons
Project Hemisphere
The Space Between
Infinity
Circle of Protections
Sessrúmnir
The 45th Parallel

VALERIE WILLIS
Cedric: The Demonic Knight
Romasanta: Father of Werewolves
The Oracle: Keeper of the Gaea's Gate
Artemis: Eye of Gaea
King Incubus: A New Reign
Queen Succubus: Holder of the Crown
Val's House of Musings: A Mixed Genre
Short Story Collection

V.C. WILLIS
The Prince's Priest
The Priest's Assassin
The Assassin's Saint
The Champion's Lord

COZY MYSTERIES

ANN SHEPPHIRD
Destination: Maui
Destination: Monterey
Destination: Lake Tahoe
Crime, Detective, and Noir

A.K. RAMIREZ
Secrets & Photographs
Memories & Scars

D.A. SPRUZEN
The Turkish Connection
The Witch of Tut

JOE DAVISON
Journey to Hell

MARK ATLEY
Too Late to Say Goodbye
Trouble Weighs a Ton
A New Day Starts Here

HORROR, THRILLER, & SUSPENSE

ALAN BERKSHIRE
Jungle
Hell's Road
Linda's Story

ERIKA LANCE
Jimmy
Illusions of Happiness
No Place for Happiness
I Hunt You

MARIA DeVIVO
Witch of the Black Circle
Witch of the Red Thorn
Witch of the Silver Locust
Witch of the White Serpernt

MARK TARRANT
The Mighty Hook

OCTOBER KANE
Nothing Will Be Left
Everything Will Burn

STEVE ALTIER
The Camping Trip
Jimmy's Curse
The Ghost Hunter

DISCOVER MORE AT
4HorsemenPublications.com